Professional Misconduct

By

Sarah E. England

Copyright © 2003 by Sarah E. England.

The right of Sarah E. England to be identified as the Author of the Work (Professional Misconduct) has been asserted by her in accordance with the Copyright, Designs and Patents Act 1988.

All rights reserved.

All the characters in this publication are fictitious and any resemblance to real persons, living or dead, is purely coincidental.

This book is dedicated to Kam, who kept me sane with her irrepressibly wicked sense of humour when we worked as medical reps together. I will be forever grateful.

Also to my husband, Don, for enabling me to quit.

And finally to my mum, for buying me a computer and believing in me. Thank you.

Contents

Chapter One 7
Chapter Two 18
Chapter Three 31
Chapter Four 41
Chapter Five 54
Chapter Six 64
Chapter Seven 76
Chapter Eight 91
Chapter Nine 102
Chapter Ten 109
Chapter Eleven 122
Chapter Twelve 132
Chapter Thirteen 138
Chapter Fourteen 151
Chapter Fifteen 160
Chapter Sixteen 165
Chapter Seventeen 173
Chapter Eighteen 184
Chapter Nineteen 197

Contents

Chapter Twenty………………………………..........207

Chapter Twenty-one…………………………….....218

Chapter Twenty-two……………………………....227

Chapter Twenty-three………………………………..233

Chapter Twenty-four……………………………....243

Chapter Twenty-five…………………………….....255

Chapter Twenty-six……………………………….....265

Chapter Twenty-seven……………………………….275

6

Chapter 1

If only the person in the toilet cubicle wasn't being so, well, full on with their bodily functions, she could have relished this moment - given these anticipation fuelled minutes the recognition they truly deserved. For how often did a girl rise through the ranks and reach the top? It wasn't every day now was it? And boy had she deserved her day in the sun, her fifteen minutes of fame. More than most, that was for sure.

Melissa leaned over the sink to get a closer look at her reflection. One of the things she liked about staying in upmarket hotels was the quiet opulence of the ladies toilets - all those neatly folded towels in a basket, bottles of luxury hand lotion and pots of cotton wool. Picking up a can of hairspray, Melissa teased her hair into big hair, then carefully applied a tad more gloss to her already gleaming fuchsia lips. Today she had to look her absolute knock-out best.

'Ah, Melissa! How are you, lovey?'

Melissa jumped. Deep in thought, she hadn't noticed Pat Hardcastle, the Company's Sales and Marketing Director, emerge from the toilet cubicle. Pat hadn't washed her hands, she noticed. Ugh! And now she was buffing up her hair and putting lipstick on. She tried not to think about all the people Pat would subsequently go out and shake hands with.

'I'm great, Pat. Thanks. Been working really, really hard, you know?'

Pat snapped her handbag shut, smiling with stretched coral lips at Melissa. Melissa waited. What was coming? Oh no, Pat was reaching out to touch her face. She kept her smile fixed, letting Pat cup her right cheek and shake it slightly, like a mother reassuring her toddler. 'That's what we like to hear,' she said. 'Nothing less than what we expect from our top representatives.'

It was times like this when Melissa wished she hadn't sold antibiotics, hadn't seen those videos on Staphylococcus Aureus and E.Coli crawling all over the skin, invisible to the naked eye.

'Now, must press on,' Pat said. 'We've got a full morning ahead of us.'

'Yes, I won't be a minute,' Melissa called, watching Pat stride out. Jeez, why do women with huge arses always wear tight trousers and short jackets? And why in peach for pity's sake? She looked at her watch - the one the company had given her last year for being the top sales rep in male impotence products - and took a deep breath. Five to nine. Good. In a couple of minutes she would see the others in her team to break the news. She had some serious gossip and it was absolutely out of the question that she keep it to herself, even if it was supposed to be confidential. 'Bugger that,' she muttered, undoing the top button of her pinstripe suit to display a hint of cleavage and lace. 'Management here I come, and not before time either.'

The contrast, as she stepped into the foyer was a sharp one - tinkling piano music and softly lit mirrors to this - a veritable rugby scrum. Melissa took a deep breath. Dear God, it was wall to wall reps: people in suits trying to out shout each other, be the one to tell the most riotous jokes and back slap the most jovially. A hundred exhibitionists and no wallflowers. How, amongst all this lot was she ever going to find the girls? Melissa stood on her tiptoes and peered over the sea of heads. Ah, there at the far end, it was just possible to make out Veronica's blond bob, head and shoulders above most of the people around her. And if she wasn't mistaken, that was Sam next to her in the red suit. At that precise moment, Sam turned in Melissa's direction and laughed, a cascade of red hair and flashing green eyes causing a ripple of male interest all around her. As per bloody usual, Melissa glowered, lowering her head and beginning to push her way through the surging crowd.

By the time she reached the girls, Melissa's cheeks were burning hotly. 'Hiya! How are you?' she shouted to Veronica, before being pulled back under the scrum, re-emerging a moment later to lunge for an air kiss. Veronica leaned back a fraction. You know, Melissa thought, it would be nice if the snooty bitch would stop smoking for five minutes. Veronica's lips had flickered upwards slightly at the corners in what was, she supposed, an effort at a welcoming smile before blowing a plume of smoke over Melissa's head.

At least Sam was as friendly as ever. Sam gave her a warm hug. 'It's so hot in here, isn't it?' she said, noting Melissa's high colour. 'Mmmm.' E.Coli on her face and now flushing. Great! Melissa began to fan herself with the training agenda she had efficiently printed off the night before, one of the benefits to being the regional training officer in addition to her sales job - she knew what was going to happen today whereas none of the others did. The thing was though, the most important thing, it would be difficult now to impart her news with all this noise going on. Ah well, she'd just have to shout over the lot of them. 'Have you heard the latest?' she shrieked.

Veronica and Sam shook their heads.

Within their immediate vicinity there was a distinct drop in volume as interested ears strained. 'The latest' was always of interest. Melissa leaned towards the two girls and yelled at the top of her voice, 'Dick's been promoted.'

Veronica's jaw, she noted with satisfaction, had momentarily slackened, her eyes slits through the haze of smoke. But it was Sam's reaction that caught her off guard. Suddenly lunging forwards, Sam grabbed Melissa's shoulders, 'tell me you're not making this up! Oh God, please, please tell me this is true.'

'Oh, it's true all right,' Melissa said with a smug smile. 'I just got back from the managers' meeting last night?'

Sam kissed her, then jumped away and punched the air. 'Yes!' she cried. 'Oh God, this is the best news I've ever had. Yes! Yes! Yes!'

Melissa's smile faded a little - some of the men were muttering something about having whatever Sam was having and making other completely unfunny remarks about Sam's bouncing bosoms. 'So anyway,' she said, pulling Sam towards her to stop her from jumping up and down. 'Like, his job will be up for grabs? And I'm going to go for it - I could be your new boss,' she added with a giggle. 'Imagine!'

'Where's Dick going then?' Veronica snapped.

'Another division, I think - something to do with a new product launch? Whatever. Oh, this is top secret, by the way. And, like, no-one is supposed to know yet so don't tell anyone else, will you?'

Veronica shook her head almost imperceptibly.

'Course not, Melissa,' Sam said, unable to stop the smile from spilling out across her face.

It really was excellent news for all of them, Melissa thought. Dick had been their regional manager for the last six months since the launch of Happylux, the company's new anti-depressant, and during that time he'd made their lives unbearable, particularly Sam's. She looked over at her radiant face now and decided that despite all the lustful looks that were being directed at Sam instead of herself, she would be a far kinder boss to her than Dick had been. In fact the whole team was going to be ecstatic.

The volume of mind numbing noise made it difficult at first to work out what was happening, but suddenly people were yelling to each other to be quiet. A short, dumpy bloke wearing one of the Launch Conference T-shirts emblazoned with the words, 'Make it Happen,' had sprung onto a chair.

'Listen everybody, listen everybody. Can I have your attention please?' he shouted, clapping insistently in the manner of a camp Sunday Schoolteacher. Quiet, please everyone. Thank you.'

Melissa kept a fixed smile on her face despite Sam clutching her arm excitedly and Veronica blowing nicotine fumes onto the back of her head. Would all that smoke dull her highlights? Really, that was something she would have to sort out if she was to supervise Veronica's work - no way could she even contemplate spending a day in Veronica's car if she insisted on smoking. She shuddered - just think of all those free radicals on her delicate complexion.

While the man in the T-shirt struggled to gain control over the good natured but raucous crowd, the three girls were quietly digesting their enormous good fortune; Dick was pushing off. Melissa caught the eye of some of the others in the team. Boy, would they be thrilled when they knew. Images of herself driving a top model Mercedes flicked into her head. What would she have - silver or black metallic? There would be a pay rise too, wouldn't there? Her colour heightened further, her eyes glistening with pleasure. She had worked so very hard for this - years and years as a rep, all the extra admin she did for Dick, the office based training for the new recruits, not to mention winning the top sales award year after year. Oh God, it was so exciting.

'Now I want everyone to go to their syndicate rooms to practice role-playing,' T-shirt man shouted, flicking through papers on his clipboard. 'Ah yes, with the exception of Dick Walton's team, who are to go directly to the conference hall for role play. On video! With real doctors!'

A roar of protest went up from the crowd - 'role play, not again, Jesus Christ,' only to be quickly replaced with comments about being positive and looking forward to the challenge as they met the disapproving eyes of their managers.

'What?' Sam's fingers dug further into Melissa's arm.

Oh dear, poor Sam. Melissa turned to give her a reassuring smile but met instead with a wall of Veronica's eye-stinging cigarette smoke.

'So can you all make your way now to where you're supposed to be? And please - let's make the most of this superb opportunity to improve and share our selling skills. Show these doctors just what Topham Pharmaceutical reps can do. Make it Happen, guys!'

As he jumped off his chair with a flourish, a noticeable ripple of panic broke out amongst the previously happy crowd. Oh my God - role playing on video! Everywhere there were wild eyes and frantic questions - what brochures? When were they delivered? Could anyone lend a spare copy?

'Twits,' Melissa muttered under her breath, before remembering with a jolt, Johnny King. She'd better get to him quickly. After all, she was supposed to be the regional trainer and if their team didn't do well, it may reflect badly on her, not just Dick.

It wasn't difficult to find him. As she'd guessed, he was with a small group of rebels in the hotel car park having a last minute cigarette. God, even with his hair sticking up and stubble on his chin, he was a bit gorgeous. Very 'James Dean,' the girls had decided one drunken evening miles away from home in yet another anonymous hotel.

'More like Nick Cotton from Eastenders,' Sam said.

'Hi, Johnny,' Melissa called, pointing to her watch with a grin. His eyes, after a moment's recognition, shot straight to Sam. Melissa bristled, fervently wishing that Sam was not still clinging to her arm.

'Melissa,' Johhny said in his flat Yorkshire accent, his gaze still fastened to Sam's cleavage. 'What's up, luv?'

'What's up, Johnny King, is that our team is supposed to be in the conference hall, like, as of now, doing role play with guest doctors?'

'Oh role play! Gosh that's something jolly different,' Johnny said, mimicking the cut glass tones of Annabel and Hector from the marketing department. Then catching sight of Sam's terror stricken face, he smirked. 'What's the matter, Samantha? Don't you like doing role-play?'

'I bloody hate it,' Sam said. 'I was in such a good mood as well, after what Melissa told us.' She smacked her hand against her mouth, 'Ooops…'

'About Dick?' Johhny asked, stubbing his cigarette end out.

Melissa narrowed her eyes. 'What do you know?'

Johnny smirked. 'Only that the fat bastard's pushing off. My worry is who'll take his place though. I mean there's only Mike really.'

'Like, hellooo…' Melissa said, pointing at herself.

'Well, we don't want a bloody woman in charge, do we, luv? I mean - best place for you lot is in the kitchen.'

As Melissa tried to whack him with her agenda printout, he dodged her, whispering to Sam, 'or in the bedroom - nudge, nudge, wink, wink. Know what I mean?'

Melissa, Sam and Johnny were the last to traipse inside, following the rest of their sombre suited colleagues into the dark conference hall. Whirring cameras and a row of serious looking customers awaited them.

Melissa's eyes went straight to Dick, his usual contemptuous sneer notable for it's absence as he watched his team trail in. He looks nervous, she thought, clocking the beads of sweat on his upper lip and the way he kept glancing over at Pat and James, the senior managers. But why? Surely his new job was in the bag, wasn't it? Rumour had it that he was going to be in charge of creating a whole new sales force for the company's trail-blazing cardiovascular drug - Dick's rise to the top was nothing less than meteoric. Perhaps though, it could still all fall through? Melissa shuddered - not only had the Government yet to license the drug, it was also imperative that the right man was at the top. The future of the company depended on it. She had to help Dick. The team had to perform well this morning. I mean, honestly, all they have to do is what they are supposed to do every working day - sell Happylux effectively to their customers. She groaned inwardly. On second thoughts….. Still, hopefully Dick would be smart and put her on first. Or snooty drawers, Veronica.

She took her place at the end of a row of seven chairs, placed there for Dick's team to await their turn at role-play. The stage was set with just one chair, a spotlight and video camera focussed on it. In front of the chair was a large desk. Behind it, relatively in the shadows, sat Dr. Fotheringhill. Melissa did a double take. Oh no, Fotheringhill, Consultant Psychiatrist, Medical Director and specialist in reducing reps to tears. They must have drafted him in specially.

She looked over at Dick, now sitting with Pat and James at the side of the stage with the other doctors. If only she could catch his eye, give him the nod that she would go first, but no, he was far too busy chuckling away with Pat. Her palms began to feel a bit clammy. Oh Jesus, he had no idea how bad his team actually were. He hardly ever came out and worked with them. It was well known that Dick despised anywhere north of Cambridge, preferring to spend his time pottering down to the office on the south coast, which suited everyone just fine. Melissa worked with them instead and they had a good laugh.

'Do you know that mean bastard stayed in the hotel last night while we all had to drive here this morning?' Sam whispered to her.

Melissa nodded. 'Yeah, I know. It took me three hours as well. He booked himself into a suite....' Mid-sentence, she realised too late that Dick was giving 'Brett the idiot' the nod. 'Oh shit!' He just had to go and pick him. What on earth was he doing? Didn't he know how hopeless Brett was? That all the doctors laughed at him and set him up?

As Brett proudly stood up, slicking back his gelled hair, she heard Johnny mutter, 'good luck mate, you're gonna need it.' Brett's footsteps echoed loudly on the polished floorboards as he walked up to the stage, tripped slightly on the first step, managed to ignore the titters from behind him and held his hand out to Dr Fotheringhill, who remained seated. Melissa cringed - this was as painful as it got. Dick was smiling. He must be telling Pat what high hopes he had for his newest recruit, his bright young graduate, she thought. What a nerve - Brett had no experience and a poor degree in sociology. This was the only company that had agreed to take him on, and that was only because they were desperate for someone to take the graveyard patch that Brett had unwittingly inherited.

Melissa's eyebrows shot up - was that Dr. Fotheringhill cracking his knuckles before he rose, albeit slightly, to give Brett a cursory handshake? She leaned towards Sam and whispered, 'he looks like he's spoiling for a fight.' Sam nodded. No doubt about that. Dr. Fotheringhill had the advantage of a superior education and over thirty years experience in psychiatry compared to twenty-two year old Brett, who had none. Everyone held their breath.

'Ah, hello there - good morning Doctor, er....' Brett squinted at Dr. Fotheringhill's name badge. He hadn't wanted to wear his glasses today and had forgotten his contacts. 'Featherdill...'

The doctor glared at him. 'Fotheringhill,' he boomed.

'Yes. Fotheringhill, ha, ha! Sorry about that. Well, hello - I'm Brett Morgan and I'm here in the hospital today…'

'What a coincidence,' said Dr Fotheringhill dryly. 'So am I.'

Melissa was aware that some people were smothering snorts of laughter. Oh poor, Brett. She glanced over at the senior managers, dismayed to see that Dick's smile was slipping, Pat's had slipped and James had his hand over his face.

'So, here we are,' Brett said with a beaming grin.

'Yes.'

Brett cleared his throat. 'Now, can I ask you what you use for depressive episodes, doctor?' he continued in an optimistic voice.

'I don't have depression,' Fotheringhill said.

'Ha, ha! No, of course not. No, I meant for your depressed patients, doctor, d'you know what I mean, yeah? You do get depressed patients don't you?'

Dr Fotheringhill stared at him.

'Well I'd be fucking depressed if he was my doctor, wouldn't you?' Sam whispered to Melissa. Everyone on their row heard her and tried not to laugh. Dick glared at them from across the room.

Brett tried again. 'Well, perhaps I could ask if you have ever tried Happylux, doctor?' he asked, concentrating on opening up his glossy sales brochure to the first page - one of twenty.

'You can ask.' The doctor yawned, not bothering to look up from his scribbling.

'Well, have you then?'

'Once or twice.'

'Oh cool.'

To Melissa the few seconds of silence that followed seemed to last for all eternity while Brett dropped his brochure, retrieved it, rifled through it, looked up to smile then rifled through it some more.

Everyone waited. Someone coughed. Another sighed heavily. At last Brett found the page he wanted. 'Aha!' he cried triumphantly, inching his chair closer to the desk. Pointing to one of several graphs, he inflected a great deal of enthusiasm into his voice. 'If you take a look at this really interesting and new graph here…Er - doctor, if you could look at this please for a minute.' Brett stared at the top of the doctor's bent head. 'This graph, doctor? It's really great…..'

'Ask him an open question for pity's sake,' Melissa hissed.

Everyone waited. Then Brett, his extensive twelve week training course seemingly having deserted him, decided to flap his brochure in the doctor's face. 'Hello!' he called. 'Over here, ha, ha! '

Melissa gripped her chair. Someone had to do something. Finally she managed to catch Dick's eye and a rare exchange of understanding passed between them.

Dick stood up. 'Okay, thank you Brett. I think everyone here will understand how difficult it is going on first, particularly with the video camera on. Well done, Brett. Thank you.'

'But…' Brett began to protest. 'But I haven't start…'

Melissa began the clapping before standing up decisively. Okay, Fotheringhill, she thought, fixing him with a stare a stuffed owl would ave been proud of. You've got me now. Come on -make my day.

Chapter 2

Relief enveloped Sam in it's warm blanket. She was safe, she had survived. It was lunchtime and oh joy, they had a whole hour to themselves. 'I'm a survivor, I'm a survivor,' she sang, spearing a cherry tomato from Melissa's plate while bouncing up and down in her seat.

'Oh belt up, Sam,' Melissa said. 'You scraped through, okay? S-C-R-A-P-E-D!'

'I know, but the worst is over. I'm so happy. I thought I was going to wet myself when I saw I'd got that bastard, Fotheringhill. Still, at least I didn't say what Johnny said.'

'Oh, please,' Melissa warned her.

'Didn't you think it was funny when Johnny said sexual dysfunction wasn't a side effect unless you counted a dry mouth?'

'At the time. Oh look, here comes the stick insect. Bernie! How are you? You look so, like …..' She searched for the right word. 'Thin.'

Sam moved closer to the window to let Bernie take a seat. Bernie was the most successful sales rep in the company by a long, long way and had been the only one that morning to completely flummox Dr Fotheringhill.

'Oooh, thank you,' Bernie said. 'I've just done fifteen minutes in the gym - you should try it, Melissa.' And then with a Tony Blair style grin to the waitress, she said, 'I only want a bowl of soup,' adding with a poignant look at Sam's chest, 'I wouldn't want to put on any weight, at all.'

Sam's smile faded a little. What was it about Bernie that always made you feel a bit worse about yourself? Weren't Irish people supposed to be charming? And if so then something had gone tragically wrong with

Bernie. Some kind of birth defect, she decided. 'Where's Veronica, Bernie?' she asked.

Bernie shrugged.

'Talking about sex, though…' Melissa said.

Sam shot her a look. 'Were we?'

'Whatever. Anyway, you'll never guess what?'

Sam's smile faded completely. Trapped halfway through lunch, escape wasn't possible and Melissa's favourite subject was coming up. Melissa looked excited. Damn, she was never going to get to the designer outlet down the road now. There it was, just five tantalising minutes away - Jaeger, Monsoon, Marks and Spencers……….

'I've met someone.' Melissa said gleefully, looking from one girl to the other for a reaction.

'Oh that's great, Melissa,' said Bernie, brightly. 'Because you've been trying to get someone for ages now haven't you?' She took a slurp of soup before continuing. 'I'm the complete opposite myself. I don't mean to go on and all, but you know I've never had so much male attention since I joined this industry. I can't handle it to be honest with you.'

Sam and Melissa exchanged a meaningful glance.

'And since I got that four wheel drive - the looks I get!' She squealed.

'What looks?' Melissa snapped.

'From men.' Bernie screamed. 'Men, I tell you. I'm not at all used to it, being a good Irish Catholic girl. I don't know what it is about me, honest to God I don't,' she said, adjusting her thigh high mini skirt.

'Hellooooo!' Melissa waved a napkin in Bernie's face. 'Can I just tell you now about this person I've met, please?' She leaned towards Bernie and Sam in a conspiratorial manner. 'He's a doctor,' she said in an excited whisper. 'I met him a week ago and he's one of my customers?'

'Oh my God, Melissa - isn't that against the rules?' Sam asked. Everyone knew that reps weren't supposed to have relationships with their customers, didn't they? Melissa was so naughty.

'Shocked are you?' Melissa said, looking at Sam's outraged face. 'Ha, ha! He's as fit as a butcher's whippet though. And... like, we've had action.'

Sam stared at her.

'He likes it from behind,' Melissa went on with a giggle.

'Do I need to know this, Melissa?'

'Course you do,' Bernie said. 'Don't be such a prude, Sam. You carry on Mel, why don't you?'

'There's more actually,' Melissa said.

Sam sighed. Why did Melissa insist on telling everyone every intimate detail of her love life? Didn't she realise how embarrassing it was? She gazed out of the window at a leaf dancing in the early spring breeze across the car park, imagining herself speeding along the dual carriageway with the sunroof down towards the outlet stores. It was her lunch break, and the need to spend some money was overpowering. But there was no stopping Melissa when she was like this.

Still, at least she wasn't trapped on a plane with her for three hours like the last time when Melissa had insisted on relating an exhaustive account of her affair with the AA man who had towed her home one night. She still had graphic nightmares of Melissa's face being repeatedly rammed against the shower cubicle glass. Mel said she thought her nose was going to be broken mid shag.

Reluctantly Sam's eyes met Melissa's. 'Is this going to be a blow by blow description?' she asked her, trying not to snigger at her own joke.

'Yes,' said Melissa. ' You'll never guess what either?' She paused for a moment, savouring the anticipation. 'He's only a pervert, isn't he?'

'A pervert?' Bernie screeched, deliberately causing several people to swivel round and stare at her.

Sam knew she'd regret this, but it was near impossible to leave the word, 'pervert' hanging in the air like that with no further explanation. 'How do you know?' she asked.

'Well,' Melissa leaned forwards conspiratorially. 'For one thing I went in to see him on Monday and he, like, asked me to have it off with him on his desk but to leave the door open to his secretary's office?'

'No way! Fecking Nora,' Bernie said.

'Why?' Sam asked.

'Well, why do you think? So, he's got the thrill of someone, like, catching us *at it,*' Melissa giggled. 'Imagine!'

Sam tried not to. 'I think I'll go and get the coffees.'

'Sit down, Sam. I haven't finished yet,' Melissa said, grabbing Sam's arm, forcing her to sit back down. 'Anyway, the other thing is that he only makes dirty phone calls, doesn't he?'

'Oh?'

'Yes. Bad ones. They're all about spanking and....'

'Melissa, really sorry. I have to go and get some fresh air. I'll see you later, okay?'

'Okay then, copulater,' Melissa said, moving closer to Bernie.

As Sam left she could hear Melissa's excited voice, 'honestly Bern, it was as big as a frigging rolling pin, I'm not joking.'

Sam picked up speed, weaving her way through the crowded dining room. With the meal over, most of the reps were now bored and beginning to circulate. A chubby, blond girl in a tight, beige suit blocked Sam's way. She was jumping up and down, shouting in a strong Leeds accent, 'I was shaking. Oh my God, it was soooo funny. I was like that.'

To the appreciation of her audience she mimicked something akin to the expression of a shell-shocked retarded chicken, and as Sam dodged what could have been a nasty poke in the ribs from the over-animated girl, she suddenly found herself smack in front of Johnny.

'Not leaving us so soon, Samantha, surely?' he said in a deliberately lascivious voice.

'Well...'

'Come and sit next to me, Sam. We're having a bet. Me and Brett say a tenner Mike gets it, and Mike's put ten on Melissa.'

'What, for Dick's job?' she asked, flicking a sly glance at her watch as she perched on the edge of his seat. 'Frankly, I'm not sure I care which one of them gets it, I'm just so bloody, deliriously ecstatic that he's going.

'What about Bernie?' said Mike, the daddy of the group, with a growl of displeasure. 'After all, she's top rep for all of five bloody minutes.'

'Bernie? Oh my God, you're joking me!' Sam felt her stomach lurch. 'But, but she's only been with the company for six months, same as me.'

'Bloody ridiculous,' Mike agreed. 'But there's talk all the same.'

'Got to watch her,' said Johnny. 'Miss Micro-Mini Networker.'

'Surely not. I mean it's not that she isn't a nice person or anything, it's just that it has to be Melissa really. Sorry, Mike,' she added, catching Mike's expression. There was something about Mike, wasn't there? Some reason he was still a rep. Some sort of scandal, she wasn't quite sure.

Mike scowled.

'Anyone's better than Limp Dick anyway,' Sam added, floundering.

'Listen Sam - I taught that arse licking bastard everything he knows,' said Mike.

Sam nodded. It was difficult to know what to say.

'It'll be Mike, d'you know what I mean, yeah?' Brett chipped in. 'He knows what he's doing, he's been a manager before. Well, Mike or Melissa, maybe. One or the other, d'you know what I mean?'

'Mike or Melissa what?' came a sharp voice. Bernie, appearing out of nowhere, plonked herself onto Johnny's lap. Wriggling and shuffling, she fiddled with her mini skirt. 'Well? Come on! Mike or Melissa what?'

Johnny sighed. 'For Dick's job. Jesus, you weigh a ton.'

'I do not. In fact, some people keep saying I'm too thin.' Her eyes flicked to Sam.

'Ah, they're just jealous,' Johnny said.

'Yes I know,' Bernie grinned. 'Anyway, what about Veronica?'

All eyes shot to Bernie. 'What?'

'Veronica,' Bernie repeated with the brightest of smiles. 'She's your man if you ask me.'

Into the stunned silence, Brett said, 'Where is Veronica, anyway?'

'Wouldn't you like to know?' Bernie said, jumping off Johnny's knee before giving him a playful slap on the thigh.

Half an hour later, the question of Veronica plagued Sam as she zoomed back from her mini shopping spree. That, and her finances. For example, it was just possible that she didn't really need the lime green and diamante sandals she'd just bought, but she could tell Simon, when he checked the statements, that he shouldn't worry because if she had spent the same amount on therapy, which she needed for this job, it would have cost an awful lot more. So she had *saved* money, in fact. Yes, and they would go with any number of outfits that she had in her wardrobe and another thing - they would last forever. Never would they go out of date, so they were an investment too. Excellent - case for the defence sorted.

But now the question of Veronica popped into her head again. Veronica always disappeared at these things. Every training session, every conference - where did she go? Perhaps she doesn't want to associate with us commoners, she thought, or maybe she's chain smoking behind a hedge somewhere? But Veronica as their next manager? That was something she had never considered. Better than Dick, yes. But even so, there was something so distant about her, so, so… She searched for a word to describe Veronica - aloof. Yes, that was it: it was impossible to imagine Veronica rooting for her. In fact it was impossible to imagine Veronica rooting for anyone - even a tiny fluffy white kitten with one eye, a limp and a chest infection.

Still deep in thought, Sam quickly locked her car and raced towards the hotel entrance. Five minutes to go before Pat Hardcastle's post prandial rant - the hardest possible time of day to keep awake. She planned it deliberately Sam was sure. But as she sprinted across the car park a car horn suddenly blasted her out of the way, the flash of metal blinding her as it sent her sprawling towards the safety of the hotel steps. 'Bloody idiot,' she shouted after what she now noticed was an Aston Martin. The elegant car swung into it's space, followed by the appearance of a tall, raven haired man easing himself out of the driver's seat. Languidly he removed his sunglasses to get a better look at her. Instantly the blood rushed to her face. Shit! It was only James Harris, their new marketing manager.

'You nearly ran over me. Sorry,' she said.

'That's okay, no problem,' said James, with eyes that swept up and down her body.

Smiling weakly, Sam turned tail and hurried into the hotel. As it was, she only just made it to the conference hall in time for Pat Hardcastle's speech. Pat, their sales and marketing director, was second in rank only to the MD. Creeping in at the back she found herself sitting next to Johnny.

'Hardass is on the warpath,' Johnny whispered, his breath hot on her ear. 'We could be here some time.'

'Oh God, I should have brought a hot water bottle and a cup of Horlicks.'

'A sleeping bag and a good book.'

'Some comfy slippers and a dressing gown,' Sam giggled.

'Shhhh!' The man in the 'Make it Happen' T-shirt turned round to glare at them.

At that point the lights dimmed and Pat appeared on stage. Gripping the sides of the lectern she pursed her lips tightly. For several seconds she said nothing, allowing the atmosphere of dread to build. And build it did. Worse, everyone knew that the more angry Pat was, the stronger her accent, which made certain people snigger uncontrollably. Pat pronounced 'York' as 'Yarke' and 'home' as 'herme.'

'The anticipation's killing me,' Johnny said dryly.

Eventually Pat spoke, almost spitting out the words. 'This morning,' she said, 'was a shambles. An absolute shambles.' She looked slowly around the room at the people she had called 'la crème de la crème of the industry' just a few months ago when Happylux had been launched. 'You're all sat there,' she said, 'wondering why your sales aren't better than they are. Well let me spell it out for you: Three Key Messages!' She waited a moment for the importance of that to sink in while the reps all looked at the floor. 'Where were they this morning? Why do you think we bother with a marketing department if you're going to ignore our marketing executives?'

'Good question,' Johnny whispered to Sam.

Sam giggled. 'Look at Annabel and Hector,' she said to Johnny, ignoring another glare from 'Make it Happen' man in front.

Annabel and Hector from the marketing department, who were sitting behind Pat on stage, did nothing to hide their sanctimonious expressions. Still visibly smarting from the realisation that the reps were not using their glossy brochures, had seemingly never even opened them in fact, they were nodding in agreement with Pat.

'That Annabel looks like she hasn't had a shag in about six years,' Johnny said to Sam, who snorted with laughter.

'Shhh!' the man in front said again.

'Right,' Pat shouted. 'Right, let's get on with it this afternoon. And this time remember the three key messages. Remember the right message to the right customer the right number of times gets the business in.' Moving out from behind the lectern she stood with her hands on her hips and shouted. 'Who wants to be a top representative? Who is prepared to go that extra mile? I want to hear your commitment and your enthusiasm. So come on - who wants to be a top representative?'

There was a shifty embarrassed mumbling from the audience. 'I do,' said a couple of managers.

'Sorry? I'm afraid I can't hear you. I said, who wants to be a top representative?'

'I do,' the collective response a little louder now.

'He's behind you!' Johnny shouted.

Pat peered into the dimness of the audience. Who the hell was that taking the Micky?

'Again!' she insisted.

'I do,' the reps yelled.

'Good.' Pat nodded. 'Now get off to work and show those doctors what you can really do. Show them that Topham Pharmaceuticals is the best company and Happylux is the best anti-depressant. Make it Happen!'

'Is that it?' Sam asked Johnny, incredulously. 'Haven't we been short changed? Shouldn't we have had another two hours of her?'

Johnny, whose thoughts had drifted off some time ago, shrugged and joined in the polite clapping which followed Pat's speech before the reps could begin to file out.

'Only five hours to go,' Sam muttered as they shuffled along, waiting for the baseball caps they were to collect at the door. The caps were green and emblazoned with the words, 'Make it Happen.' Some of the reps dutifully put them on as they made their way to the syndicate rooms for more role play. Many would wear them for the whole day, some turning up to future meetings in them, screeching into the car park in their hot hatchbacks dressed in a suit with 'Make it Happen' hats perched back to front on top of their heads.

Dick kept his team waiting. After throwing paper darts at each other and generally messing around for a while, they decided that perhaps they should get on with the work they had been set without him.

'Where is he, anyway?' Sam asked.

'There'll be an issue. Someone's in trouble,' said Melissa.

'He's probably just sucking up to Hardass as usual,' Johnny said, putting his feet up on the table. 'Come on Brett, me lad, buck up - get the video on for us, mate.'

A couple of minutes later they began to watch the video they had had made of them that morning, starting with Brett. They were supposed to be analysing their performances and improving their technique by sharing ideas and using constructive criticism.

'God, you were fucking crap there, mate,' Johnny was saying as Dick walked in. They all turned to look. Dick's face was puce. A large vein had risen in the shape of a fork to the right of one malevolent eye.

Immediately Sam's stomach screwed itself up into a hard knot. Oh no, what now? It couldn't be her this time, surely? But for once, his eyes had not gone straight to her, but to Bernie O'Reilly, who on hearing the click of the door, had jumped to her feet and rushed to the flipchart.

'Ah Dick, we were just saying we have loads of work to do.' She beamed at him, displaying a row of tiny, sharp teeth.

'Sit down. Yes, you most certainly do,' Dick snapped, marching up to the flipchart and flicking the sheet that was now full of doodles over in an aggressive manner, so aggressive he knocked the stand over and ripped the paper. Somebody sniggered. Whirling round, Dick's black eyes immediately shot to Sam.

Jesus, Saddam Hussein's got nothing on him, she thought. Her heart began to pound faster and faster until she thought it might explode. Everyone was looking at her, thanking God she supposed, that it wasn't them he was going to humiliate.

'I'm going to be working with all of you *intensively* starting from tomorrow, after this morning's frankly shit performance,' he said. No one spoke as he allowed the unhappy atmosphere to deepen further. Dick's glare remained on Sam. Then in a much quieter, more patient voice, as if he had to use every fibre of self control he possessed, he addressed her personally. 'Now, what are you doing tomorrow, Samantha?' Carefully, as if it were a prized possession, he retrieved a glossy black diary from his briefcase, which to date, had been virtually unsullied by appointments with his team.

Tomorrow? Tomorrow? Sam's face burned crimson. Sheepishly

she opened her own diary and looked at the words, 'hairdressers 10am, lunch with Carol 1pm.' 'I'm in Derby tomorrow,' she said truthfully.

'Excellent. Well in that case I will meet you at Junction 25 off the M1 motorway at eight. I trust you have plenty of good quality calls organised?' Dick stared her down.

'Yes,' she said in a small voice, praying he wouldn't ask for the details.

But Dick was far too intent on his own diary, methodically crossing out the words, 'golf club,' and inserting the words, 'Sam, 8am, J.25,' instead.

'Now, Veronica,' he snapped. 'Friday!'

Sam looked at Veronica. It was a wonder how the woman stayed so unruffled. Would anything ever fluster her? And what about Melissa? Melissa was doing her nails for God's sake, albeit discreetly, under the table. Bernie was smiling happily, no dementedly, Sam decided, probably awaiting the month's sales results which would undoubtedly show herself still at the top.

And then there were the lads - useless Brett, yet still the apple of Dick's eye, plodding Mike and finally Johnny, the thinking woman's bit of rough. Johnny was swinging back on his chair with a dreamy look on his face, his soft, hazel eyes half closed. Sam smiled involuntarily, letting her thoughts wander. Actually, he was quite sexy. He had the look of a naughty schoolboy, forever rebelling and shooting lascivious looks at the women, yet at the same time appearing utterly in control of everything, and he most definitely had the body of a fully grown man. Blimey, he's miles away, she thought - look at him, and with Dick on the rampage too.

'Johnny, what do you think?' Dick snapped.

Johnny's eyes flashed open. 'Yeah, totally agree with you mate.'

Dick stared angrily at him. 'I said, and I repeat - is Monday morning all right for you?'

'Yeah, cool, mate,' Johnny said.

'Jammy sod,' Sam muttered under her breath. Why did it have to be her that got Dick tomorrow? How could she possibly sort out any appointments before then when she was stuck here all day? Not to mention the fact that she had two early mornings on the trot now. Oh no, it was going to be a total disaster, wasn't it? Another one.

Chapter 3

Veronica pushed her Gucci sunglasses up onto the top of her head and dialled James on his mobile. Gosh, it had been nothing short of a minor miracle that Sam hadn't seen them together yesterday. It was early afternoon and she was lunching alone in a busy, upmarket café in central Leeds, surrounded by other people with sunglasses on top of their heads.

'Hello, Bunny Bumpkins, it's me,' she said to him in a little girl voice, pouting slightly even though he couldn't see her.

As soon as he spoke, that familiar thrill shot through her. His was the voice of an upper class English pilot - irritated, slightly bored even, at having to speak to the passengers. 'Yah,' he drawled.

'Have you missed me, Bunny?'

'Of course.'

'What are you doing?'

'I'm in a meeting.'

'A lunchy type of meeting?'

'Yah.' She imagined him looking at his watch, calculating whether he had time for another pint or not.

'Bunny - are you sure we weren't seen yesterday? I mean, Sam saw you in the car park but I don't know if she saw me. Have you heard anything since, any rumours or anything?' It was absolutely unthinkable that anyone should have seen them together. How could she possibly explain it?

'No. Although actually, hang on a sec.' She could hear him moving around, then the sound of traffic as he stepped outside. She held her breath. 'Squishy, hi! Sorry darling - I'm with the MD. Actually,

Squishy, I did hear an amazing snippet about one of your colleagues. Is it Melissa? Yah, Melissa. Pat told me yesterday she'd had to have a word with Dick after her speech yesterday because some woman had rung Head Office and made a complaint about her, wanting to speak with Dick about the matter.'

'Oh?' Veronica wasn't one for gossip, but with things the way they were just now, well, as her father always said - information was power, and James was usually a good source. James had fingers in all sorts of pies. James was just…..well, James was just fab and brill.

'It's incredibly funny, Squish. Because this woman couldn't get through to Dick, she had to leave a message. The receptionist, Belinda, you know Belinda, don't you? Well, Bel writes it down and hands it to Pat. We've all read it. It says, 'please would someone tell Melissa Crow to stop shagging my husband?'

'Oh golly, how awful! Who was this woman?'

'She wouldn't leave her name.'

'Gosh, no wonder Dick was in such a bad mood yesterday - if I was him I would've had an absolute blue fit.'

'Was he? He was in amazingly good form at lunch time - pretty good laugh as usual. He's such a card, isn't he? No, I think the problem is if Melissa isn't suitable to take Dick's place as manager then who is? Look, Squishy - simply got to dash, okay? Love you….'

'James, I need to know more. What do you mean, 'Melissa take his place?' Won't there even be an interview for this job?'

'Squish, I don't know any more. I'll find out, okay?'

Veronica stared at the phone after he had clicked it off, positive that at that precise moment James was dashing back into the pub for one last pint. He was such a pet, though, and how incredibly amazing that he should come back into her life like this. He and her older brother had been at private school together. The first time Rupert had brought James home for a weekend, fifteen year old Veronica discovered that she did, despite the rumours, have hormones just like everyone else. One moment her world was Lacrosse and Gymkhanas, the next it was James gazing at her through the tennis nets with an intensity impossible to misinterpret. Something about him - maybe the twitch of his sensual lips as he watched her, or the way his dark, secretive eyes constantly sought her out - had stirred a desire in her so strong it had woken her in the early hours. She couldn't sleep. She had to have him.

In the end, Daddy had taken him aside and had words about it. Veronica was shipped off back to boarding school, written off as just another skinny teenager with a bad case of infatuation, a subject which provided endless amusement for her parents and their friends at dinner parties. But oh how much she had adored him. Her heart picked up a beat remembering how she had lain awake at night yearning for him, imagining his muscular body on top of hers, the photograph of him playing polo placed firmly under her pillow until, years later, it finally fell apart.

Yet, incredibly, here he was back in her life. It was fate, had to be. He must be here to help her get out of this pitiful sales job and up to where she belonged. It had been such a shock to her, this hard world of commerce, when as a high achieving young graduate and after a stint in NHS management, she had joined the multi-billion dollar pharmaceutical industry only to find herself having to grovel every day to customers.

She toyed with her lunch - a few lettuce leaves and a radish 'drizzled with Chef's special dressing' - and then lit a cigarette.

'You're not eating much, love,' the waitress said in an exasperated voice. The restaurant was filling up.

'I can't or I'll bloat,' Veronica snapped, her irritation rising once more from this morning's minor humiliations.

Last November she'd had to queue up early in the morning in the dark and the rain with dozens of other reps, just to make the one annual appointment possible with a group of doctors who were high on her list of 'must sees.' Unfortunately they were high up on every one else's list too, and each rep was given just the one appointment for the following year if they queued up for it on that particular day. By eight-thirty in the morning all the appointments would be gone.

So, when her hard won seven-thirty a.m appointment came around for all four doctors in the practice that morning, she'd hauled herself out of bed at five, and driven up to North Yorkshire with grim determination. She would see these doctors and she would get their business. She would switch them from whatever anti-depressant they were currently using to Happylux. This was her chance. All the way up in the car she had told herself this. It would so be worth it, and after yesterday's news it could be sooner rather than later.

But as she swung her BMW into the GP's car park, another rep suddenly screeched up alongside her, parking diagonally across two spaces in a nasty looking Vectra. Veronica looked across at the woman driver - a rep, she decided, no doubt about it - designer sunglasses, full make up and a desperate look on her face. Yep, a rep. And if so, then what the blazes was she doing arriving on the same day as her? No way would the woman have got an appointment that coincided with hers. The system here was strict - just one rep per week. They were the rules for goodness sake.

Veronica quickly jumped out of her BMW, not bothering to check her pre-call objectives on her laptop, and shot round to the car boot for her briefcase. But not quickly enough. The other rep, a chubby middle-aged woman in a bright red suit, leapt out of her Vectra already equipped with hers, and raced up the steps in front of Veronica, fat knees pumping as she ran, panting and gasping, determined to get there first.

I'm going to lose my appointment, Veronica realised with a surge of panic. I will not run, I will not run. I simply will not stoop to that level. With an outward calm an Oscar winning actress would have been proud of, she walked in after the red-suited woman and presented her business card to the receptionist at the desk, who was still giggling having witnessed the scene.

'Ah, are you the rep with the appointment?' she asked, gazing up at the tall, expensive looking blond in front of her.

'Business Executive, actually,' Veronica said, pointing to her card details with a long, manicured fingernail.

'The rep then.'

'Mmmm.'

'Right, well as I've just told the other lady, I'm afraid that two of the doctors are off sick, one's had to attend an emergency, and the one who's left is already run off his feet, so I'm afraid there's no one for you to see this morning. All right?'

Veronica stared at the woman.

'I can make you one for early next year as a special favour, luv,' the receptionist said as she opened the diary. 'You know, since you turned up and everything. You'll need to get here early though, you've only to be a few minutes late and a rep turning up on spec can go in instead. So - how about, let me see, seven-thirty in the morning on the second Tuesday in January next year?'

'Lovely,' Veronica said with an unnaturally bright smile. 'Next January you say? Well, I so should be free. How very kind. And perhaps if I camp out all night?'

'Not at all,' the receptionist said, looking up from the diary with an equally bright smile. But Veronica had gone, already screeching out of the car park amid a cloud of exhaust fumes.

She was gripping the steering wheel, her thin lips bloodless, a cigarette clenched between her middle two fingers. A quick glance at the clock on the dashboard told her it was just a quarter to eight. 'Bloody, bloody hell,' she muttered. There wasn't another surgery for miles around - that was the only one in this small market town - all she could do was bomb back to North Leeds, although most of the doctors were by appointment only. Her sole chance of seeing anyone at all was Dr. Prakash - the only doctor in town who saw all the reps and all the patients who asked him to - a victim, it could be said, of his own niceness.

Dr. Prakash had a surgery that was sandwiched between a fish and chip shop and a launderette in a part of Leeds well known for drug pushers and prostitutes, and already there was a queue of patients stretching all the way down the road. Some had brought packed lunches. Dr Prakash would see them all.

By the time he saw Veronica she had been waiting for four hours, enduring the last hour in his small, hot waiting room squashed up against some seriously under washed people. One elderly man had spent half an hour coughing up thick, green phlegm into a handkerchief, a woman had changed her baby's full, particularly rancid nappy on the floor in front of everyone, and the toothless person jammed up tightly next to her had methodically worked their way through an entire family sized bag of toffees.

'Ah - lovely to see you, Amanda, Julie, er - Veronica. Yes, Veronica,' Dr Prakash said as he welcomed her into his chaotic surgery, warmly clasping her hands in his. 'And how are you? I was only thinking about you yesterday, and wondering how your beta-blocker was going?'

'I sell the anti-depressant, Dr Prakash - Happylux.'

'Ah, very, very good. Now, would you like a cup of tea?'

Veronica thought about the hygiene aspect and declined. Besides customers always put incredibly revolting milk in. 'Thank you, no. I have to get off to the hospital soon. I just popped in to see if you had tried anyone on Happylux yet.' She smiled - he really was such a sweet man.

Dr Prakash thought for a moment 'Happylux, you say? Is this a joke name?'

'No. Do you remember last time we talked about the reduced side effects with this one compared to the others?'

'I think this is a joke name.' Dr Prakash waggled his finger at her as if she had tried to catch him out. 'Ha, ha! You know, Victoria, you look a lot like someone I have seen - someone very famous. Hmmmmm.'

'Really? How amazing. Look, could I just perhaps show....'

They were suddenly interrupted by Dr Prakash's secretary, who popped her head round the door. 'Dr Prakash - you have another two patients to see and you have four reps. Do you want me to tell the reps to go?'

'No, no. I will see them all,' he said. 'Now, Victoria, who is it that I am thinking of? Help me out here. Who? Who?' He closed his eyes, stroking his chin thoughtfully.

'Look, I so appreciate how busy you are, doctor. Perhaps if I just leave you this information booklet this time? As you can see, the three main points are....'

'Aha! Yes! I've got it - you look like Fergie! The Duchess of York.'

Veronica froze. 'What?'

'Exactly like her, yes you do.' He clapped his hands together delightedly. 'That's it, you could be twins.'

'I so don't think so, Dr Prakash. Here, have this leaflet.'

Veronica fled, unable to control her rage.

Another glance at the clock on the dashboard - she'd been lucky, the car had still been where she left it - told her it was twelve-thirty. She still had time to see if the Consultant for Care of the Elderly at the local hospital was available for a chat. He had flirted with her quite unashamedly the last time she'd seen him - it was possible he would give her five minutes if she showed up on spec. She put her foot down. A couple of minutes later she was eyeball to eyeball with his receptionist. 'And you are?' the woman asked coldly.

Veronica brought herself up to her full height and presented her business card. 'Veronica Ball - Business Executive.'

'You'll have to wait until the end of clinic,' the receptionist snapped, refusing to take the card or even to look at it. 'Okay?'

'Okay, but would you mind just asking the doctor now if he is actually going to have time to see me, so I know whether or not to wait? I mean, the clinic is already terribly over run, and if he's rushing off at the end, I might have waited for nothing.'

'Oh, I'm far too busy for all of this.' The receptionist adopted a flustered and pre-occupied appearance, suddenly picking up bundles of files and re-arranging them. 'Just take a seat and we'll see,' she said, already peering past Veronica to the person behind her.

Veronica hesitated.

'Okay?' the receptionist said in a sing-song voice that defied argument.

'Thank you so much.' Veronica looked around the waiting area, shuddering with distaste. The clinic was packed wall to wall with elderly people in wheel chairs or on trolleys. Some were calling out, not sure where they were, others clutched catheter bags or x-rays. Many were in nightdresses, some stained, or anonymous white theatre gowns. One poor lady had been wheeled in on her bed and left there - a tiny, withered hand tried to grab at nurses as they scurried past.

Feeling suddenly conspicuous in her pinstripe suit and patent stilettos, Veronica found a plastic chair at the back of the room that didn't look too dirty, snatched up an ancient copy of 'Hello' magazine and prepared for a long wait. An hour and a half later, she suddenly became aware of an eerie quietness. She put her magazine down, realising with a start that she was alone. She looked around in panic - oh bloody hell, the clinic was empty. Damn, that article about J-Lo's beauty routine had been simply too involving. What now? The last patient had gone in some time ago but the question was - did they come out?

Approaching the reception desk again, Veronica noticed the frosty receptionist in the back room and tried to get her attention with a polite wave, but Frosty turned her back and continued chatting. Thankfully another marginally friendlier looking woman appeared clutching a bundle of files.

Veronica twitched her lips up into a smile as best she could. 'Is Dr. Wright still here, please? Only I've been waiting for him for hours.'

'Sorry, luv, he's gone. What did you want him for?'

'I'm a business executive.'

'Oh, a rep. Well you should've said. I thought you were one of the patients sat there.'

Veronica opened and closed her mouth but no sound came out. One of the patients? Was the stupid woman blind?

'Do you want me to see if his secretary will see you?' the woman asked.

'His *secretary*? Why?' Veronica spluttered.

'I can't promise, mind you - you might need an appointment.'

'Oh this is ridiculous,' Veronica snapped. 'I am so not making an appointment just to see a secretary.'

So now, safely in the designer café, she picked at her lettuce and ruminated on how much longer she would have to humiliate herself daily by accepting the crumbs these people threw at her - stupid people who couldn't even speak their own language properly half the time: 'Sat there,'she snorted to herself. 'I was sat, we was stood.' Didn't they do grammar at school? Had they even been? For goodness sake, how much longer would she have to ingratiate herself with them?

She lit another cigarette and inhaled deeply. And more to the point, she thought, what was she going to do about her little problem at home? Because once she got Dick's job, and make no mistake she would, then her husband, Greg, would have to be swapped for something else.

Chapter 4

The following Tuesday morning found Sam bombing down the motorway in the outside lane. Late again. That manicurist would kill her. She flashed a stupid person out of the way. Christ, why were thick people allowed to drive cars? It was so bloody irritating. She flashed them again. The person in front stuck a finger up, refusing to move over. Plus - they quite clearly had a mobile phone clamped to their ear. 'Moron,' she muttered, wondering what she could do to prevent the full scale fury that was threatening to engulf her. Distraction was required urgently. Hmm, maybe she could ring Melissa on her car phone - it was still only quarter to nine and Mel wasn't picking Dick up until nine-thirty.

Poor Melissa was worried. She'd been told that there had been a complaint made about her but she didn't know what it was. Dick was going to talk to her about it today. Lucky old Mel, Sam thought with a wry smile as she tapped in Melissa's number.

'Mel, it's me,' she shouted to make herself heard above the noise of the road. 'Look, before you pick Limp Dick up, I just thought I'd give you a quick ring to say, don't worry about that ponsy, fat bastard....'

'Sam!' Melissa screamed. 'Stop! Er, hi! Er, he's in the car with me.'

There was a second or two of silence while all three absorbed the impact of what Sam had just said over the car phone system loud and clear.

'Are you still there, Samantha?' came Dick's overly polite voice. 'Hello?'

'Er, hello Dick. Look, Melissa - don't worry about that awful doctor, okay? Sorry about my language, Dick - just trying to give Melissa some moral support, that's all. Bye.' She pressed the 'end' button with trembling fingers, suddenly sweaty and slightly dizzy. Oh Jesus, what had she said? Had he bought her explanation? No, surely even he wasn't that dense. She switched the phone off altogether and pulled into the inside lane, deep in thought.

Melissa had told her she wasn't picking him up until nine-thirty, that she was meeting his train for pity's sake. Talk about being well and truly shafted. It wasn't as if she wasn't in enough trouble with him as it was after last Thursday, the day after the training day from hell. Because she'd had no appointments booked, he'd followed her around all day from eight-thirty in the morning to five in the afternoon like Dr Death holding a scythe over her head. She had lurched from rejection to rejection, desperately trying to get to see a doctor. Any doctor. In the end they had seen just one locum GP in the entire day, someone she had never laid eyes on before, and an out and out misogynist if ever she'd met one.

'I know all about Happylux,' the doctor said, casting a smug glance Dick's way. 'What else have you got?'

' Er, nothing. So…'

'Actually I think you've got a damn cheek bringing out yet another anti-depressant. Do you know how many there are on the market?'

'Erm, well, about seven new ones and….'

'Dozens. And there was nothing wrong with the old ones. So, what good reason do you have for bringing out yet another and wasting our time?'

'Well Happylux is better on side effects…'

'None of my patients get side effects.'

'But, surely…..'

'So thanks for coming then,' he said, standing up.

'But, Happylux…'

'As I said, I know all about it. I'm a busy man. Good -bye.'

He shook Dick's hand and then shunted them to the door, with Sam just managing to chuck a couple of Happylux pens at him before it closed firmly in her face.

She and Dick walked silently out of the surgery, down the path to the car park. She knew he wouldn't make it any easier for her And she wasn't disappointed.

'So,' Dick said, swivelling round to face her the second they were in her car, 'what could you have done differently there, do you think, Samantha?'

Sam sighed, wishing with every fibre of her being that she didn't have to look at him close up like this. His huge bulk and coffee breath had her trapped in her seat. 'I could have asked him a question,' she said in a small voice.

'And?'

Sam racked her brains. Eventually she said, 'I should have used the sales brochure.'

'And?'

Dick's black eyes bore into hers. A wave of exhaustion hit her head on. She fought with heavy eyelids, battled with a yawn. And then she remembered, 'Oh yes, the key messages.'

'Quite. The key messages, Samantha. At every call. It is your job to see at least ten customers a day, and you must repeat the key messages to each and every one of them. Okay?'

'Yes,' she said meekly, nodding and trying to look positive.

After that she had walked around the hospital corridors with Dick's presence weighing ever heavier on her. He sighed and made notes even while she was talking to the secretaries and receptionists. After two further hours of rejections - everyone was busy or off sick that day, it seemed - a brain wave suddenly floated Sam's way - hey, maybe she could play on Dick's love of food to stall for time? There was a superb Italian place not too far away - by the time he's had a plate full of pasta and a rack of lamb or something, an hour would have gone. Then she could drive really slowly to her main psychiatric hospital where she had a few secretarial friends. It was just possible that she could get through this.

But when they got to the restaurant, Dick decided he wasn't hungry. Just a salad, he snapped, would be fine. The waiters were super efficient and in twenty minutes flat they were done.

'So,' Dick said, tapping his fingers while she slowly sipped her second cappuccino. 'Where do you have planned for us next, Samantha?'

'Don't you want to go through the sales figures on the laptop?'

'Not today. Why, do you?'

'Well, not if you don't.'

'Don't you think it's more important to actually have some sales to put into the sales figures?'

'Yes, of course.'

So that was that then. She drained the last, by then stone cold, dregs of her coffee, visited the toilet to re-apply her lipstick for the third time, and took as long as possible to pay the bill. Finally, with a self-enforced, renewed optimism, Sam drove Dick to her psychiatric hospital. Hopefully her friend, Carol, would find her a junior doctor to see. Then, God willing, Dick would push off.

'Doesn't this car have a fourth gear, Samantha?' Dick asked her.

'Oh, it doesn't like it.'

'It's a brand new BMW - of course it likes it.'

Reluctantly she pushed the car up into fourth, still managing to keep the speed well below thirty miles an hour on the dual carriageway.

Eventually, they arrived at the psychiatric hospital. Sam found a space about half a mile away from the entrance, and then rummaged around in her car boot for a good ten minutes before deciding that it simply wasn't possible to string this out any longer.

She looked at her watch - two-thirty. If Carol could find her just one junior doctor to see, she would be saved. She rapped on Carol's door before bursting in with a flourish. Carol's desk was empty. Not just unoccupied, the cover was over her computer. Oh no! Oh, yes - of course, it was Carol's day off, wasn't it? That was why they had arranged to meet in town for lunch that day. An irritated looking woman at one of the other desks looked at Sam askance as if she'd never seen her before in her life.

'But I was here last week,' Sam said with a nervous laugh. 'Remember?'

The woman shook her head so Sam decided to try someone else. She looked around, noting with dismay that there were only two temps.

'The doctors are all up on the wards or in clinic, I think,' said one.

The other shrugged her shoulders. 'Don't ask me,' she said,

Sam looked over at her one remaining hope for the day - Dr. Douglas's secretary. As Dr Douglas never saw reps, she had never bothered asking to see him before. But Dick was here - she had to. Very tentatively, Sam walked over to her desk, trying to ignore the fact that the woman was neck deep in paperwork, clearly typing her dictation notes and fielding phone calls at the same time. She waited, a pleasant smile fixed on her face as she scanned the photos and postcards surrounding her desk. Eventually, the woman looked up at her with a raised eyebrow.

'I see you like Mel Gibson,' Sam said, acutely aware of Dick scribbling furiously into his notebook. 'Did you see him in Braveheart?'

'Yes and yes. Is there anything else only I really am busy?'

'Well I would like to see Dr Douglas if at all possible.'

The woman laughed. 'No chance - he's never seen a rep as far as I know and I've been here for twelve years.'

'I have a free book he might like.'

'Sorry love, there's no point in even asking - he'll just bite my head off.'

'Oh, okay - thanks, anyway. We'll just wait in the main reception area then, shall we? Maybe one of the junior doctors in clinic will be free.'

The secretary nodded almost imperceptibly, immediately turning back to her computer screen, while Sam and Dick walked over to the Psychiatry for the Elderly reception area, incongruous in their business suits amongst the patients.

The second they sat down, Dick turned to Sam and said, 'so what is your business strategy with regard to Dr Douglas, Samantha?'

'It's to not see him.'

'I'm sorry? Your business strategy for one of your most important and influential customers is, and I repeat, 'not to see him'?'

'Yes. Well, what else can I do if he won't see anyone?'

'Help me to understand something here, Samantha. You see, you should at least be aiming for something. We don't pay you your exorbitant salary and have you riding around in a BMW at our expense just for you to *not* see the customers, you know.'

'I know.'

'I'm going to share something with you now - I find your attitude very aggressive. You are a very aggressive person, are you not, Samantha?'

'No.'

'Yes you are. '

Sam looked around helplessly. Oh God, what could she say to him? And then, out of nowhere came her saviour - in the form of an officious looking woman with a clipboard.

'The doctor will be with you shortly,' she said with a bright smile.

'Oh, thank you,' Sam said. Thank God in heaven and all the angels.

'While you're waiting and for your information, there's a drinks machine just here and the toilets are down the corridor,' the woman added. 'Okay?'

'Thank you,' Dick said.

'Oh, I didn't put them there just for you,' she laughed. 'They were there already.'

'Okay, thanks anyway.' Dick smiled tightly at her joke, his smile quickly fading as he noticed an old lady in a brown cardigan, an orange dress and turquoise slippers making a bee line for him.

The old lady squeezed herself in between Sam and Dick, sitting so close to Dick that her thigh rubbed against his. 'Are you married, luv?' she asked him with a toothless grin.

'Er, yes, thank you,' he replied politely whilst inching discreetly away from her.

'What's your name, luv?'

'Dick,' he replied through gritted teeth, trying not to breathe in the overpowering smell of ammonia.

'Oooh, Dick - you're lovely, you are. Isn't he?' she said to Sam. 'Isn't he lovely?'

'Gorgeous,' said Sam.

At this point, the old lady put her hand on Dick's knee and Dick stood up. 'Right, well - I think we've probably done all we can for today,

Samantha,' he snapped.

'But, we have a doctor to see,' Sam said, stricken. For goodness sake, she thought, a whole day of work and just when I get the chance to see someone he wants to leave - typical!

Dick looked at his watch.

'Look, I'll go and see if I can find that lady with the clipboard,' Sam said. 'I'll check how long we need to wait.' Approaching the out-patient reception desk, she explained they had been waiting for half an hour now and wondered how much longer they could expect before the doctor would see them.

'Who told you that you could see someone?' the distracted receptionist asked her.

'The lady with the clipboard - she's got dark hair and…' Sam racked her brain trying to recall what the woman was wearing, and then it hit her, 'oh shit, slippers.'

The receptionist burst out laughing, turning to her colleagues. 'Maud's been at it again - led this young sales rep a right merry dance. Sorry, luv,' she added to Sam. 'I'll take her back up to the ward.'

Dick stalked out at a faster pace than was strictly necessary with the old lady's happy sing-song voice ringing in his ears, 'bye-bye, Dick,' she called. 'Bye-bye lovely Dick.'

Wordlessly, Sam drove him back to the Holiday Inn where he had left his car. He'd shot off without so much as a backwards glance, and the last she saw of him, he'd looked extremely hacked off. The entire day had been far, far worse than she could ever have anticipated.

And now, heaven only knew what would happen to her after what she'd just called him over Mel's car-phone. Sam pulled into the Beauty Salon car park and nervously switched the phone back on. Immediately it beeped - a message was waiting. Oh God - it would be him. She would get a warning or something. Oh God....

Still, better get it over with, she thought, dialling in to pick the message up. 'Hi, Sam,' came a cheerful Irish voice. 'It's Bernie here - Bernie O'Reilly! Can you give me a ring as soon as you get this message, pleeeeeease? Byeeeeeeee'

Sam groaned, punching Bernie's name on her mobile as she ran into the salon. 'Bernie? Hi, it's Sam.'

'Oh Sam!' Bernie cried. 'Oh Sam, I just don't know what to do. Dick's sending all these text messages and e-mails about having to see ten doctors a day and I'm finding it so difficult. I just thought I'd ring you for some advice about coping with the pressure, you know, with you being so much *older* than me and all?'

'Well you can only do so much, can't you?' Sam said as the manicurist hurried her into a cubicle. 'Yes, sorry, I know I got held up. Er, the red I think, mmm.'

'Helloooo, helloooooo, anyone there? I'm still here,' Bernie's voice shrieked out of the handset.

'Yes, sorry.'

'Where are you?'

'Oh, just here, waiting for an appointment. So, look, don't worry about it - just delete the texts and e-mails before reading them.'

Bernie gasped. 'Sam, I don't get up at six in the morning and work until seven at night for nothing, you know? This job is everything to me, everything.'

A thought occurred to Sam - perhaps she'd better actually read these messages from Dick. 'Got to go, Bernie. Call you later, okay?'

After Sam ended the call with Bernie, she noticed with dismay just how many texts from Dick there had been over the last few days - and all with exactly the same message: 'Ten doctors a day multiplied by the three key messages = business.' Sam bristled. Was it was just possible that she wasn't doing enough here? For the first time in months she decided it might be best if she read the management's e-mails as well, just to see how desperate things really were.

Tapping into her laptop with gleaming red nails later that afternoon, the true horror of the situation was revealed. There were league tables for exactly where you were in the company with regard to sales and also for the number of customers you were seeing compared to everyone else. The information was available to all so everyone knew what everyone else was doing. 'Oh hell, I'm at the bloody bottom again,' Sam wailed. 'Wait a minute, though, who's that at the top?' She did a double take - there in big red letters was the name, 'Bernie O'Reilly,' with a call rate of twenty five doctors a day.

Sam jumped up, sending her chair flying. 'Twenty five?' she screamed at the computer. 'Twenty fucking five? A day? That lying little baggage. Aaaaah!' It wasn't possible. Something was going on here. There must be someone she could call about this, but who? Mel? No, not after this morning, and besides she would be the manager soon. Veronica? Oh Christ, no - hardly Samaritan material was she? Then it hit her - Johnny.

Yes, she would call Johnny, something she rarely did. In fact, she had never called him - probably because there was something about the way he looked at her, something mocking, his eyes always flicking towards her chest, that put her off. Sexual, she thought, yes, it's like he had sex with me in another life and he can remember all the details but I can't. The thought made her smile as she pressed his name on her mobile.

'Sam!' came his lazy voice. 'How're you doing?'

'Sorry to bother you, Johnny - you're not rushing into a call or anything, are you?'

Johnny sighed. She could hear a rustling noise, a newspaper? and the distinctive click of a cigarette lighter. 'I've got five minutes, sweetheart,' he said. 'So, what can I do for you?'

'Oh thanks. It's just this daily call rate business that Dick's banging on about every five minutes. I'm actually a bit worried about it because I'm at the bottom and, well, so are you. So, I wondered, you know, if you were concerned at all, and also how in God's name is Bernie O'Reilly getting to see twenty five doctors a day? It's bloody impossible. How is she doing it?'

'Oh that old chestnut - fiction, my dear.'

'What? Are you telling me Bernie O'Reilly's making it up?'

'Yeah. Well, what do you think?'

'It never occurred to me - that's dishonest! Oh my God. How do you know? Are you sure?'

'I've got a mate who caught her at it, and there's quite a bit of gossip going around about her. She's a very busy lady, by all accounts.'

'Oh? What gossip? Do other people know about all this?'

'It's quite funny really. My mate's wife is a nurse in one of Bernie's hospitals and apparently everyone runs and hides when they see her coming. Anyway, one day his wife's just coming out of a meeting when Bernie lunges at her and tries to pin her to the wall with a brochure, you know, like she does? His wife gets away but when he checks his laptop later that night, he sees that Bernie has recorded her as a full customer call complete with notes!'

'When all his wife said was, 'hello?''

'Well, not even that, more like, 'get off me!' ha, ha! And worse than that - she's been seen sitting on the patients' beds, selling Happylux directly to them - to mentally ill patients!'

'You have to be joking? Isn't that against the rules?'

'Just a bit. If the doctors catch her she'll be skinned alive.'

'But, how will she get away with all this? I mean, she's at the top of everything - sales too.'

'Well she probably will get away with it. I've seen it happen before. In fact, I wouldn't be at all surprised if she got a promotion soon.'

'But that's so unfair.'

'Yeah, well - shit happens,' Johnny said in a bored voice.

'What can we do?'

'Nothing, Sam. Do not get involved. Believe me.'

A wave of rage rushed through Sam as she clicked off the phone. So that was what was going on. Christ, it was all so unfair. Hmmm, why hadn't she thought of this herself, then? It was bloody brilliant.

Sam paced. Yes, she could make it all up. Invent a totally fictitious account of her daily work. She need never compromise her retail therapy again. It was so obvious. Everyone must be at it. Deep in thought, she barely heard the click of the front door. 'Oh, Simon!' she said, whirling round as he strode in. 'You gave me a shock.'

'I do live here, you know, darling,' he said, nuzzling her neck as he ran his hands all over her body.

'What do you want for tea?' she snapped, trying to pull away from him. One of the many problems with Simon was that he smelled of hospitals, nicotine and instant coffee. And why couldn't he give up smoking? If he really loved her like he said he did, then he would. You'd think he'd know better being a bloody doctor, she thought.

'Why don't we go out? A Chinese or something?' he suggested.

'What? Out? Er, no - I've got a bit of a headache actually. I think I'll just make us some omelettes if you don't mind.'

'What's the matter? You're pretty grumpy - is it time of the month again?'

'No,' she said, pushing him off a bit more roughly than she had intended. 'I'm just not in the mood to go out, that's all.'

'Fine,' he snapped. 'Well, whatever you want, my sweet. Your happiness is all that matters to me, you know that, don't you?' He gave her a little pat on the rump, saying more softly. 'I'll be upstairs in my study. Call me when it's ready, will you?'

As he went upstairs, and behind his back, Sam stuck a finger up at him. Pompous bastard, she thought. He always had to make her feel like the little woman and they weren't even married yet.

Chapter 5

Dick and James, on the back row, were becoming increasingly frustrated. 'I wouldn't mind but this has cost us nearly sixty grand,' James whispered to Dick.

Dick nodded silently - it took an iron will to even be civil.

They had hired an entire art gallery plus it's auditorium for this - the highly prestigious medical launch of their new cardiology drug. There would be a whole new cardiology sales force too - Dick's baby, Dick's future. And here in this auditorium sat the cream of cardiology in the UK - the big wigs: professors, research scientists and medical directors. What this audience thought would influence everybody else when they got back to their hospitals and universities. Articles would be written. Recommendations would be made. Or not.

It was always a gamble, but Dick and James had been sure enough about this product to spend the money. And there was huge money at stake: millions of pounds had been invested in the research and development so far. Tens, if not hundreds of millions could be recouped. This had to work.

So, it was a bit irksome that the main speaker of the day was rip roaring drunk.

The Consultant Cardiologist, trialist and author of several clinical papers on the said subject, had, in an uncharacteristic lapse of judgement, decided to have a gut full of red wine and whisky with an early lunch on the plane up to Glasgow from London. As he was being introduced by the highly revered and deeply sombre Chairman, and everyone settled into their seats for what would undoubtedly be a groundbreaking presentation, the Consultant Cardiologist giggled, tripped down the steps, and proceeded to put his youngest child's crayon drawings onto the overhead projector.

'I might as well show you thish,' he said. 'In fact, thish ish a lot more interesting than whatever else I could show you. Tee hee.'

There were murmurs and embarrassed giggles from the audience, what was left of it, that was - some had gone shopping and a fair few were on the golf course. About half of the remaining number would depart after tea break at three o'clock, leaving only the few who had a conscience or who couldn't get fired up enough to do anything else.

'Thish is a donkey,' said the Cardiologist in a splutter of mirth.

Embarrassed giggles turned into exclamations of shock as the presenter began to slide down the lectern in hysterics: 'Good Lord! Oh, I say!'

'It's a donkey,' the doctor giggled. 'In a hat. Ha, ha, ha…'

Sprinting onto the stage with a surprising display of agility, the Chairman hauled the Cardiologist up by his elbow and marched him off stage, his expression one of quiet determination.

'Right, do we have the next speaker at all?' He cast around valiantly, as he handed the giggling doctor to his secretary for removal. A large man in a very tight suit got up. 'Ah, excellent. Good show. Ladies and Gentlemen - may I present Professor Douglas Alexander Hartwell.'

A couple of people in the back row tittered together - 'Hartwell in cardiology! Ha ha!' as Professor Hartwell stood up and walked over to the lectern. He then proceeded to deliver a scathing, humiliating and highly damaging attack on the new product which had just cost Topham Pharmaceuticals ten years of research, and upon which they were relying for the future of the company.

'Oh Christ Almighty,' James said to Dick as the reality of what the Professor was saying began to sink in. 'Look at them - they're even taking notes. I wouldn't mind but all those statistics he's reciting are out of date.'

'Well it would have been all right if the last speaker hadn't been pissed,' Dick snapped. 'He was the one with most of the new evidence and work that's been done since this lot. Professor Hartwell was supposed to have been set up to look like a complete prat.'

'Well, at least the chap who's on next should set things to rights,' James said. 'Thank God.'

'He can't make it.'

'Tell me you're joking,' James hissed.

'I told you - Professor Hartwell was supposed to be sandwiched in between all the new evidence to support our product. It was supposed to be a superb set up job. How could I have known…..? '

'So, what you're telling me here is that we have absolutely nothing to counteract this pile of outdated claptrap? That we have most of the cardiology hierarchy in the UK here today, and this is all they're going to get? '

Dick squirmed a little in his seat. Damn, damn and damn. What about his job prospects now? 'At least there's tonight,' he suggested hopefully.

'Ah, yes.' James reflected for a moment on the five star hotel bill and the flights for fifty doctors and ten company personnel he was going to have to pick up at the end of all this. Trying valiantly to keep the snarl off his face, he glared at the Professor. 'I'm going to have to wine and dine this bloody fat bastard tonight as well,' he muttered.

Still the Professor droned on. He had overheads, he had a Powerpoint presentation, and most of all he had time, his lecture having been extended due to the other speakers' cancellations. By the end of his two hour talk, he had managed to entirely condemn the new class of drugs to which Topham's belonged, even going so far as to recommend another product entirely - one which he had personally been involved in the research of (and been paid for). The audience dutifully and respectfully continued taking notes, and the case for the prosecution won hands down, uncontested. There were no further speakers for the day.

There was, of course, full attendance for dinner and drinks that evening. Suddenly the customer numbers swelled. James sighed and mentally signed off a small fortune. One young registrar, who had only been asked because his consultant had dropped out at the last minute, was shouting for double Jack Daniels all round. He sat with his back to the representative sitting next to him.

'I always try to get as much drink down my neck as possible at these things,' he said loudly. 'They can't exactly say they won't pay the bill, can they?'

Bernie, the rep being cold shouldered, managed a tight, bright smile and made a conscious effort to relax her tightening shoulder muscles. The evening had started off well enough with the old small talk, but as time had gone on and the drink flowed she found herself being the butt of a few less than subtle Irish jokes.

'Oh, I went to medical school with an Irishman,' said a red faced man with a public school accent, opposite her. 'Shared a room with him, yah! He used to get plastered every night. Ha ha!'

Bernie struggled with her rictus grin.

The man with the red face went on: 'we had this incredibly sparse bedroom - you know, just a couple of beds and a kettle. Ha ha! Anyway, one night he comes back after his usual skin full, completely paralytic - ha ha! And he falls onto his bed and slips quietly over the side, getting trapped between his bed and the wall.'

There were titters and sniggers from the listening doctors.

'Yah!' red face said. ' He broke his arm, poor chap, but he didn't know that because he was unconscious. Anyway, we found him the next day and took him to Casualty, but it was too late - gangrene had set in and he had to have his arm amputated.'

'Oh no,' everyone said. Was this funny?

'Yah, and do you know what the Irishman claims is the moral of the story?'

'Not to get paralytic,' everyone said.

'No. He said the moral of the story is - always make sure your bed is pushed tightly against the wall.'

'Oh, ha ha!' Everyone roared with laughter.

The smile, which was beginning to ache with the effort required to keep it there, froze on Bernie's face.

'Here's a story for you,' a man with a beard chipped in. 'When I worked in Dublin a few years back, we used to get this tramp into Casualty every time the weather got cold and he needed a warm up and a bed. Well, one night we were really busy and in he comes, waving his bottle of spirits and saying he had chest pain. But we were rushed off our feet, so we had to turn him away, you know, thinking it was the same old routine and besides - we had no free beds. Anyway, would you believe it - he only goes and dies on the way out. He was found in the morning on the hospital driveway, stone cold, his arms stretched out towards the gates as he fell.'

'Selfish bastard!' someone said.

'Exactly, it was going to look really bad for us with him going and dying right outside like that. So what we did was this - we turned his body round to make it look like he was just coming, not going.'

As a burst of laughter exploded into the room, Bernie excused herself, deciding to nip to the bar for a nightcap before retiring to her room to watch Sex in the City and do some texting.

Whoops! Too late to do a U-turn. 'Ah, the Irish minx!' A large, red faced man who she recognised as one of the Topham's top customers, loomed over her in a cloud of whisky fumes. 'So sexy, Irish gals, I always say.'

'Will I get you a drink at all?' she asked him, squirming out of reach. Jesus, the man had hands as big as spades and way too many of them.

'Put it on your expenses, Irish minx, and make it a double.' Beckoning to the barman, he barked, 'another double whisky over here please and whatever the little lady's having. Oh, and,' turning to Bernie. 'It's room?'

'306,' she volunteered just as he slapped her on the rump.

Bernie jumped away. 'You'll be taking too much of a liberty there, doctor. Now I'm away to bed, okay?' For goodness sake, did the man not realise she was a good Irish Catholic girl. And besides, she had to do her exercises, and return twenty three phone messages. Bernie liked to ring as many people as possible on a daily basis, leaving them all messages to ring her as soon as possible. Networking - you couldn't beat it.

But as she attempted to sprint out of the bar clutching her G&T, a black cloud descended by the name of Dick. 'Bernie! Where are you going?' he smiled.

Bernie smiled back. 'Dick, I've so much work to do - phone calls…..'

'He looked at his watch. 'Why aren't you with your customers, Bernie?'

'Oh but I have been, Dick,' still smiling broadly.

'It's only ten o'clock and they might need drinks. You were

brought here to look after them and you only go to bed after they have all gone.'

'But they want to go clubbing and some want to go to the red light district,' her smile now struggling.

'Well you don't have to take them to the red light district but if they want to go to a club then you will take them, understand?'

Bernie nodded. Ah, shit!

And so it was, that at three o'clock in the morning, after several hours in a Glasgow nightclub, Bernie, flagging just a little, hailed a taxi to take her back to the hotel. She swung open the door, mobile phone in hand - at last she could pick up her messages - just about to clamber in, when a pair of spade like hands suddenly grabbed her from behind.

'Aha! The Irish minx! Trying to escape, were we?'

Bernie squeaked in protest as the drunken cardiologist she had encountered earlier in the bar, pulled her onto his knee and slammed the taxi door shut behind them. She was alone with him.

'Come here, Minxy,' he growled, lurching towards her face with blubbery wet lips while his hands flew up and down her legs.

Bernie slapped him away. How many hands did the man have? There was one in her hair, another crawling up her left leg, another round the back of her mini-skirt, fiddling with the zip. 'Look, now would you let go…..'

'What's the matter, Irish foxy, minxy lady?' the doctor slurred as his rubber dinghy mouth tried to swallow her face whole.

'Oh nothing at all,' she shrieked, swotting at him frantically. 'Now would you stop……..oh Holy Mother of God!'

Narrowly missing her mouth, the doctor got a face full of Bernie's hair in the tussle. 'Aha! Like a bit of a chase, do we?' he cried, lunging for her again.

Bernie gave him a big shove. 'We'll not be much longer now, will we?' she called out to the taxi driver in a pleading voice.

'Almost there, sweetheart,' came a cheery reply.

The second the taxi rolled up in front of the hotel, Bernie flew out, shot up the steps looking somewhat dishevelled, and straight into the lift, leaving old Spade Hands to stumble out onto the pavement .

On reaching her room, she quickly washed her face, undressed and slipped into bed. Now, at last, she could get her messages and do some texting under the sheets. Although maybe not, sleep was kicking in. And that was when she heard it - tap, tap, tap.

Bernie's eyes flew wide open. What was that? She listened, straining her ears. No, there was nothing. Must have been my imagination, she thought, drifting away. But then it came again - louder and more insistent this time. Reluctantly she felt herself begin to surface once more. Who was there? She waited - no, nothing. There was no one there. Perhaps she had been mistaken and it had been a dream after all. She pulled the bed clothes around her and snuggled under the covers.

Rap, rap rap! Rap! Rap! Rap, rap, rap!!

Nope - it was no dream. 'Oh God, please help me!' she whimpered. 'It's him, isn't it? Oh, please make him leave me alone. Hail Mary, Mother of God - please don't let him be able to get in. Please.' The knocking stopped. She lay stock still, not daring to breathe, listening.

Eventually there was an angry thud on the door. 'For Christ's sake, it's only me,' boomed the unmistakable voice of the drunken doctor.

'Oh, well if it's only you it won't matter, will it? I'll just shag you then will I?' she whimpered, pulling the covers back over her head in the hope of getting at least a couple of hours sleep.

The flight home was at six-thirty in the morning in order for her to do a full day's work on her return, which was tough even for Bernie.

But she vowed to tell the others she'd had a great time for two reasons: firstly to keep up the image of success at all times, and secondly so someone else would volunteer to go away with the customers instead of her next time.

The following morning saw James Harris clutching his coffee cup and staring out forlornly at the planes as they took off and landed at Heathrow. God, how he hated customer meetings. Two days was far too long - in future he would have to send someone else. That would leave him free to tootle down to the village pub at lunchtimes with someone from marketing. Topham's head office was in a huge industrial complex on the south coast and he would normally be heading there after landing at Heathrow, but today he was meeting Katrina, his fiancée, who was flying in from Japan. They were going to do breakfast together before she left for Paris and he for Head Office.

His eyes were scratchy, and he noticed with annoyance that his Armani suit was seriously crumpled. Putting on his Gucci sunglasses he settled down with a fresh polystyrene cup of coffee and lit a cigarette, looking for all the world like an advertisement for aftershave.

Thankfully Katrina's flight was on time. God she's ugly, he thought, as he watched her strut confidently towards him after her long haul flight. She had white boots on and carried a Burberry bag. On seeing James, she gave a squeal of delight and a funny little skip. He tried hard to smile, really hard.

Katrina was Japanese, whippet thin, young, rich and very, very clever. He'd first been attracted to her when he'd seen her from the back in the dark at a company function. She had looked amazing - long black hair and the tiniest butt he had ever seen. So it was nothing less than tragic that when she turned round her face had borne a remarkable resemblance to a short sighted, buck toothed camel. He'd flinched, but then someone told him that her father was the Managing Director for the whole of Topham Pharmaceuticals in Asia. And he fancied working from Bangkok quite a lot.

He gave her a light peck on the cheek as she approached with outstretched arms, gently averting his mouth away from her protruding teeth. 'Darling!' he cried. 'Let's go and do croissants and coffee shall we?'

She beamed at him. 'Sure. Whatever you want, James.'

James smiled, then abruptly hugged her close to his chest so he could look over the top of her head at a young, redheaded girl who was wiggling past in tight, white jeans. That girl looked amazingly like that sexy piece in Dick's region, he thought - mmmm, ding-dong…..

Katrina, unhappy that her face was being squashed, pulled away and swung round just in time to see the girl he was watching. She turned and gave him a questioning look.

James shrugged. 'Sorry, sweetie - I thought she was someone I knew. Come on - let's go.'

Chapter 6

Dick had to drive back from the launch conference. It was a long way back from Scotland. Bored, he picked his nose and wiped it on the upholstery of his BMW 5 Series. He'd made two stops at 'Little Chefs' already and run out of chocolate. So, what could he do now to pass the time? Ah yes, his personal favourite - he would call his team one by one and arrange to work with them for the day, giving little or no warning. This was a perk of the job - they would squirm and pretend they were delighted he was coming out with them for the day, and he would chuckle to himself. They must think he was really, really stupid. So, who first? It was six-thirty in the evening just when they would be relaxing. Perfect. He would call Samantha.

Sam had been having dinner with Simon when Dick's call came. Simon had gone to a lot of trouble to make a lasagne with organic lamb and aubergines.

'Fucking bastard, arsehole, shitbag,' she said, glaring at her plate of food.

'More wine, darling?'

'I hate him. I really and truly hate that bastard.'

'Obviously. Look, can't you just forget him for one evening?'

'I can't though, can I?' she snapped. 'It's all right for you, everyone bows and scrapes when you get to work in the morning: doctor this, doctor that. You don't know what it's like. I've got to get up at six-thirty in the morning now because of him, and he'll be in my face until five o'clock. And I have *no fucking appointments!* Again.'

'Sam, I really am getting a bit fed up of this. All this pressure and obsessing over numbers and sales and managers. Where is the sexy, carefree girl I first met? You can give up any time you like, you know -

God knows I earn plenty. Or you could go back to nursing if you wanted some pin money.'

'Aaaaagh!'

'Or do something else then - have baby.'

'No.' She couldn't be expected to give up her car, the money, the …..money, and well, the money. An alarming vision of herself trapped at home with a demanding baby that would be sure to look like Simon popped into her head. And no way would she ever go back to nursing. Never. Sam glared at him defiantly.

'Have it your own way,' he said quietly, beginning to clear away the plates in the manner of a martyr.

'My own way?' Sam laughed disbelievingly. Why could he never see her point of view? 'My own way, you say? Have - you - any - bloody - idea - what I have to go through each day, Simon?' she shouted, picking up the dirty saucepans one by one and throwing them into the sink. Satisfyingly, Simon winced. 'Well, have you?'

She watched as he reached for his cigarette packet.

'You just don't care, do you?' Tears began to prickle. She blinked them away furiously.

Simon sighed and looked at his watch.

'Oh, I'm sorry. Am I keeping you from something?'

'Oh shut up Sam. Stop bloody nagging, woman,' he said, calmly lighting a cigarette and sauntering into the sitting room. A second later the TV was on and the sound of racing cars screaming round and round a track filtered into the kitchen along with the acrid stench of nicotine. He'd be lying on a beanbag, his nose inches from the screen.

Forgetting she had no shoes on, Sam stepped outside just as it began to spit rain. There was nowhere to sit in their tiny back garden apart from some stone steps. Cooling off rapidly, she put her head in her hands. She couldn't go back to nursing no matter how bad things got. Not ever. All that compulsory night duty, working over weekends, bank holidays and Christmas, the bed pans, the wet beds, the colostomy bags that needed emptying, the infected wounds that had to be drained and the perpetual stink of disinfectant and shit. Anger boiled again, unprompted, as she remembered those endless nights where her own life felt as if it had been put on hold - forever trapped in a parallel universe of chronic tiredness, darkness and incontinent patients.

She just hadn't thought it through really, had she? She'd pictured herself as a Barbara Windsor type character in 'Carry on Nursing,' sitting on beds having a giggle and getting chatted up in the canteen by handsome, earnest young doctors. Enemas, catheters and denture washing hadn't really come into it.

And then there had been the not inconsiderable matter of the sputum pots. Oh God, those sputum pots - the daily round of inhalations for the chest infection patients who were supposed to 'cough it all up' into a tiny, polystyrene carton. Sometimes the sputum was thick and green, and if they missed the pot it would sit, pulsating, in a solid glob on the bedspread waiting to be oozed back in. The pots, when full, would be heavy and warm. And every time sputum pot duty fell to her, she'd retch in the sluice afterwards.

Mind you, there had been the funny times too - like that night a bloke had been admitted via Casualty with a vibrator stuck up his bum. The operating surgeon had extracted the still vibrating vibrator, popped it into a plastic bag and clipped it to the end of the patient's bed. When the poor bloke woke up the next morning he had a crowd of giggling fellow patients and a few nurses standing round his bed peering at it. Incredibly, it had still been going. They'd nicknamed him Duracell Man. And then that woman who had sworn she had absolutely no idea how she'd come to sit on a glass bottle. She'd slipped, she said. As you do.

Sam smiled, nearly laughed, and then realised with a start where she was - a mad woman with no shoes on, sitting in the back garden in the rain, laughing to herself. No, there had been good times, but she wanted more for herself. There was a whole world out there - she wanted to smell of perfume, wear a suit, go out for Sunday lunch, wear her hair how she wanted it, heels and lipstick, to be called Sam and not Nurse. Nursing, she realised, was a vocation and it wasn't for her. Probably it never had been. There really was only one way to go now and that was forwards, which was why she would put up with having to work with Dick again tomorrow morning, and why she would smile at rude receptionists and pretend that medical sales was her very life blood, that her customers' every word mattered deeply to her and she was happy, no delighted, to wait for two hours to see one doctor who might give her just five minutes of his time. If she was lucky.

And by seven o'clock the next morning, Sam was about to get lucky, although she didn't yet know it. Simon had left early, always a bonus. She had a shower, then spent half an hour sipping tea and staring in at the contents of her wardrobe. She needed more stuff. There was absolutely nothing in there that she could possibly wear today. What she wanted was a chic trouser suit in beige, but she only had one in black or navy - far too dark for the time of year. She did have a skirt in beige but that meant a problem with the legs business - it was too warm for boots, Damn it, too chilly for bare legs and strappy sandals, and flesh coloured tights were an absolute no-no. Flesh tights and she would look like her mother. Oh dear, what to wear, what to wear….

By half past seven desperation won over and she threw on the black trouser suit with a white top, in a temper because it just was not what she felt like wearing today. Damn that man, making her rush like this. Now she didn't feel right and she would be late.

Time was of the essence. Flying out of the house, she jumped into her car and set off for the hotel Dick had picked, which just happened to be at the most remote corner of the territory she covered. Another of Dick's specialities - 'meet me at the crack of dawn at a venue involving the longest possible drive.' In fact, this one was so far away it bordered Bernie's territory. Bernie! Sam, aware of a frantic beeping noise as she backed out of the drive, looked down. There, flashing away on her car phone, a message waited for her: 'Please call Bernie O'Reilly as soon as you get this message - urgent.' It had been left at seven - fifteen.

What, Sam fumed as she drove with her foot flat to the floor, was so blasted important that the woman had to have her call returned 'urgently?' She punched Bernie's name in on her phone. It rang and rang.

Eventually Bernie answered. 'Oh Sam, hi! Just a minute. Look, I'll have to get back to you.' Bernie was shouting above what sounded like a football crowd. 'I'm just starting a conference - they're all coming in. I've got two hundred doctors and over three hundred nurses coming today and they're all arriving now. It's pandemonium, I tell you. Then I've an appointment with the Medical Director at six, and tonight I'm taking all the junior doctors out for a meal.'

'Okay, bye,' Sam said, wasting no more time. Obviously it couldn't have been that important. Ten to eight. Damn. She was never going to make it on time. The phone rang again: Dick. Oh great, now she'd have to tell him she was going to be late.

'Hello, Dick,' she answered in a low voice. But as she listened, a feeling of euphoria swept through. 'What's that you say? You're stuck in stationary traffic? Oh dear, how awful for you, what a disappointment, yes. You could be stuck there for hours yet. Uh huh, yes, best turn round, mmmm.' There was a God! Hallelujah!

Yes, you bastard, Sam thought, stuck there for hours but waiting until the last possible moment to phone me so I would definitely have had to drive all the way out here. Still - freedom! Oh happy days. And as she was up and now in a fantastic mood - she may as well pop into the nearest surgery to see if there were any doctors who might see her before their clinic started. With a happy, sunny smile, Sam parked in the near empty car park and sauntered into a brand new health centre she had never visited before. And luck, it seemed, was on her side today - the new Australian locum doctor would see her immediately.

'Thank you for seeing me. I'm Sam Farmer from Topham Pharmaceuticals,' she said, handing a huge guy in red braces her business card as she was ushered in.

'Hi Sam. G'day. Take a pew, why don't you? Now, what can I do for you?'

Wow! What an unusual guy. The warm welcome was a shock. And my, oh my, what a big boy he is, she thought. He must be at least twenty-five stones in weight yet so young, and so, so - blond. He looked like a gigantic baby in braces.

She was just about to speak when he said, 'Can you get me to any conferences, Sam?'

'Sorry?'

'I want to go to a conference. I want to be wined and dined, Sam. I've just come over from Australia and I need a bit of hospitality, mate.'

'How long are you here for, doctor?'

'Probably about a year? I've been here before and I wouldn't mind staying to tell you the truth. Believe it or not, I actually like it here although it's a bit third world compared to back home.'

'Is it? Ah well, that's great. It's possible I could find you a place on one of our UK based meetings. We will be running some more workshops on depression…'

'The thing is here, Sam. Would you be able to get me a woman?'

'Pardon me?'

'A woman. Would you be able to get me a woman on one of these things?' he asked, leaning forwards with a intense look on his face.

'I think you might have to find your own, er, woman actually, doctor,' she said, blushing. 'But I can probably invite you to our next depression workshop. I think it's in Milton Keynes. Shall I put you on the list?' Yeah like right at the bottom of it. What did he think she was, a pimp? 'So, have you got any experience in using Happylux at all?'

'Sweetheart, you get me on this conference - nice hotel mind, and plenty of booze - and I'll use Happysox for you.'

'Happylux.'

'Happylux. No probs, mate. Now you make sure and be in touch about all this, right?'

'Yes, no problem mate, er, doctor.' Sam shook his hand as she left, promising to get back to him about the conference.

There was always a catch, wasn't there? If the doctor wanted to see you and was really, really nice then he wanted something, right? That familiar sinking feeling threatened to pull her down again. No, she was on a high. Luck could still be with her. She would ask at reception to see if any of the other five doctors might see her today as she could see them all drinking coffee and chatting in the back room. Good, they hadn't started yet.

'Male or female?' came a male voice over the intercom after the Receptionist had relayed Sam's request with the requisite, 'you don't want to see a rep today do you, doctor?'

The receptionist, a severe looking woman in her fifties with a beehive hairstyle and a blouse with a pussycat bow on it, looked Sam up and down in the rudest possible manner, and said, 'female.'

'Good legs?' Sam wondered if the man knew she could hear all this.

'She's wearing trousers.'

'Blond?'

'Redhead.'

'Would I like to see her, do you think?'

'I don't think you've got time, Malcolm, and she has seen the locum.'

'Oh I'll give her five minutes. I'm feeling generous today - show her in.'

'The receptionist stabbed the intercom button, glaring at Sam. 'Now, don't be any longer than five minutes with him or I will personally make sure you never get in here again, okay?'

'Fine, yes. Thank you,' Sam said, hoping Malcolm was worth the humiliation she had just endured.

'Sit,' Malcolm barked without looking up from the newspaper he was reading. She sat. The room smelled musty and was piled high with papers and files. Malcolm took a loud slurp of coffee. Then the telephone rang. 'Christopher, old boy! Yes plenty of time, fire away. How are you?' he bellowed, staring at Sam's body. Up and down his beady eyes travelled, and up and down again. Ten minutes later, he glanced at his watch. 'Look, I'll have to go, old chap. We must find time to grab a round of golf one of these days. Yes, ha, ha! Indeed.'

'You're going to start clinic now, aren't you?' Sam said as he replaced the receiver.

'I'm afraid so. What is it you wanted to flog anyway?'

'I wanted to *discuss* Happylux with you.'

'Oh yes. Can't use it here, though - too expensive.'

'But it isn't. If you could find a few minutes to look at the admission figures for patients on anti-depressants, you would see how more patients stay out of hospital on this one. I'm sure you would see how cost-effective it is. Patients like it, you see - they get fewer side effects so they keep taking it and are therefore less likely to relapse and end up in hospital. Oh, yes, and it works quicker too.'

'That's what they all say,' he said, standing up to usher her out of the door. 'Tell you what, though, have a word with our practice manager. She might be your best bet.' He scanned her body again and smiled. As Sam left, he buzzed through to the practice manager and asked her to arrange a meal out for the staff with Sam one evening next week.

On her way out, Sam noticed the receptionist glaring at her and suddenly remembered that she was only supposed to have been five minutes. Damn - she'd been in there ages even though it wasn't her fault. Perhaps she could smooth things over by explaining about the phone call and leaving a few presents? God knows she needed to get rid of some stuff, she'd got a garage full - couldn't get the car in there anymore.

Smiling hopefully she walked over with a fistful of Happylux pens and post-it pads. 'I'm so sorry, I know you said…'

'What part of 'five minutes only' did you not understand, exactly?' the receptionist snapped, expertly siphoning off the freebies into her handbag.

'His phone rang, I barely got to speak.'

'Really? I let you in there out of the goodness of my heart and you betrayed my trust. Look at the queue now! Don't ever expect to get in here again, okay?'

Sam opened her mouth to speak but the receptionist had already picked up the phone, furiously pressing the keys on her computer while she listened. Another phone rang. Irate patients tapped on the glass window. Sam gave up.

Watching her go, the receptionist smiled to herself as she spoke to the practice manager. 'No I'm sorry the representative has gone. No, she didn't leave a card either. I don't know which company, Sue. I know - dreadful manners.' Over my dead body, she thought as she watched the beautiful redhead in her well cut suit walk past the waiting room full of screaming children, and out into the sunlight towards her expensive company car.

Sam jumped into her BMW. Her car phone was flashing. There was a message: 'please call Bernie O'Reilly. Urgently.'

'It can wait,' Sam snapped. First things first - retail therapy was required. And so it wasn't until much later that afternoon, when Sam was driving home with a boot packed full of goodies, that Bernie finally got through to her.

'Oh Sam, something terrible has happened,' Bernie wailed.

'Oh no, what?' Sam said. Like she cared? For pity's sake, she'd had to get up this morning and she'd had a hard day in the shops.

'I think I'm in trouble,' Bernie hissed.

'Why are you talking in a funny voice? Where are you?'

'I'm crouching behind my exhibition stand. This is the first time I've had a moment. The thing is - one of my customers is threatening to report me,' Bernie said.

'Report you? What for?' She really could not wait to hear this.

'He says, oh God, Sam this is terrible. You can't tell anyone else, okay? I just need some advice and all.'

'Go on.'

'This doctor says a patient of his asked for Happylux and practically detailed the product to him. The patient knew all the comparative data and all the trial work. He knew more than the doctor, which was pretty impressive considering he was supposed to be mentally ill.' Bernie's voice had risen with panic.

    Sam clamped her hand over her mouth to stop herself from laughing.

    'I'm so worried, Sam. The ward nurses told this doctor they had seen me selling Happylux to the patients, sitting on their beds and all - with my sales brochure.'

    'Is it true?' And were you in your mini-skirt? she wanted to ask.

    'Well only a bit. Nothing that would, you know, harm anyone. I'm under so much pressure. I had to do something, so I did.'

    'Bernie, we're all under pressure and it's totally against the rules. Surely you knew that?'

    'Well they did say we were to use our ingenuity…'

    'What's the doctor going to do now?'

    'He said he should report me. He told me he was really disappointed in me and that I should have known better. He said he wants to ban all reps from the hospital completely. I was just begging him not to report me. Holy Mother of God, I was pleading with him in the end, just pleading. I was practically on my knees.'

    A huge wave of laughter threatened to engulf Sam. She struggled with her reply for a moment, picturing Bernie clinging to the doctor's legs, being dragged down the corridor as she clung on, still pleading with him. Eventually she composed herself. 'Do you think he's going to?'

    'I think he might let me off but I'm going to have to watch it from now on.'

    'Mmmmm. Well at least you've learned the lesson now.'

    'I suppose so. Look, thanks for your listening ear, Sam. It's just the pressure, you know?'

    The pressure weighed heavier than ever on Sam as she drove

home in the spring sunshine, her sunroof open, the radio on. But, she thought, there was pressure and pressure, wasn't there? There was the pressure she had endured as a nurse to get the momentous list of tasks done by the end of the shift. And then there was this - a different kind of pressure - to see ten customers a day when she had all on to see one, and having to actually sell stuff in order to keep her job. And what about the pressure of looking like you were enjoying it all? Putting the happy face on while you were being rejected and insulted was possibly the biggest pressure of all.

Yes, I can see why Bernie's done it, she thought, and she'll probably get away with it too, if I don't tell anyone else, like Melissa for example. Not that Mel's got a leg to stand on with all her indiscretions, and anyway, Bernie said she had learned her lesson didn't she?

So Sam decided to keep the information to herself, just like Johnny said.

Chapter 7

That evening, while Sam was furiously throwing carrier bags into her wardrobe before Simon got home, Melissa was masturbating on the spin cycle of her washing machine.

'I always come quickly for a woman,' she'd said to Sam, earlier on the phone. Sam had told her she was in a hospital but the background noise had sounded more like a shopping mall to her. 'I think Bruce was a bit surprised - like, I can do it four or five times in a row as well,' she went on.

'Is Bruce this perverted doctor you were telling me about?' Sam said in a distracted voice.

'Yes, he's a consultant psychiatrist, actually. He came over last night for dinner but we didn't quite get around to eating it if you know what I mean?'

'I think I can guess.'

'Anyway, we did it in the bathroom, the bedroom, the kitchen, the living room and on the stairs?'

'Uh huh.'

'We did it in, like, every corner? Are you listening, Sam?'

'Uh huh.'

'But then do you know what he said, the cheeky sod?'

'No, of course not.'

'He said how disappointing it was that all women lose their bodies once they're over the age of twenty-five? And I'm twenty-eight! Then he left - said he didn't like sushi, that it was, like, crap and he was going for a take-away?'

'That's awful. I notice he said that about women's bodies after he'd managed to do it five times.'

'Yes, and then this morning when I was in his office waiting room...'

'You were there this morning after what happened the night before?'

'Oh yes. Anyway, this morning there was, like, this other rep waiting for him? She's the Brazilian one I told you about - all tight blouses and thick, red lipstick? Well, she told me she gives him blow jobs twice a week in the car park.'

'I just don't believe this.'

'It's true, Sam.'

'How do you feel about that?'

'Well I don't know if I believe her - she's such an old tart and she's married. Whatever. And do you know what she said? Guess! She said that South American women are, like, much sexier than English women and that they know how to please a man whereas we don't have a clue.'

'The bitch.'

'Yes. I think he sleeps with other women too.'

'Blimey, he is busy.'

'Oh yes, he's obsessed with sex, you see. He said he can't think of women as people at all - only as pussy?'

'Oh, he's sick. Still, at least he's in the right job to cure himself.'

'He's as fit as a butcher's whippet, though, Sam. Where are you, by the way? I can hear jazz music.'

'Oh, just here. So what are you going to do now you know he's a sick pervert who's screwing everything in a skirt? And he's your customer, Mel. You shouldn't be doing it with him anyway, should you?'

'Mmmm. Well if he pesters me to death again I'll have to say no, I suppose.' That Sam had a cheek speaking to her like that.

'Just don't go to his office anymore, it's easy. In fact, if you like, I could cover him for you in future?'

'No!'

'Well, I know what he's up to and I can at least do the job we're supposed to be doing. It's a good idea - think about it.'

Melissa bristled. 'No, I'll handle him,' she said firmly. 'Anyway, the reason I've phoned you, Sam, is to ask if you will co-sponsor a meeting at the Post-Graduate Centre with me on Friday, you know, to split the budget and make sure we get to speak to everyone? Some of the juniors are on your rotation and it's hard for me to, like, cover them all?'

'Will Bruce whatshisname be there?'

'Pilkington. Yes.'

'I see. So, I'll get to have a look at him, will I?'

'Mmmm. Well that's part of the reason - if you can, like, talk to the others, then I can handle him?'

'Okay, Mel. I'll see you Friday then. Twelve o'clock okay?'

After Melissa had put the phone down she wondered if she had done the smart thing there. No way did she want super sexy Samantha Farmer going in to see her drop dead gorgeous, dreamboat doctor, even if he was sexually incontinent.

The spin cycle was reaching it's peak. Melissa closed her eyes and thought about some of the fantasies Bruce had revealed to her last night. He wanted three in a bed and he wanted yoghurt, Mars bars and video cameras. She sent herself on the washing machine as she thought about what he might do with these.

It was odd about the dirty phone calls, though. Now, those were becoming increasingly alarming. Was it possible that Bruce Pilkington might really be borderline ill? Sort of sexually, seriously disturbed or even dangerous? With a frisson of delight, Melissa considered some of the things he was now asking her to do - ooh, the thrill of it all….

Melissa had been a rep for Topham Pharmaceuticals ever since she had graduated at the tender age of twenty-two. She had six years selling experience now under her belt, including the last two years as the field trainer, in addition to her responsibilities as a rep. She had her own house - part of a selective mews development with an exclusive courtyard, in an upmarket village on the outskirts of Hull - and she'd filled it with all the 'must have' accessories. Melissa had decking, she had an Aga with multi-coloured tiles above it, a Belfast sink, a wet room, and now she was having a pond built in the back garden.

But there was something missing. This, surely, was not all there was? A visit to her mother's hideously suburban bungalow usually spurred her on: a reminder that a person can never have too much excitement. And she had given this company everything they wanted, excelled in sales and played by the rules, well roughly speaking, and now it was her turn - she would settle for nothing less than management. They owed her.

Jumping off the washing machine, Melissa considered her options - a position of power would be sexy and it would be hers without a doubt, and soon. But it would also be quite nice to have a man on a more regular and reliable basis - on tap as it were. This was actually a bit of a problem. First there was so little spare time to go on the pull, and secondly most of her friends now had partners and children, and only wanted to have girls nights in, while their little kids watched inane videos and everyone talked about nappies and teething.

So, what to do? An internal conversation ensued: either she was going to have to control the wayward doctor with the sex problem, or……….hmmmm, what about Johnny King? She'd tried to hit on him a few times now, though. Remember at the last conference when she'd asked him to come to her room for some training manuals? He'd knocked on the door five minutes later and she'd opened it wearing only a towel, which she had let slip to the floor, saying, 'ooops.' He'd looked away, the idiot, which had been something of a disappointment. Still, at least he had seen her naked body, and make no mistake - he had seen it all. And next time he would definitely know what she meant when she asked him to come to her room for some training manuals, wouldn't he? Besides, wasn't he divorced? Wouldn't he be desperate for a bit?

Melissa sighed. Men didn't take subtle hints like eyelash fluttering and come hither looks - waste of time. A girl could spend months doing all that, then while she wasn't looking, another woman would come along and wham. And let's face it, there was always another woman. Men thought they did all the running, did they?. Uh, Uh! The women sorted it out between them and no mistake.

Melissa fed her cat, Louis, made herself some toast, watched the early evening news and then settled down to do at least four hours work preparing training sessions for the office, and sales and activity graphs for Dick. Dick always asked Melissa to do these for him each month, convincing her it was necessary as part of her development in becoming a manager. It took her around two hours each time. Dick would then present them to the senior management as his own work.

The lurid phone call that cropped up about half way through her work schedule that evening was a welcome distraction.

'Stop pestering me,' Melissa said. 'Yes, red ones. A thong, actually.'

A thought suddenly occurred to her - what if this wasn't really Dr Pilkington? Oh my God - she might be turning on some greasy old man in urine stained trousers with food spattered down his string vest. He might have a single yellow tooth protruding from his mouth, rheumy eyes and advanced halitosis. If so, she had just agreed to lick strawberry yoghurt off his private parts. Melissa felt a flutter of fear - she was a single woman living on her own after all. Dialling 1471 showed her that the caller had withheld his number. Perhaps she had better check with Bruce at Friday's post-graduate meeting just to make sure that these calls really were from him, then they could go on with their game.

The Post-Grad. Administrator was a wiry, little woman answering to the name of Marlene. She had a good heart and always put her back into whatever it was that she did. And today, Melissa could see that she was cross. 'There are people who are starving in this world you know,' Marlene snapped at the junior doctors who were complaining about the food. 'You come here, get a free lunch and all this extra education from people you could learn a thing or two from, and then all you do is complain.'

The young doctors rolled their eyes, toying with their egg mayonnaise sandwiches and sausage rolls.

'Now go and speak to those nice young ladies who paid for it all, and make yourselves useful,' said Marlene.

They grimaced, reluctantly dragging themselves over to Sam and Melissa's exhibition stand, which was emblazoned with banners, leaflets and give-aways bearing the brand name, 'Happylux,' in bright red letters: Happylux pens, Happylux tissues, Happylux clocks, staplers, mugs and cushions.

'So, what are you flogging then?' one of them said to Melissa. His mates smirked.

'A dead horse,' she said, and laughed.

The doctor stared at her, devoid of humour. 'What?'

'Right,' said Melissa and tried again. 'Happylux. Have you heard of it?'

'Yeah, but we never use the stuff. It kills people.' More smirks.

'I see, and, like, what brings you to that conclusion, doctor?' she asked him as politely as she could. He was spoiling for a fight, the little bastard - he knew it and she knew it.

'There was an article in the Lancet last month about it. I'm surprised you didn't know about that,' he said. 'And we've had several old people die when they've been on that stuff.'

'Well it is a sad fact that, like, old people do die eventually? It comes to us all, doctor.' Melissa smiled fleetingly. 'It really is highly unlikely that it was the anti-depressant that caused their deaths, actually. As for the Lancet article, we have had a response printed to that work? I think you'll find that the study you're talking about had several major flaws in it. It was only, like, a one tailed trial for a start, and you may have noticed that it was sponsored by our main competitor? Happylux actually has a very good track record and over one million ……..'

Melissa stopped talking. She'd lost him. He didn't want to know. She watched as he made no attempt to disguise the fact that his eyes were roving around the room, and he quite obviously wasn't listening.

Eventually his eyes returned to her face, glazed. 'Sorry, you were boring me to death with something,' he said.

'Whatever. Here, have a pen,' she said and left him there, thinking he was lucky she hadn't poked him in the eye with it.

'One day I'll hit someone,' she said to Sam. 'It's not as if they know all this stuff either - I bet that little shit knows virtually nothing about depression in the elderly. I wouldn't want him anywhere near my grandmother, that's for sure. Can you imagine….? Sam? Hellooo?' She waved her hand in front of Sam's face.

'Mmmmm. That wouldn't be 'Bruce the Perv' over there, by any chance, would it?' Sam asked, nodding her head in the direction of a tall, muscular man with black hair and piercing blue eyes. 'Dear Lord, no wonder he's got a sex problem - women must have been throwing their knickers at him since he was about twelve.'

Melissa followed Sam's gaze, only to realise with stomach lurching dismay, that Bruce Pilkington was visibly, mentally undressing Sam, practically raping her with his eyes. Heat shot into Melissa's face. She turned away quickly, pretending to shuffle some clinical papers around on her stand. 'Calm down,' she told herself. 'He does that to everyone. It's you he wants, not her. Keep calm. When you turn round he'll be looking at you again.'

Horribly, irresistibly she couldn't help casting a sly glance over her shoulder to check. But his lustful gaze was still undeniably on Sam, openly appraising her body, his eyes lingering on her breasts, staying there. Under some kind of masochistic compulsion, Melissa turned to look at Sam, whose face was now as crimson as her own. 'He fancies you, the bastard. I knew he would,' she said, her eyes filling with unbidden tears.

'Look, you can keep him, Mel - he's dangerous. I don't want him. It should be bloody illegal to look at people like that, anyway.' Sam shot off towards the kitchen to talk to the caterer, uncomfortably aware that Bruce Pilkington's eyes were glued to her rear end as she did.

'You know,' Melissa said to Sam, following her into the kitchen. 'Dick has asked me to give you a special training day?'

Sam whirled round. 'Oh?'

'Yes. Is Monday all right for you?'

'Fine. As long as it's you and not Dick, I don't care. Shall we meet in that gorgeous Italian café I told you about? There are loads of sexy waiters, Mel.'

Melissa softened. 'Yeah okay, and we'll have a bit of a lie in.

Would, like, eleven o'clock, suit you?'

Dick had told Melissa that Sam's call rate was virtually non-existent: the average pensioner saw a doctor more often than Sam did. He suspected that Sam was not going to work, nor, when she did, was she selling Happylux effectively. In short, the project was to 'manage her out of the company.' This project was to be Melissa's, as part of her 'development in becoming a manager.'

'I'll have my coffee hot and strong,' Melissa said with meaning, to the Italian waiter with the sultry, come-to-bed eyes, when she and Sam met the following week. 'And one of those sponge fingers dipped in please?'

Despite himself, the smooth Italian's cool expression dissolved a little as Melissa eyeballed him unblinkingly.

'That's got him going,' she said to Sam as the waiter swaggered off to get the ladies their coffees. 'He won't be able to, like, stop thinking about me now.'

They opened their laptops and leaned over them, looking exactly like two serious business women.

'I had a dirty phone call last night,' Sam said, watching Melissa closely.

'Really?' Melissa's huge eyes widened. Something told her she wasn't going to like this.

'Yes. It's the first one I've ever had and I couldn't quite believe it actually - I was just having my beans on toast, when all of a sudden the phone rang and it was knickers off this and bend over that....'

Melissa paled a little. 'Er, what were the exact words, though?'

'It was horrible, it really shook me up.'

'Yes, yes,' said Melissa. 'But what precisely did this person say? Did he, like, go on about spanking bottoms and things at all?'

'Mmmmm.'

'Jesus! I knew it. He must have picked up your business card last week at the Post-Grad meeting?'

'So it's Pilkington is it?'

'It must be, yes. I've had my dirty phone caller traced and all the calls go back to his hospital, although they say they can't pinpoint it to an extension, but it's a bit of a fucking coincidence if it's not him, isn't it?' Melissa's face burned indignantly. She had assumed that those special phone calls were just between the two of them. How dare he fantasise about Sam as well. Hmmm, it seemed increasingly likely that Johnny King would be the lucky recipient of her charms now.

'I'm not interested in him, Mel,' Sam said, picking up the vibes. 'I wouldn't want that kind of a bloke anywhere near me. If I was to be unfaithful to Simon, which I'm not going to be by the way, it would be with someone classier than that.'

Charming, Melissa thought. 'Like who?' she said.

'Oh, no one,'

'Go on! You know my little secrets. Who is it you fancy?'

'Well, only a little, but - James Harris actually. I wouldn't do anything, though.'

'Why ever not?

'Melissa!'

'You should learn to live a little, Sam - you're far too much of a prude.'

'No I'm not - I just don't want to hurt Simon.'

'So you would if you could get away with it then?' Melissa asked with a grin. 'Well, well, well. You and James. Whoever would have thought it?'

'You're not going to tell anyone are you, Mel?'

'Mum's the word. Now, let's have a look at these sales figures of yours. 'Ooooh deary me....'

Mmmm, Melissa thought, how very interesting. She wasn't altogether sure she liked Sam all that much now she came to think of it. For instance, she didn't like the way those two men in the corner of the cafe were staring at Sam with their mouths open, or the way that man earlier had opened the door for Sam and then let it swing back in her own face nearly giving her a black eye, while Sam said, 'thank you,' and he said, 'you're welcome,' in a lascivious voice. And she certainly didn't care for the way the waiter was attending to Sam with sugar and biscuits, completely ignoring herself.

'That'll do now thank you,' she snapped. 'We're trying to work.'

They went, in the afternoon, to see a consultant psychiatrist in one of Sam's hospitals, where they drank tea and invited him to a conference in Turkey, an invitation he was only too happy to accept.

'Are you going too?' he asked Sam, staring at her mouth and then at the top button of her blouse with eyes that seemed drawn as if by magnets, unable to stop himself.

'No, she's not,' said Melissa, smiling in her most flirtatious manner. 'But I will be.' She made eye contact with the young doctor and held it there, making sure her message hit home.

'Oh, right,' he said, looking a little flustered. 'Well maybe next time, Sam, eh?'

Sam opened her mouth to speak.

'Don't worry, doctor, I'll look after you,' Melissa said with a big smile.

After leaving the consultant, the two women clattered noisily down the hospital corridor in their power suits and high heels, leather briefcases and car keys waving around in total contrast to the poor souls rocking and muttering to themselves on the steps as they strode past.

Melissa speeded up. She hated these places - hated having to wait in public areas where mentally ill patients pushed right up against her waving a cigarette in her face. Last week a woman in an ancient dress and slippers, who looked as though she hadn't washed her hair in years, and whose fingers were dyed a deep yellow from nicotine, had rushed up close to her and said, ' you look nice.'

'Thank you,' Melissa said to her, still walking.

'You've got lovely hair,' the woman said, reaching out to touch her.

Melissa had tried not to flinch and said, 'thank you,' again.

'And you've got lovely legs,' the woman called after her as she stalked off down the corridor. 'You can see your blue veins at the back though,' she added, loudly.

And she loathed having to engage in conversations where social conventions were irrelevant, the threat of violence hanging over her should she answer in a way not quite to the questioner's liking. Like the time a big man in army gear and reflective sunglasses (in winter) had pinned her to the wall outside a secretary's office and asked her if she was waiting for the doctor.

'Yes,' she'd said, in a small voice.

'Well - I - was - fucking - well - here - first, okay?' he shouted, jabbing his finger into her shoulder on each syllable, his face only millimetres away from hers.

But worst of all, was having to go up onto the wards. It was all right for Sam, she had been a nurse, but sometimes things could be a bit confusing in Mental Health. She had once spent half an hour arguing the case for anti-depressant use with a highly articulate young man who insisted that psycho-therapy and eating fish could cure all mental illnesses. His arguments had been rational and based on current theories on the matter. She'd produced paper after paper to discuss with him, and had even got as far as inviting him to a seminar when two giggling young blokes, one with a pony tail and the other in combat gear, came into the office and said, 'come on then now, Michael. You've had your fun. It's time for your medication.' And then with a brief nod to her, 'Sorry love. Ha ha!' But now, as Sam and Melissa marched past a bloke flashing his wares through a burgundy chenille dressing gown, calling after them, 'come up and see me anytime, luv - ward 33. I'll be out soon,' a chill had grown between the two women.

'I think we ought to have a full day working together properly,' Melissa said to Sam once they reached the car park. 'Your sales are going down. In fact, you have a negative growth rate and you're growing at below the rate of the competition in your area. Do you know what that means?'

'Yes, of course,' Sam said, looking somewhat taken aback. They are outstripping me.'

'Any ideas why?'

'No.' she said miserably, looking away across the hospital grounds at a man mowing the grass. That seemed like a nice job……

'Well, like, how much selling did you do in our last call, for instance?' Melissa asked her.

'It would have been inappropriate.'

'Inappropriate? Sam - we're, like, paying for him to go to the European conference? Of course he isn't obliged to use our product but he's got to use something, so why shouldn't it be ours? You didn't even ask him!'

'I feel embarrassed, it feels like a hard sell, a bribe. And he was so nice, you know, with the tea and everything….'

Melissa looked away and took a deep breath. 'Well it isn't a bribe. He has to use something doesn't he? Our product is the most cost effective and patients like it. It works. What's the problem?'

Sam said nothing.

'Right. Well, I suggest we go out and do lots of selling practice over the next few days. What do you think?'

Sam managed a weak smile. 'Okay. Thanks, Melissa. I know you're trying to help me, ' she said, leaning forwards to kiss her on the cheek.

As Melissa drove home she ruminated on one or two things. First off - she was a successful sales person, and she was powerful in her role as a successful representative and regional trainer. Secondly, she would soon be a manager, so she would have to pull her socks up and show senior management just what she could do. It was no longer good enough to just meet the reps at lunchtime and talk about sex and stuff. It was important to differentiate herself and demonstrate her training abilities, which had
shown themselves to be questionable at that training day they'd had recently. Things would be changing from now on. Melissa Crow was someone to be reckoned with.

Oh and another thing, she muttered to herself - that was the very last time she would ever sit there feeling sexually inferior to Sam Farmer. The very last time.

Chapter 8

A balmy, blossom filled morning in May with the air full of promise and the hazy sky just beginning to give way to a deep, intense blue, found Veronica Ball pursing her lips and glaring at the queue outside Betty's Tea Shop. She really had done her best today, but despite asking at every single surgery in Harrogate, not a single doctor had agreed to see her. She hesitated - it had only just turned twelve o'clock, yet already the queue snaked down the street. Veronica did not do queuing. So, foregoing her little treat of a cup of Darjeeling with a slice of lemon, she jumped back into her BMW and bombed back to Leeds, cursing under her breath. Everyone had been busy. She so accepted that, had been quite prepared to wait or be very brief, whatever. But was it really so bloody necessary to speak to her as if she was pond scum? What was it with these people?

God, how amazing it would be not to be a rep. anymore - not to have to smile a zillion times a day at incredibly ordinary people who just stared back at you. There so had to be a way out of this - something else she could do to help herself. And whatever it took, she would do it.

She stubbed her cigarette out and turned on the air-conditioning. There really wasn't any point in agonising. She had done her best - it was just that her call rate was hovering around eleven a day and Bernie O'Reilly was at twenty-five. Management set so much store on these things. James had said activity was almost as important as actual sales. No, no - she would not dwell on it anymore. It was time for some relaxation - she moved to switch on Radio Four, then decided against it. No, first she would call James.

His rich, double cream voice boomed into her car as she drove. 'Squishy! How incredibly amazing - I was just thinking about you, darling.'

'Really, Bumpkins?' A thrill fluttered through her. 'Are you missing me terribly?'

'Terribly, heart-breakingly.'

'We could so be together more often if I got Dick's job, though, couldn't we, Bunny? Wouldn't that be wonderful?' She sighed loudly. 'Still, I suppose Melissa or Mike will get it.'

'Not necessarily, Squish. Pat's got a massive problem with Mike, search me what it is, and Melissa's been a very naughty girl.'

'Oh yes, the phone call. That's nothing though, surely? It'll blow over - nothing to do with her job.'

'She could get away with it, we'll have to see.'

'Interestingly I heard that Bernie O'Reilly might be in the running too. Now that I so can't believe, can you, Bunny?'

'Yes indeed. I think Pat is considering her actually.'

Veronica nearly lost control of the car. 'What?'

'Well she is at the top of all the sales and activity leagues, you know. She's an incredibly hard worker and everyone at the office likes her. One or two of the chaps fancy her rotten - excellent pair of legs.'

'Bumpkin - she has *no* medical background, no experience and she's only been in the company for six months, like Sam. You so have to be joking. The woman used to sell lingerie at parties for God's sake.'

'If it's any consolation, I'm thinking the same as you on this one, Squish. You're my main contender.'

'So you would back my application then?'

'Yah - absolutely'

Veronica reverted to her little girl voice, 'thank you, Bunny. I do love you.'

Thank Heavens for James - he was the one person she could rely on in this company. Gorgeous, sexy James - he would simply do anything for her now they had found each other again. The memory of his gleaming, muscular body writhing around on top of hers was totally on her mind as she drove through Leeds city centre towards the Victoria quarter, a smile still hovering around the corners of her lips. It really was all to play for now, she had an incredibly good chance of getting exactly what she wanted.

Her spirits soaring, Veronica switched off the air conditioning and opened the car window instead. Immediately the sound and smells of the city hit her - booming stereos, beer, fried food. How wonderful, alive and exciting it all was - lunch at Harvey Nicks might be nice, and then maybe some light shopping for the forthcoming conference in Spain. It was going to be particularly important this year to make the right impression - a management style one. The aim was to look sophisticated and professional, yet remain highly alluring and sexy. No easy feat. She would need to get some more shoes and maybe a new briefcase too. Oh, and she'd better check her passport.

Suddenly the traffic came to a halt and a crowd surged across the pedestrian crossing. Veronica was forced to put the handbrake on. She sighed, pushed her sunglasses on to the top of her head and rested her elbow on the window ledge. And then she saw him. She did a double take. There her husband, Greg, was sitting outside a pub with his arm around a young blond girl. He was, laughing and joking in the sunshine, smiling rapturously into the girl's face, in exactly the same way he used to look at her in fact - as if he wanted to eat her alive, couldn't wait to devour her. She knew that look, it was absolutely unmistakable, impossible to misinterpret.

Someone tooted their horn. There was the pressure of traffic behind her as the lights changed, the absolute need to keep going with the flow on the busy ring road. She tried in vain to get another look in her wing mirror. Time enough to make sure it was Greg, time enough to take in the name of the pub, and time enough to take a snapshot view of the girl - very young (nineteen?), very blond (curly, permed?), very tanned, very slim, tight jeans exposing hip bones and navel, her arms wrapped around Veronica's husband as if she'd known him all her life.

As Veronica turned the corner she saw him slip his hands down the back of the girl's low-rise jeans and pull her towards him. The girl laughed, tilting her head slightly as he moved to kiss her lips. Then they were out of sight.

It wasn't entirely unexpected - she had known something wasn't quite right -he had been that bit more distant of late, a little less attentive, a little cooler. He hadn't wanted to discuss holidays. He'd forgotten their anniversary, rushing out to grab a box of chocolates from the newsagents downstairs as soon as he realised. Chocolates for God's sake! As if she ever ate chocolates. All the signs had been there, yet they still hadn't prepared her for the gut-wrenching shock of actually seeing him with another woman. And one at least ten years younger than her at that.

'Fucking bastard,' she spat, gripping the steering wheel ever tighter as she manipulated the bends in the multi-storey car-park. Dear me, someone's tyres were screeching. A woman with a small child glared at her. An old man in a trilby pointed at her accusingly.

'Calm down, Veronica,' she told herself. 'Calm down - what was it feisty, American women said? Don't get mad - get the money.'

She parked and took several deep breaths. Right, first she would have the lunch she had planned for herself, but not at Harvey Nicks. No - somewhere far, far more expensive. She chose an exclusive bistro popular with media types and business men. The menu was certainly tempting, and Veronica perused it with interest. Then, ignoring the pan-fried armadillo with chef's special dressing, and the octopus on a bed of celeriac drizzled with chef's special jus, she ordered a rocket salad with a glass of white wine while deciding what to do next. And as she pushed the lettuce around her plate, plots and plans began to form in her mind. By the time she had drained her glass and mauled her leaves to a point of no return, she knew what she had to do.

First she went to the building society and drew out ten thousand pounds from their joint account. And then she spent it. She thought it would take days but it didn't. The money disappeared remarkably quickly and she began to understand why Victoria Beckham needed so much of it. So there she was - just another elegant, classy blond, laden with designer carrier bags, snapping at the sales assistants.

'What do you think of the new Russian peasant look, madam?' a chirpy young girl with a pleasant enough face, in the Gucci section at Harvey Nicks asked her.

'Suitable for Russian peasants,' Veronica snapped, rifling aggressively through the classic black trouser suits. What she wanted was a pair of slim fit, black trousers. Veronica had a thirty-six inch inside leg measurement and she intended to exploit that fact to the maximum.

She could have been a model if she'd wanted: her mother had taken her as a gangly seventeen year old to a modelling agency, thinking it would help Veronica appreciate the value of money if she could earn some of her own to support herself through university. But there had been a problem with the photographer. First, he had given her too many orders, and secondly there had been so much smiling involved it hurt her face.

In less than ten minutes, she bought an immaculate black trouser suit together with black leather, high heeled boots and a matching leather bag to die for - the exact opposite of the peasant look. Veronica simply did not do poor. The bill totalled just over two and a half thousand pounds. Then she moved on to Versace.

She got stuff from Versace, Dolce and Gabbana, Armani, Donna Karan, Prada and Miu Miu. She got bags, shoes and make up, luggage, perfume and music. She got so much stuff she could barely carry it all back to the car. In just over three hours she had spent ten grand - exactly the same amount her husband had planned to spend on the speed boat he had been saving up for. And only then did she begin to feel a bit better. Cheap at the price really, she reasoned - a divorce would cost him a whole lot more. Greg should be grateful.

Mission accomplished, she took the booty back to their luxury waterfront apartment, poured herself a glass of chilled white wine as usual, and then another, and then another. She lit a cigarette and sat on her leather futon looking out over the city. There was no one she wanted to call, or could call to discuss the matter with. It was a warm evening, the beginning of summer, the sky a mixture of pinks and corals, blues and lilacs. The sounds drifting up to her were of people drinking outside bars, clinking glasses with each other, telling jokes - sudden bursts of laughter filling the air - sounds of summer, of hope. Veronica closed her eyes for a moment. She and Greg used to share this time together when they were newly married and everyone thought they were such an amazing couple - so glamorous, so absolutely right for each other. When he was faithful. When he loved her. The lying, cheating skunk.

Leaning out of the window, she surveyed the scene - young men in their shirt sleeves were drinking beer from bottles outside the café beneath her, enjoying the last of the evening sun while they watched gangs of giggling girls saunter past in short skirts. Suddenly a Porsche screeched to a halt directly in front of them and the passenger door flew open. Everyone watched as a young woman staggered out, crouched down and vomited heartily into the gutter. Another woman shot out from the driver's side, dressed in a leopard skin jacket and a short, tight, red skirt.

'Are y'all right, pet?' she shouted to her friend.

The first woman doubled over and noisily retched again. She gagged a couple of times, then wiped her mouth with the back of her hand. 'Aye, I am now,' she said, jumping back into the Porsche.

Veronica wrinkled her nose and closed the window. It really was quite true what Mummy had always said - money and class did not always go together. There were some things a person so couldn't buy.

Her wine glass was empty again. May as well finish the rest of that Chablis, she decided, while she was waiting for her little problem to roll up. Greg the dentist, had already started to pay for his misdemeanours, but he would pay one hell of a lot more yet for crossing Veronica Ball than he would ever have dreamed possible. She had not been nicknamed Veronica Ball-breaker at school for nothing.

While Veronica poured herself another glass of wine, the lads in the team - Johnny, Mike and Brett - were having their weekly business meeting in the Slug and Pellet.

'Have you heard about the new nurse we're getting?' Mike asked the other two over the noise of the football match.

Johnny and Brett shook their heads, their attention fixed on the wide screen above the bar. 'Go on, you stupid bastard,' Johnny yelled, shaking his fist at the TV.

'It's about time though, isn't it? I mean we're the only team without a nurse adviser. No wonder our sales aren't as good as the others when we've had no one setting up depression clinics for us.'

'Cool,' Brett said.

'No way should he be sent off. No frigging way!' Johnny stood up, shouting at the screen along with most of the other blokes in the bar.

Then he noticed the expression on Mike's face. 'Sorry, mate. What was that?'

'Oh nothing - just a new nurse joining the team.'

'Oh. ' With the football match temporarily suspended while an argument ensued between the referee and a manager, Mike, Brett and Johnny drank their beer.

'So…' said Mike.

'Cool,' said Brett.

'Ah, well,' said Johnny.

Brett looked around him, searching for something to say. In the end he said, 'I hear Sam Farmer's having an affair,' that being the first thing to pop into his head.

'Sorry? What?' Mike and Johnny stared at him. 'Who with?'

'Shit, I thought everyone knew, d'ya know what I mean? Melissa rang me yesterday, yeah? You know - wanting to come out and work with me, yeah? Said she'd just been out with Sam, and her sales were really crap, and she had to have loads of extra training, d'ya know what I mean?'

'Go on,' Mike said.

'Well it was just that she said something about Sam relying on her relationship with James Harris more than her limited talents. So I asked her what she meant, and she said that at the end of the day, yeah? all she was going to say was that it was hard work that matters not who you sleep with.'

Johnny was finding it quite hard to speak normally. 'That's not true,' he said. 'Sam wouldn't be unfaithful to Simon, no way.' He stared angrily at Brett. Stupid bastard must have got it wrong.

'Melissa said it was common knowledge, d'ya know what I mean?' Brett persisted.

'I'm saying nothing,' Mike said.

'That must be a bit of a strain for you,' Johnny said.

Mike smiled. 'Yeah well, I've seen loads of girls lose their jobs that way. It's never the manager that goes, always the female rep, and they certainly don't get promoted. Once word gets out that they're the company bike, no one takes them seriously.'

'What about sleeping yourself to the top, though?' Brett said, his eyes wide. 'I mean, at the end of the day, right? The women have got that advantage, haven't they? It happens all the time, d'ya know what I mean?'

'Well I'd sleep with James if I thought I'd get promoted,' Johnny said, taking a slug of beer. He looked up at Mike and Brett's shocked expressions, and grinned.

'Would you?' Brett said.

Johnny laughed. 'Did I ever tell you about that time our very own regional trainer invited me to her room to examine her documents?'

The others shook their heads. Mike began to smile.

'Oh yeah - Mel asked me to come over and when I got there, she opened the door and let her towel slip. I'm not kidding, mate - I swear on my mother's life.'

Brett gasped. 'Was she naked?'

Johnny grinned. 'Do you know, it's funny really, but all I could think was - bloody hell, that needs a good trim.'

Mike shook his head incredulously. ' I just couldn't go for that. I'd rather have a cup of tea and a biscuit.'

'I think I might have to give her one to put her out of her misery one of these days, though' Johnny said.

'She might be your next manager - could be a smart career move,' Mike said. 'Anyway, talking of managers, what do you think

Bernie's chances really are for getting Dick's job?'

'Pretty good,' said Brett.

'Depends on what gets out,' said Johnny, dragging lazily on his cigarette.

'Like what?' Mike said.

'Oh this and that,' Johnny teased. He knew what Mike was after, he wasn't born yesterday, but he didn't care that much either. He took another drag. 'All I know is that a mate of mine, and I told Sam this, told me that Bernie makes up her calls and sells Happylux to the patients so they'll ask the doctor for it. She sits on their beds with her sales brochure - its bloody unbelievable, mate.'

'All you know? And Sam knows too? What Bernie is doing is against the ABPI code of practice, and Sam is withholding information as well.'

'Er, so am I, mate,' Johnny reminded him. 'And no-one can prove it, remember.'

'Hasn't she been reported?'

'No, Mel said….'

'Melissa knows?'

'Yeah, well, we talk.' Johnny looked at the floor, trying to avoid Mike's heated gaze on him. Of course, Mike had once been a manager hadn't he? Once a company man, always a company man.

Brett looked from Johnny to Mike, and then from Mike to Johnny. What was all the fuss was about? Most reps did dodgy things didn't they? Although by the look on Mike's face, he could be wrong on that one.

Eventually Mike said, 'Right, we'd better get on with some work. I wondered how you two were fixed for running some local evening meetings. We could do one in each of our areas and invite all the doctors to all three.'

'Yeah, good idea mate,' said Johnny, groaning inwardly at the huge amount of extra work that would be involved. 'But who's going to organise it all?' Immediately they both looked at Brett. 'Would be good experience for you, mate,' Johnny said.

Mike nodded. 'All you've got to do, Brett, is book a couple of hotels or restaurants and ask some consultant psychiatrists to speak on a really interesting topic, like psycho killers or something, and then do a mailing. We'll help you with the mailing.'

'Cool,' Brett said, wondering not for the first time, if he'd been shafted.

Chapter 9

Melissa, waiting in the reception area of the Holiday Inn, looked at her watch for the third time in less than five minutes. It was now eleven o'clock and the new nurse, Trisha, was nowhere in sight. Damn, damn and damn again - where the hell was she? Two hours late was not a joke, and worse, the woman didn't have her mobile phone yet so she couldn't contact her. She would give her ten more minutes and then leave.

Frankly, today was not a good day to mess Melissa around. It had not been a good weekend. Not good at all. She ordered another pot of tea and some more biscuits to pass the time, while she ruminated yet again on the matter of Bruce Pilkington. They had agreed that he would come round to hers for a meal on Saturday night. Fuelled with excitement, she had decorated the house with scented candles, bought several seductive CDs, and prepared trout and Arctic Roll for dinner. Oh the anticipation - soaking in her Edwardian Slipper bath in warm, soapy water up to her neck, dressing carefully in a satin slip dress - so easy just to slip off again, reclining on her cream leather sofa to the sound of Norah Jones. Yes, the anticipation had certainly been the best bit because Bruce Pilkington had never showed up. Nor had he called. Nor had there been an answer from his mobile phone. Distraught, Melissa had finally given up and gone to bed alone. Never again would she be able to play Norah Jones without thinking about Bruce Pilkington and what might have been.

Sunday had been spent at her mothers, trapped with her cackling coven of neighbours, rueing the day she had ever told her mother about Dr Pilkington. Why, oh why, did she never learn her lesson?

'Tell Elsie all about your young man, Melissa,' her mother insisted, with what Melissa was certain was a malevolent gleam in her eye.

'Oh please, mum,' Melissa hissed.

'Elsie, our Melissa's going to be married to a doctor - a consultant in what was it, Melissa? Come on - tell Elsie what he does.'

'A doctor?' Elsie gasped in amid a clatter of tea-cups. 'Well, of course, our Frieda nearly married a dentist at one time. Did I ever tell you about that, Maureen?'

'Mmmm,' Melissa's mother said. 'But she didn't marry him, did she? What is it Frieda's husband does?'

Elsie froze. 'He's not her husband.'

'Oh, of course - I remember you telling me now. It's just that I always assume - you know, with her having five children.'

Envisaging handbags at dawn, Melissa found herself saying, 'let's look at bridal brochures, shall we, Mum?'

Worse, this morning she had left home at eight o'clock in order to meet Trisha, who had just joined their team, and had stopped for petrol on the way to the hotel. Just as she got out of her car, she realised that she was the object of a discussion between a couple of bald, fat blokes standing by a lorry.

'Not *too* bad,' one said, as if he assumed she must be deaf.

'Eight and a half weeks?' the other one asked.

'Nah - four and a half, more like.'

'Minutes? Ha, ha.'

'Just about worth one, though.'

'Nah, not my type.'

'Bastards,' Melissa fumed, assaulted by an array of pornography as she walked into the petrol station to pay. 'Every last one of them.'

And now this: she looked at her watch again - quarter past eleven. Oh it was absolutely ridiculous. How much longer could she pretend to be busy on her laptop?

Trisha was supposed to be with her all week because Dick had said he had to go to the office for an important meeting. Melissa was to show Trisha what the reps did, how to approach the GPs, and get her involved in discussions on setting up depression clinics. The team had never had a nurse to help them and consequently there were very few depression clinics in their area. This was important to all of them because if patients weren't being diagnosed then how could they get treatment? And more to the point, Happylux?

Melissa had four appointments booked that morning - Trisha would have made several excellent contacts - yet she had been forced to cancel every single precious one of them. She began to pace - five more minutes, no more. Damn and blast the bloody woman.

She was just about to go, when at twenty minutes past eleven Trisha walked in. Melissa stopped pacing and stared. No, this could surely not be her. 'Tell me I'm dreaming,' she muttered under her breath. A tiny, frantic looking blond woman with her hair partly pinned up in grips, blinked short-sightedly into the gloom of the hotel foyer. Melissa's eyes travelled south: Trisha had on a black mini-skirt which barely covered her knickers, long black boots and a little yellow jacket. My God, she thought, she looks like a hooker who's made an effort to be respectable for school sports day.

The first rule in medical sales is that the representation is sober - it's a serious business, after all. Melissa had been advised that 'funereal' was best, if in doubt, after turning up to her training course six years ago in a cream skirt she was reliably informed you could see through - this after four days of wearing it. Most of the women opted for trouser suits in black or grey, although there were a few individual attempts to spice things up. However, no one had as yet gone as 'individual' as a mini-skirt with thigh high boots.

'Hiya,' Trisha said in a breathy voice.

Melissa looked pointedly at her watch and waited.

'Oh, I'm so sorry. I really am, please don't be too angry with me, please. I tried so hard. I've been up since six o'clock and I've been driving since seven.'

'Four and a quarter hours? Like, where have you come from ?'

'Sheffield.'

'Did you, like, take a detour to Scotland or something?'

'Oh that rings a bell - Scotch Corner actually. Look, I am so, so sorry, I really am. I'm afraid I'm not used to the motorways and things. I've been working on the wards for so long, and my husband used to do all the driving, and now he's left me for another woman.'

Oh God, Melissa thought, now she's going to cry. It should be me that's bloody well crying. And what the hell was that on Trisha's left shoulder? It looked like.... ugh, it looked like a sick stain. 'Right, well we'd better get you a cup of coffee hadn't we?' she said. 'And then perhaps if we just, like, sit and chat about the product, since it's so late? I can tell you what we do, and this afternoon we'll go and see a couple of my hospital doctors to, like, give you an understanding of how the depression clinics will help secondary care? Okay?' If in doubt, Melissa reasoned - go straight down the one hundred percent professional route and do not deviate.

'Fine, yes. Thank you,' said Trisha in a more relaxed voice. She smiled widely at Melissa. 'I knew you'd be kind as soon as I saw you. Are you a Taurus by any chance?'

Melissa battled with the pleasant expression on her face throughout lunch while she learned all about Trisha's divorce, her three young children, how her colleagues at the psychiatric hospital had been constantly angry with her. It hadn't been her fault that the ward had been set on fire and one patient had stabbed another one while she was in charge. Then there had been that incident recently with a psychotic man holding one of the nurses hostage on the roof. Again, Trisha had been left in charge, and only for a ten minute tea break. Anyway, she'd got lucky: Dick Walton had got chatting to her at one of the national nurse conferences and offered her a job on the spot.

'Did he really?' Melissa asked through gritted teeth. Well, that made a mockery of what he'd said about interviewing the length and breadth of Yorkshire but never being able to find anyone of sufficient calibre, didn't it?

Later that afternoon in the hospital car park, she continued to battle with her expression while she watched Trisha, who could barely see over the top of her steering wheel, struggle hopelessly to park the Volvo estate she had been given. In a cloud of exhaust fumes, Trisha jerked the car back and forwards in tiny jolts, each jolt bringing her closer and closer to the car on her left side. Eventually she had to have it parked for her by a workman who had spent the last ten minutes watching her with a mixture of concern and superiority. Melissa fumed inwardly, tapping her foot as she waited, having expertly swung her Audi into a space nearly quarter of an hour before. Now they would be late.

'My hero,' Trisha giggled, as the rather attractive workman in the hard hat handed her car keys back to her with a flirtatious grin. 'I adore men in hard hats don't you?' she said to Melissa, trotting breathlessly after her into the hospital.

'Mmmmm,' said Melissa.

'Oooh, this is like home from home for me,' Trisha continued. 'I'm having so much fun now I'm with you.'

'Really?' Melissa snapped, pounding down corridor after

corridor towards the outer fringes of the hospital. Eventually their surroundings became noticeably gloomier and less well kempt, seconds later they were in the psychiatric unit. Melissa knocked sharply on a large, oak door, hoping she hadn't missed her appointment with the consultant psychiatrist. But luck was on her side - the consultant swung the door open.

'Well, hello,' he said, his eyes zooming down to Trisha's boots. 'Can I offer you two ladies some coffee? I'm afraid it's only instant.'

Melissa's mouth opened and closed. That was unusual - she had never, ever been offered coffee here before. What a nice surprise. But as she opened up a perfectly pleasant discussion about depression clinics, she became increasingly aware that Trisha was staring intently at the doctor with her huge baby blue eyes, frequently crossing and uncrossing her shapely legs. Melissa's sidelong glance of irritation went unnoticed however, because the doctor was transfixed, having totally lost the thread of the conversation several minutes beforehand.

'Hello....' Melissa called, flapping diagrams and graphs in front of his face.

The doctor, still smiling at Trisha in a glazed sort of way, jumped. 'Sorry, you were saying?'

Bloody woman, Melissa fumed. She would definitely not be having her for the rest of the week. Trisha would be palmed off soon and no mistake. At three o'clock she armed her with explicit instructions on how to get home, and waved Trisha off. Then she called Sam on her car phone.

'Hi, Sam! Listen - would you mind having the new nurse with you tomorrow, and, like, for a few days actually? She's really nice.'

'Oh,' Sam said in a dull voice. 'Okay.'

'Great, thanks - you're a star. I'll have to, like, give you her home number because she hasn't got her mobile yet? If you ring her this evening, she should be there? Well at some point, anyway. Whatever.'

'Wasn't she supposed to be with you all week, though?' Sam said. 'I mean, I'm not best placed to give her all the help she needs am I?'.

'Mmmm,' Melissa said. 'Actually, I think it's, like, a good idea if she gets to see the whole spectrum. Plus she'll, like, get to know some of the team before the conference?'

'Okay.'

'Like, hello? It isn't up to me to do everything in the team, Sam - we've all got to pull our weight.'

Sam sighed heavily. 'I know. Sorry. Oh dear, oh look - I think my signal's going, I'll have to go now. Bye.'

Melissa glared at the dead phone. Oh yes, that reminded her - she really must write up Sam's report.

Chapter 10

The night before Melissa's call, Simon nuzzled up to Sam on the sofa. He kissed her neck, ran his fingers through her hair, and whispered in her ear with hot breath, 'I want to make mad, passionate love to you - right now.'

'Get off I'm watching Coronation Street,' she snapped.

'But how can you resist me? I'm not working - I'm all yours for the whole evening.'

Sam looked at him. His glasses were speckled with bits of something - what could it be? It looked like chip fat, and he had a rather offensive looking line of spittle which ran from the top lip to the bottom. It was always there and it annoyed her. 'Well I have to go out and you know I do,' she said, removing his hand from her left breast.

'Ring and cancel,' he murmured, putting it back on again.

'I can't.'

'Of course you can.' His fingers fumbled excitedly with the buttons on her blouse. 'And just think - in six months time you'll be my wife.'

'Uh-huh.' She slapped at his hand.

'You'll be an AB one then, like me.'

Sam sprung forwards. ' A what?'

'An AB one - you know, social class? As I'm a doctor you'll move up a couple of classes when you marry me.'

Sam stared at the slappable smirk on his face. 'Have I just been insulted? I'm not quite sure, perhaps you could *help me out* with this one.'

'Don't be ridiculous, I'm only saying….'

'How could you insult me like that, you, you…..bloody

hypocrite. I thought you said you were a socialist? In fact I'm surprised you haven't grown a beard and bought yourself a Volvo the way you go on, and now here you are bragging about class. Still it makes a change from bragging about money, I suppose.'

'At least I've got some money. At least I don't spend it all.'

'Neither do I.'

'No? Well, what was it you were smuggling in when I got home then? Again. Let's have a look, shall we?'

'Don't change the subject. Leave me alone. It's my hard earned money and I'll spend it how I damn well like.'

'Really? So how come I pay the mortgage and all the bills while you plead poverty?'

'Because it's your house.'

'Sam, we're supposed to be a partnership. So come on - where's your half? Come on - I want some money from you.' He grabbed at her wrist, staring angrily into her face.

'Stop it. I can't pay you, I haven't got anything,' she shrieked. Oh, this was too much. She ran upstairs, slamming the bedroom door behind her, and threw herself prostrate onto the bed. Please, please don't let him come up - he was so in her face, him and his bony fingers, always mauling her to death. And if he didn't get his way then he'd stalk off in a temper - as if she should be on tap all the time for his amusement or something. It wasn't as if he was interested in whether or not she was happy, only if she was going to get her bra off or not. Well, she was sick of it - sick, sick, sick. What a bastard! And another thing - it was hardly as if it was worth it when he did get his own way - five little whimpers and a wet patch. What more could a girl want? And anyway, how dare he ask her for money when he'd just bought himself a brand new sports car. He'd never had to worry about anything in his entire life.

Oh Christ, though, it was a good job he didn't know what a mess she was really in. She had four credit cards and six store cards - all completely full. The only thing left to plunder was her expense account with the company float in it, and that would have to be used for clothes for the conference next month or she'd haven nothing to wear.

After several minutes, she rolled onto her back to listen. Good, all was quiet, he hadn't come after her so that must mean he was going to drop the subject. She would address it at some point. But just not yet. It would be nice, she decided, just to lie here for a bit and think, to sleep.

'Sam?' The bedroom door flew open.

She sat bolt upright with a start. Simon stood silhouetted against the hallway light. 'I think we should have a proper discussion about this, don't you?' he said, moving slowly towards her.

As he drew level, she looked into his accusing eyes and said, 'push off.'

'Just how much have you been spending, Sam?'

'Not much.'

'Right, so I can have a look in your wardrobe then, can I?' he said, striding towards it.

'No. Stop. No, you can't. It's none of your business. Look, you have to stop this, I'm going out in a minute to see customers.'

'What are you frightened of? If you've nothing to hide you won't mind me taking a look at what you threw in here less than half an hour ago, will you?' he said, flinging open the wardrobe's double doors.

Sam ducked as carrier bags and boxes shot out like bullets. Oh for goodness sake, she could have told him there was a certain way you had to open that door. Clothes, shoes, coats, boots and bags were stuffed into every last crevice, not a single square centimetre of empty space remained.

Simon paled as he turned to glare at her. 'What the hell have you been doing?'

'Happy now?'

'Oh fucking ecstatic. Listen, tomorrow we're going to sit down and work out our finances, Sam. This has got to stop. How much in debt are you, anyway? A thousand?' He looked at her questioningly.

Sam met his eyes defiantly.

'What, two thousand?'

Still she stared at him.

'More? More than two thousand?'

She stood up and walked over to the bedroom window, her back to him. Why couldn't he just push off and leave her alone?

'Five?' he asked in a trembling voice.

'About that,' she muttered under her breath.

'What?'

'I said, about that.'

'Do you know the exact figure, Sam?'

There was a moment of uncomfortable silence, and then she said, 'fourteen.' The word came out louder than she expected and it hung in the air between them. When she eventually turned round, Simon had gone.

She picked up a shoe, his, and threw it at the door. Everyone was hounding her. She'd had Melissa out with her for several days recently due to this intensive extra training exercise, and it had been very stressful. Worse, she'd been forced into saying yes to loads of evening meetings because Melissa was there, ever present, hovering over her shoulder when she'd been asked. This was very tiresome because she normally avoided evening meetings with doctors like a killer virus. Oh well, there was no hope of getting out of tonight now. It was just to be hoped she had something decent to wear, that was all.

And in a way, it was a relief to go. An hour later Sam was waiting in a downtown Indian restaurant, on her own in the back room with all her Happylux leaflets, while the screen projector whirred away in anticipation. It might not be so bad, she thought, in fact she might even enjoy herself. Who knows what's round the corner?

The agreement was that the psychiatrists and junior doctors from the local psychiatric hospital would listen to a short presentation on Happylux, Sam would pay for their meal and then they would go on their own sweet way to do whatever they wished. It should all be over in two hours maximum. And at least, she consoled herself, she would have a few psychiatrists names to put into her computer for once - some compensation for missing Coronation Street and that programme on people doing up houses for profit.

An hour later, she was still waiting.

'You a rep?' the smiling waiter asked her.

'Is it that obvious? Or do most of your customers bring a projector with them?'

'Oh dearie me, this always happens - the doctors that come here are always late.' He shook his head sadly. 'The poor rep usually has to sit here for hours. Never mind, luv, cheer up. Do you want some poppadoms?'

An hour and a half later, just when she had decided to start packing up, a young couple burst breathlessly into the room. 'Oh, where is everyone?' the man said, rubbing his hand up and down the girl's back as he spoke.

'I don't know - they were supposed to be here at seven for my presentation. Anyway,' Sam said, holding out her hand. 'I'm Sam from Topham Pharmaceuticals. We haven't met have we?'

'No - Tim Bradbury. I'm one of the medical students and this is my girlfriend. She *is* a nurse so I hope you don't mind,' he said, leaning over to kiss the girl lustily.

Sam watched in dismay as the two wrestled with each others tongues. Had she invited these people? Were they in a position to prescribe her drug? She bit down her rising temper. This was exactly why she didn't do these bloody evening meetings - you always ended up paying for a pack of students to have a free meal. Damn and damn Melissa.

Presently another couple arrived, then a group of girls, laughing and shouting, followed them in. 'Sorry we're late everyone. Where's the rep? Oh - there you are. Could we get some drinks over here, do you think please?'

'I'm Sam,' Sam said, stepping forwards. 'And you are?'

A dark haired girl lit a cigarette and said, 'oh we're all students. We so knew you wouldn't mind. I think some of the psychiatrists will be along later - we last saw them going into the Spearmint Rhino though, so I wouldn't hold your breath. Better put the vindaloo on hold, ha, ha!'

Sam packed away her Happylux leaflets, unplugged the projector, and went to sit quietly at the end of the table, letting the students' inane banter ricochet over the top of her head. She picked at her onion bhaji. The very second this lot finished their main course she was out of here. Ten minutes max.

Suddenly a loud cheer broke out. Sam looked up to see that two of the psychiatrists had finally rolled in. One of them she recognised as the elusive Medical Director from forensic psychiatry who never saw representatives. Well, what a coup - at least she had some justification for the meal expenses now.

He slipped into the seat next to hers, smiled wickedly and said, 'so, lady rep - which is your favourite vibrator? The Rabbit? Oh no, let me guess - you prefer the real thing.'

Sam, about to take a sip of wine, spluttered.

'Tell me your wildest fantasies then,' he said, his head drunkenly lolling onto her shoulder.

'Selling lots of Happylux,' she snapped, determined to get the name in at the very least.

'No, don't be silly,' he whispered in her ear. 'Do you know what mine is?'

'No.'

'Sheep.'

'Oh please!'

'Really. Ha, ha! I want to *be* a sheep - they're so lovely and woolly, don't you think?'

Well, this was psychiatry for you, Sam thought, casting around in vain for a normal person to talk to. She took another sip of wine, wishing she could finish the bottle. In one.

'Why don't you come and see me tomorrow? I'll show you round,' the Medical Director suggested.

'Really?' Sam blinked at him. Blimey, this was a stroke of luck. How had he got from sheep to this all of a sudden? Perhaps he was sobering up?

'Yes. I'll show you round our unit for the criminally insane. Then we could do lunch, maybe?'

'How lovely.' Sam smiled broadly. Okay, maybe the evening had been worth it after all.

'So, are you coming on to the party with us?'

She reached for her bags. 'No, but thanks anyway. I'll pay the bill and see you tomorrow. Bye everyone,' she called.

'Oh, bye,' a girl said. 'Who was *she*, everyone?'

Full of anticipation, Sam arrived at noon the following day for her tour of the forensic unit. 'I'm here to see the Medical Director,' she said to the receptionist, the same one who told her he wouldn't see her two weeks ago. 'I have an appointment.' She put her briefcase down while she waited. What a lovely place, she'd never noticed before - lots of potted palms and comfy sofas.

'Hello, excuse me?'

Sam turned back to the receptionist with an expectant smile on her face.

Sorry, dear. There's no one here,' the receptionist informed her. 'Everything's had to be cancelled this morning - they're all ill.'

'What? *All* of them?'

'I'm afraid so. Would you like a token so you can get out again? I'm afraid you won't be able to get out of the car park without one of these.'

Sam's pleased smile faded. 'Oh, right. Okay, thanks.' Christ, wasn't that just typical of her luck? But as she bent to pick up her briefcase, the double doors behind her suddenly swung open with a flourish, smacking into the walls on both sides.

'Ah, there you are! Come on up to my office, will you?' a voice boomed.

Sam jumped and spun round. There he was - the Medical Director himself, holding the door open for her. Clearly he hadn't been up long - he was still in his overcoat and his hair was standing on end. But still….

'Thank you,' she said with a grateful smile.

'Sorry about that,' he said, bounding up the stairs two at a time in front of her. 'I'm afraid we had an all nighter last night - still drinking brandy at five this morning…' Three flights up and they were in his office. Immediately he reached for the keys to his desk, pulled out a flask of something and took a swig.

'Thank you for seeing me,' Sam said, trying not to breathe in the overpowering stench of stale alcohol fumes. 'It's really kind of you.'

He shrugged and lit a cigarette. 'Hang on a minute, just let me open a window - we don't want to go up in flames, do we? Now,' he said, throwing himself onto the couch, 'See that up there?'

Sam looked to where he was pointing. A head and shoulders plaster cast adorned with a black woolly wig and black rimmed glasses stared back at her.

'Er, yes?'

'Put them on, will you? And then we'll go walk about.'

'Sorry?'

'Come on, I insist. Everyone has to wear the wig and glasses if they want to come on one of my tours.'

'You are joking aren't you? I can't walk about like that - I'll look like Groucho Marx.'

'No tour no lunch,' he said, taking another swig. 'Your call.'

Tentatively, she took the wig and glasses down, and put them on.

'Excellent,' he said, suddenly bursting with renewed energy. 'Now, let's go and see my maddest patients first, shall we?'

Trailing after him onto the wards, it was impossible to ignore the hysterical laughter. Great hoots and guffaws followed them everywhere they went. 'Have you met my latest recruit?' he asked the sniggering nurses, while Sam's face burned.

He'd even insisted she keep the wig and glasses on during lunch in the canteen, by which time most of the other psychiatrists had arrived. They talked to her as if it was quite normal that she had them on, only splitting their sides with shrieks of laughter after she'd gone. Although not before she heard them.

Sam headed straight to the shops. Tears stung her eyes as she drove off - oh dear God, she could never, ever go back there again to those mad bastards. Never. Only spending a serious amount of money she didn't have could save her sanity now. In fact, it would serve them all right if she came back as a patient herself in the not too distant future.

She screeched into the car park and began to wander aimlessly round the shopping mall. What could she buy? She must get something - something to make her feel better. But it was not to be. She flicked through racks and racks of clothes in an irritated manner - everything was for teenagers and skinny ones at that. Which grown woman in her right mind, for example, would wear these groin revealing pink hipsters?

Sam stared at the monstrous pink pants for several seconds, before realising that she couldn't move. Put them back, she told herself. But no, nothing happened - an enormous wave of tiredness had engulfed her like a general anaesthetic, and there was nothing she could do to stop it. She fought with heavy eye lids, struggled desperately to stop them closing. She grabbed wildly for the nearest clothes rail as her knees buckled. Voices crowded in on her, the lights were too bright, a small child's screams too piercing. There was only one thing to do - she had to get back to her car, and home as soon as possible.

Once safely in the car, she closed her eyes for a few minutes, letting nightmare thoughts race through her mind. What was happening to her? She was going to lose her job, wasn't she? What would she do if they sacked her? If they said she just wasn't cut out for the corporate world? There were no answers, nothing obvious. Try not to worry, she told herself. Nobody else worried themselves to death - look at Johnny. Relax, relax.

And it was at that moment that Melissa's call had come. Great, so now she had another problem - she had to have this person, this nurse tagging around with her all day tomorrow - bloody Trisha somebody. There was no response from Trisha's phone until ten o'clock that night. Simon was on call at the hospital and Sam had planned an early night. Sighing with exasperation she decided to give Trisha's phone one more try before turning in. Trisha sounded agitated. There were kids crying and arguing in the background. But they agreed to meet at eight- thirty the following morning at a motorway hotel just outside Chesterfield. At least, for once, she an appointment to go to. Hopefully she would be able to string it out.

At ten-thirty the next morning Sam was still waiting. Now, had she got this wrong? No, she reassured herself, they had definitely agreed on eight-thirty, she was not going mad. The problem was one of communication, that was all, because Trisha had no mobile phone. She tried Trisha's home number - maybe she was ill? But it rang and rang. She looked at her watch - quarter to eleven. It would be a push now to make her appointment on time. Sam waited. Eleven o'clock arrived. Right, well there was no longer any option other than to cancel her one and only appointment.

And it was then that irritation kicked in. Christ, she was in enough trouble as it was. Where was the blasted woman? Should she call Head Office? Perhaps she should phone Melissa for some advice. Yes, that's what she would do. She tapped in Melissa's name on her mobile and waited, only vaguely aware, at first, of the strange apparition that had appeared in front of her. No, surely not - this could not be her, no way.

The two women stared at each other. They were the only two women who were alone and obviously waiting for someone. Trisha looked at a beautiful woman in a black trouser suit holding a silver phone. She looked at the luscious red curls framing an exquisite face, the porcelain skin, the bright green eyes, the lip-glossed full lips, and then the expression she was used to seeing on people's faces when they had been waiting for her - the totally hacked off but trying to conceal it one. Tentatively, Trisha tried a smile.

Sam stared back at Trisha, her eyebrows somewhere up near her hair line as she took in the long, blonde hair, which was fastened up in parts with grips, while the rest fell down. She took in the white platform shoes - Spice girls circa 1995 - and the long floral dress, which had a couple of buttons missing at strategically important points and a large blackcurrant stain down the front. Worse, the dress was entirely see-through and you could actually see her striped knickers through it.

'Trisha?' she asked, thinking, please no.

'Hiya,' Trisha said, rushing forwards with little steps like a pony. 'Before you say anything, I'm really sorry I'm late, but I got lost.'

'From Sheffield?'

'Yes. I went towards Chesterfield like you said but I couldn't find the bypass and it was only when I saw the signs for London that I realised I'd gone too far. I really am sorry. I will get the hang of this one day.' Trisha stared at Sam with her huge, baby blue eyes.

'Don't worry, Trisha, we all have days like that. Shall we get you a coffee? Then we can try to see some doctors. I can't promise anything, mind you.'

'Oh thanks, Sam. You're all so nice.'

Sam gave Trisha instructions on how to get back to Sheffield shortly after lunch. Then she called Brett.

'Brett, hi! Listen, Melissa says we are all to work with our new nurse this week, Would you give her a call tonight and fix up for tomorrow?'

'Oh cool. No probs. D'ya know what I mean?'

'Great, thanks,' Sam said. Thank the Lord God Himself for useful idiots.

Chapter 11

Pat Hardcastle and James Harris were again discussing who should take over from Dick, on a temporary basis at least. It was now pretty urgent since they'd had word via Alistair McCraw, the MD, that the licence for the new product in cardiology was imminent. Dick would be moved quickly into his new position as National Sales Manager, and therefore a stand-in for his region was required urgently. There would be time later to recruit for the permanent position.

They were in Pat's office on the top floor at Head Office - a modern complex, which closely resembled an airport terminal from the outside. The vertical blinds were drawn against a breezy blue sky. The air conditioning hummed.

'How about Bernie?' Pat suggested. 'She would breathe life into that group - let's see what she's made of.'

'You have to be joking, Pat.' James wondered what planet Pat was from sometimes. She was like the New Labour Government, he thought - all ideas, radical proposals and pledges which sounded great but were actually going to cause maximum distress and chaos to the people down below. Living in her ivory tower she forgot about follow through, and if complaints surfaced later then people were just stupid. Or worse - the big No-no: Negative. They would then, of course, have to be 'managed out.'

'Look, wouldn't Melissa be the obvious choice for an immediate take-over?' he asked. 'She stands in for him anyway, and she's an incredibly good regional trainer. She works amazingly hard. We can see how she fares, and then run the assessment centre after the annual conference. It would look a bit odd if we bypassed Melissa, you know.'

'Melissa! That woman's a total liability. Haven't you heard all the rumours, James? Surely you must have noticed her behaviour towards men. I want to get her off that training position all together, not give her any false hopes.'

James, who was actually pretty used to women throwing themselves at him, had not noticed Melissa's behaviour being any different to any other woman's. He sighed heavily and leaned back, putting his feet up onto Pat's desk. 'Pat, rumours are just that - rumours. We can't crush the woman's future simply because of one person's complaint. Look - she knows what she's doing and she's an amazingly low risk factor here. We could at least give her the chance to run things for a few months - to prove her mettle, yah?'

Pat scowled at the soles of James' polished shoes.

James, noticing the look, removed his feet from her view. Drawing up his chair, he leaned forwards and smiled winningly. 'My dearest Patricia - you absolutely know that Bernie only has six months experience. The resentment would be simply huge. Look, what about Mike? Again just as a temporary measure - I think the others would accept him.'

Pat's eyes darkened. A rash began to spread up her neck. 'Over my dead body!' she snapped. After that... *incident*, Mike isn't getting anywhere near management ever again - not if I have anything to say about it, anyway.'

'When does the poor guy get a second chance, Pat? It was ten years ago now, wasn't it? You so can't punish him forever.'

'Oh I can.'

'Well it has to be Melissa then. If you gave it to Bernie, even on a temporary basis, we'd probably get resignations left, right and centre.'

'Is that a bad thing do you think? I mean we are talking about

Dick's region here, James.'

'You're an amazingly cruel woman, Pat.' James smiled at her in what he trusted was an irresistible manner. It usually worked. He waited.

Eventually Pat returned a semblance of a smile. 'Oh go on then - Melissa it is. But don't give her any false hopes. Stress that it is only temporary and she will have to apply for the job just like everyone else.'

James relaxed. Excellent, it had all gone to plan. Pat was, of course, absolutely right about Melissa - she was a liability. That gave Squish a fighting chance. 'What actually happened between you and Mike, anyway?' he asked her, as they strolled out to the coffee machine.

'Oh, you don't want to know, luv.'

James smiled his sympathetic smile. She would tell him sooner or later, of that he was certain.

And so Melissa Crow had one of the best days she'd had in years. Today she was supervising Bernie. Bernie had a huge meeting planned for an entire hospital. She had engineered matters so that she was the only rep to sponsor the hospital's annual meeting in the Great Hall. Normally there would be at least a dozen reps. This time there was just Bernie. Bernie would be able to record all one hundred and fifty doctors plus many hundreds of nurses as sales calls that day. Her call rate should soon be racked up to a staggering thirty-two customers per day: not just a record breaker for Topham but for the entire industry.

Melissa waited for her at the main entrance. Bernie had squeezed in a breakfast presentation in the junior doctors' Mess before meeting her. 'I'll be right with you, so I will,' she shrieked down her mobile phone a few minutes earlier, over and above what sounded like a rugby brawl. Melissa checked the time - eight forty-five. Bernie was truly mind boggling. Bernie, she knew, sent herself off to sleep to the tones of various self-help tapes, instructing her sub-conscious mind to overcome all difficulties, focus on her goals and channel her energies, which were considerable. Melissa had indeed witnessed Bernie's abundance of energy. Long after all the other reps had gone to bed at meetings and conferences, Bernie would still be up - drinking, dancing, and networking on full power. That's when she was generally at her most lethal, zooming in on managers, moving in for the kill when the competition had thrown in the towel and gone to bed - exactly the right time, she knew, to pick off the tired and the drunk, those who suddenly found themselves isolated and vulnerable.

Bernie had to succeed. Confiding in Melissa on a long coach journey to Gatwick Airport one morning she'd chatted away to stop Melissa feeling travel sick and told her she was one of eight, all of whom had been born into poverty in Southern Ireland. She was the runt of the litter, the little sister who had not yet achieved anything outstanding and she was absolutely determined that she would. To Bernie, everything was a challenge that she could overcome: there was no such word as 'no' in her vocabulary. At this point Melissa had been violently sick. But of course, Bernie was to sales what a stripper was to a rugby club. Bernie, frankly, was a star.

'Hi, Mel!' Melissa whirled round. Bernie, dressed in a mini-skirt and high heels, grabbed Melissa's arm and man handled her into the hall. 'Now would you be a darlin' and get this exhibition stand up for me? I've a lovely man somewhere bringing in all my boxes.'

Melissa pursed her lips. Erecting the huge exhibition stand was a job two grown men would struggle to do, yet Bernie had disappeared and she had just ten minutes before the customers would start arriving. There was little choice other than to get started. She began to struggle with the scaffolding and heavy boards, glancing round a few minutes later to see Bernie's 'lovely man' weighed down with crates. A hump backed, near dwarf sized pensioner with rheumy eyes and buckling knees staggered after sprightly Bernie, who was giving him sharp directions as to where he should be putting everything.

'And when you've done that, there's a load more in the car boot,' she said to him with a big smile. 'So, Melissa - Holy Mother of God, what are you doing here? Come on now woman, we've got five minutes, so we have.'

The two women rushed around in a whirlwind of leaflets, spotlights, and Happylux tissues, pens and clocks, finishing with seconds to spare.

Melissa, a slight sweat having broken out on her forehead, glared at Bernie. 'If you'd met me at eight thirty like we planned....'

'Oh, hold on a moment, Mel.' Bernie lunged towards a small doctor who thought he had managed to grab a pen and escape without having to talk to the rep. 'Hello, there! Did you get all you wanted just now? Where are you from, doctor? Did you come far today?' Bernie asked him with a huge grin.

'I only really wanted the pen and, er, I'm from just across the corridor, actually,' he said, inching away as best he could.

'Oh, wow! That's very interesting. Very interesting indeed.' She placed her hand on his wrist, and then got straight to the point: 'So, how much Happylux have you used so far this month exactly?'

'What? Er, none so far, sorry.'

'None? None?' Bernie screeched. 'But why ever not? What's wrong with it? Are you trying to put me out of my home and onto the streets?'

'No, of course not…...'

'Now you come on over here and I'll show you exactly why you should be using Happlux as your first line treatment for all your patients every time. I promise you I will have you totally convinced.'

'But I'm not in psychiatry and I haven't really got time…...'

'Oh, you don't need to be - everybody's depressed these days. Now come on, you've got five minutes, doctor. Now would you be taking a look at this poor woman in the 'before' photograph,' she said, thrusting a sales leaflet in his face. 'Did you ever see anything in your life as miserable as the poor soul? Imagine what her life would have been like without Happylux. Now look at her in the 'after' photograph following a course of Happylux. See the difference? Could you deny your patients that chance in life, doctor?'

By the time she had finished with him, Bernie had an agreement from the doctor that he would be using Happylux from now on, would be telling all his colleagues about it, and would also be speaking to some GPs for her next week.

Melissa and Bernie watched him run towards the door, stethoscope and papers flapping madly. Bernie turned to Melissa with a smile of satisfaction. 'Now,' she said. 'If we do another ten each like that before lunch then we've done a good day's work.'

'Right. Well, I am, like, only here to observe, you know?' Melissa reminded her.

Bernie smiled. 'Mmm, but there's nothing to stop you from rolling up your sleeves, surely? We all work for the same company, Mel. If the company does well, then we all do well.'

'Of course,' said Melissa, disappearing to answer her phone. Bernie was such a nice person, so energetic and bubbly. So, why did she always feel so depressed whenever she was with her? 'Yes?' she snapped into the phone, without having noticed who was calling. 'Yes, it is Melissa. Sorry, I'm, like, a bit tied up right now? Oh hello, James! No, not in that sense, ha, ha! I wish, ha, ha! Sorry, what was that?' A smile of pleasure began to spread across her face. 'Really? Well, yes of course, I would be more than happy. What now? Today?'

She marched quickly back to Bernie. 'Well, it seems we have a new manager,' she said over the heads of several nurses who were hoovering up freebies straight off the stand and into carrier bags with well practised expertise.

Bernie, who was trying to hold things down, shrieked, 'hold on a moment, would you, Mel? No, not more than one clock each. I'll have to nail them down, so I will.' Once the nurses had moved on, she grabbed Melissa's arm and pulled her round the back of the exhibition stand. 'What? Who?'

'That's why you should have, like, shared this sponsorship with other companies, Bernie, isn't it? It's not fair on the doctors and nurses - there isn't enough stuff.'

'Are you mad? And give the competition a chance? You must be joking. Now what was that about a new manager?'

'It's me,' Melissa said triumphantly. 'I must be, like, the youngest one they've ever had? Certainly the most glamorous, anyway. I can't believe it, can you?'

Bernie smiled widely. 'Oh, that's fantastic news. Well done, Mel. Well done, you. You must be thrilled.' She threw her bony arms around Melissa's neck and gave her a sharp hug.

'Oh I am,' Melissa said happily. 'Listen, I've got to tell the rest of the team, and then I've to drive to Head Office? You can manage can't you, Bern?'

'Yes, yes. Now, would this position be permanent at all?'

'Not exactly.' Melissa's voice lost a fraction of it's joy. 'The job will be advertised at some stage. But they have to do that, you know.'

'Oh, but you'll get it anyway, of course.'

'There are no guarantees, Bernie.'

'Oh, but you will, Mel,' Bernie said. And then added, 'there's no one else anyway. Not unless you count Veronica, that is. Mike won't get it because of all those rumours about what he did in the past, and his sales are no great shakes, and the rest of us don't have the experience.'

'Hello…' Melissa said. 'I heard you were the main contender.'

'Me? Little me? Now where on earth would you be hearing that from?' Bernie beamed delightedly. 'No, Veronica's your competition. She's got three years experience now, and she's got her marketing certificate, and she did all that time in the NHS doing their statistics and analysis if you remember?'

Melissa shook her head, frowning slightly. She hadn't. 'Oh, right,' she said in a much smaller voice altogether.

'No, Veronica's your woman. I'd watch her very carefully if I were you,' Bernie continued gleefully.

'Thanks.' Melissa grabbed her mobile and walked out to the car park. She had a matter of hours in which to inform everyone before rushing home to pack her bags for the pre-conference meeting in Southampton. 'Yes, ' she shouted down the phone to each member of the team. 'I'm, like, your manager now?'

'Cool,' Brett said.

'To be expected - well done,' said Mike. 'Got to go - people to see and all that, you know how it is?'

'Mel, that's fantastic,' Sam squealed. 'No more Dick - this calls for a celebration.'

'Gosh, that's amazing,' Veronica said in a dull voice.

Yes, Melissa thought, it certainly is amazing. Well, she'd saved the best until last. Now she would call Johnny. What an exciting conference it would be this year. She took a deep breath, her high spirits returning rapidly. Everything was going her way. And this year she had two reasons to feel excited about the conference: firstly she was now a manager and soon everyone would know it, and secondly she was going to give Johnny King the ride of his life. Bruce Pilkington had gone on holiday to the Philippines and she did not expect him to come back disease free, therefore Johnny was definitely her next target, which was why she had so cleverly leaked the information that Sam and James were an item. Good old Brett, the useful idiot strikes again, she thought with a chuckle as she pressed Johnny's name on her phone.

'Johnny, hi!' she said in a breathy voice.

'Mel - hope you've packed your bikini, sweetheart. I hear we're off to Malaga the week after next.'

'Ooh, ha, ha! Well, I've got a thong and a cut off T-shirt, actually?'

'Sounds interesting.'

'Yes. And I've got, like, an all over tan as well?'

'I see.'

'Mmmm. You'd need to examine my body very carefully if you wanted to find any white bits.'

'Would I indeed?'

'Yes. And I've got some more good news for you. You sound out of breath. Where are you?'

'Nowhere. So what's happening?'

'Guess who's, like, your new manager as from now?'

'Veronica?'

'What?'

'Er, Mike? No, let me guess - that cute little blond from region two?'

'Johnny! No - it's me.'

'Oh, well done, Mel.'

'You sound disappointed.'

'No, I've just lost a bloody tenner, that's all.'

'But we can work together now, can't we? I could, like, give you loads of extra tuition? What are you doing, by the way? It sounds like you're in a gym?'

'Ha, ha! Listen, thanks, sweetheart. By the way, is it true about Sam and James Harris?'

Melissa bristled. Why did he always have to bring Sam into every single conversation they had? 'Yes, yes. As far as I know. They fancy each other like mad, apparently.'

'That's a shocker, isn't it? I thought Sam was getting married?'

'She is. Anyway, I'll see *you* very soon, Johnny King. On the beach - in my thong!'

'Yeah. Look forward to it. Well done, Mel.'

Melissa smiled as she clicked off the phone. What an incredibly steamy conversation that had been. Oh yes, Johnny King was interested all right. This was going to be the most fantastic conference ever.

Chapter 12

The image of Melissa as her manager was one Veronica found disturbing. Now listen, she told herself - it is so not important, okay? It would have looked like an incredible fix if anyone other than the official regional trainer had been asked to be the manager's stand-in, wouldn't it? It was absolutely fine, it really was. The important issue now was to focus on her own potential for the permanent position. That, and surely the most pressing issue of the moment - what to do about that philandering cad of a husband of hers. Still, that's what happened when your mother chose your husband for you.

Veronica had met Greg at a society wedding. Her mother had poked her in the ribs and whispered, 'Greg Henderson-Smythe,' with a discreet yet meaningful glance at a tall, clean shaven young man in glasses. 'Marjorie and Arthur's only son. He'll inherit well.'

Veronica looked over at Greg Henderson-Smythe. He was certainly handsome. At that precise moment he turned around and smiled at her. He had brilliant white teeth like a Hollywood movie star. 'Gosh,' said Veronica.

If only she had waited for James.

She was back in her apartment early today, downloading the conference details. It was a wonder, she thought, that they bothered sending pictures of the golf course and the swimming pool, not to mention the local bazaars - they never got time to make use of any of these so called 'exciting facilities and excursions.' Veronica deleted them quickly and noted the flight times instead. As usual, she thought - budget airlines and crack of dawn departures - no expense spared at Topham Pharmaceuticals again, then. The agenda looked pretty gruelling too. Still, at least James would be there - compensation enough for any girl.

After a quick glance at her new e-mails and a cursory whip through the latest sales figures, she closed the computer down and poured herself a glass of wine - the first one of the day - which wasn't so bad really, she'd got to three o'clock. Now, all she had to do was think what to do about Greg. Think, think, she told herself, concentrate, focus.

Images of the evening her unsuspecting husband had finally arrived home to discover her ten thousand pound blow out, were still startlingly fresh in her mind. Oh, of course, he'd denied everything. She'd been cold, really cold from waiting for him, mulling things over and over, her skin mottled blue, when he'd eventually rolled in. She could hear him whistling, 'Money is for Nothing,' as he kicked off his shoes and locked the door behind him. Jauntily he strolled into the apartment, calling, 'hi, darling, I'm home. God, it's dark in here. Darling?' There was a moment of silence before he suddenly noticed his wife sitting in total darkness at the window, clutching a wine bottle, staring unseeingly into the night. 'Er, everything okay, sweetness?' he asked a tad nervously. She'd turned then and fixed him with a look that Linda Blair in the Exorcist would have been proud of.

'What? What's this?' he asked, putting his hands up in the air as if he had no idea. Slowly his eyes flickered to the designer carrier bags and boxes, stacked artfully into a mountain shape on the dining room table. He tried not to stare at them, wrenching his alarmed expression from the money screaming bags, to his cold, strangely silent wife at the window. She lit another cigarette 'Something wrong, Sweetheart?' he ventured.

'Should there be, Greg?'

'Well, I swear I don't know.'

'Hmm. Perhaps we could start with where you were at

lunchtime?'

'Did you see me with my students? Is that it?'

Veronica raised an eyebrow. 'Do go on.'

'Well, I don't know. Something's upset you, obviously.'

'And what might that be, do you think?'

Greg shrugged and thought for a moment. 'Aha!' He slapped his forehead as if he had just remembered something. 'Oh, of course, of course - we were all outside the pub, drinking and messing around. Were you driving past? Is that it?'

Veronica nodded.

'Well, it must have been Heidi you saw me with, then. She's one of my students. She's from Denmark and she's struggling with her course work - so I took them all out for a drink and well, you know how young girls are? She just had one too many so I had to take her home. Nothing to worry about. Really.' He walked over to Veronica, smiling a, 'you silly thing, you,' kind of smile.

'You took her home?' Veronica snapped, stopping him in his tracks. 'And this took you how long, exactly?'

He fell to his knees and reached for her hand. 'Look, darling, you've got to believe me - I love you and I would never do anything to hurt you,' he said. 'Heidi does have a bit of a crush on me, it's true, but I was only being kind to her, that's all. Once I'd sobered the stupid girl up, I just made her a coffee and then tucked her in. Honestly, nothing happened or ever would. Veronica, you are the most beautiful woman I have ever seen. You are my life. Your happiness means everything to me. That girl is nothing, a nobody.'

'Tucked her in?' Did this man think her head was buttoned up the back or something? Veronica's eyes narrowed to slits.

'You have to believe me, darling - I love you with all my heart.'

Gaining confidence, he moved closer and began to kiss her softly.

Veronica turned her head so that he got a face full of hair, stubbed out her cigarette, and said, 'I understand, Greg. Really, I do. But we are married now, you know?'

He sighed. 'I know, darling.'

'And we promised to love, honour and cherish each other didn't we, Greg?'

He nodded meekly. 'Look, Veronica I really am sorry, okay? But there was absolutely nothing in it. There's nothing to go on about. Come on - please, can we start again? I love you, you know that. We can't let something as, as...' He searched desperately for the right word. 'As *silly* as this hurt us - we've got so much together.'

'Silly, you say?' Veronica said.

'Well when I say 'silly', darling, I meant....'

'As long as you understand, Greg, about the honour and cherish bit.'

'Oh, of course I do, darling. Of course I do.'

Veronica smiled - a frosty, hurt, little smile. Greg smiled - a warmer, 'I knew you would forgive me' sort of smile, and they hugged each other briefly.

Greg was the first to pull back. Gesturing towards the mountain of expensive looking carrier bags on the dining room table, he ventured, 'so er, what's all this then? Looks expensive.'

Veronica shrugged. 'It is.'

His face darkened a little. 'That's not like you, sweetheart?'

'No, but then it's not like me to have to witness my husband fondling a young girl in a public place, is it?' And anyway, she thought, I only drained the joint account, not my own.

'Of course not, darling. But we've covered that now, haven't we?' His voice took on a weary tone. ' I just need to know how much you actually spent today, that's all. You know I've been stashing away for this speedboat I want.'

'Mmm. Well I spent what you stashed - ten thousand.'

'Ten? Fucking hell.'

She watched anger flash across his handsome features, and smiled her little girl smile. 'Not a problem is it, Greg? I mean, we are talking about our marriage here.'

'Of course,' he said in a constricted voice. 'Well, let's hope that's an end to the matter then, shall we?' Turning away abruptly, he got up to close the windows. 'I'll get us a take-away, Veronica. I'm starving.'

Veronica nodded.

'The usual? Some bean sprouts?' he asked.

'Just half a portion.'

Later, feeling bloated from the bean sprouts, Veronica ran herself a bath and sank gratefully into the hot, foamy water, watching her skin turn from shades of blue to lobster pink. As her body temperature rose and her muscles relaxed, she closed her eyes tightly, fighting the burn of threatening tears. It was true - he had slept with that girl. Did he think she was a total fool? For several seconds her eyes stung while she struggled to gain control of herself. 'Oh, stop snivelling for God's sake, Veronica,' she muttered, echoing the words of her mother over twenty years ago when she'd been left at boarding school for the first time. 'Chin up, and all that.' She would have two more minutes of this self indulgence, that was all.

Quickly she towelled herself dry before wrapping up in a long, white towelling robe and applying a skin serum to her face. Would he want to make love to her? she wondered. Carefully she brushed and flossed her teeth, then padded to the kitchen for a glass of water. After checking that the front door was locked, she made her way to the bedroom. What happened next would almost certainly tell her everything she needed to know. Hmm, interesting - the bedside lamps were still on - he must be waiting for her. Softly she closed the door behind her and walked over to the bed, the sight of his dark hair against the white pillow sending a familiar thrill through her body.

'Greg?' She slid in beside him. 'Greg?' she whispered.

But if she had been expecting a resurgence of passion she was to be disappointed - Greg had been sound asleep.

Yes, he'd taken her for a fool all right. But it was no use dwelling on it anymore - what was done was done. She poured herself a second glass of wine, still deep in thought. She was right about him, of that she was sure. Because there were other things too - certain indisputable facts which queued up in her mind for analysis. First, he'd been home late every single night this week. And secondly, they hadn't made love in over two months. For such an intelligent man he wasn't covering his tracks very well. Veronica stretched her long legs out on the leather futon, the seeds of a plan beginning to form in her mind. Never underestimate the enemy, Daddy always said. Well then, Greg, she thought, your mistake.

Chapter 13

When Johnny phoned her, Sam had been crying. She was sitting at the kitchen table tapping into the latest sales league tables as instructed.

'Oh, please, please don't let me be right at the bottom again,' she whispered. Suddenly the screen flashed and there it was before her. She squinted at it nervously as if it was a horror movie, her heart beat already picking up speed. The fist name up was Bernie O'Reilly. The woman was two hundred percent above her sales target. Quickly Sam began to scroll downwards. She passed Veronica's name, then Mike's. A little further down there was Melissa's. Still she scrolled, until finally, just as the page was running out, she saw her own name - highlighted in red along with a few other people who had not hit their sales targets - right at the very bottom.

Her hand flew to her mouth. 'Fuck.' It was far worse than she'd expected. For pity's sake - couldn't at least one of her miserable doctors prescribe the stuff? Oh well, there was no point in staring at the thing any longer. Better download the conference flight details - at least that should be a pain free exercise. Up they popped. She reached for a pencil and began to jot them down, then did a double take. Hang on a minute - what was this? The early morning flight from East Midlands airport meant she would have to get up at four o'clock in the morning.

Well, things certainly couldn't get any bloody worse, could they? she thought, snapping the pencil in half. Still, all there was left to look at now was the conference agenda. At least this was the good bit - when you were on conference you didn't have to go out in the cold trying to see doctors. You could have a bit of a rest. It wouldn't be so bad. She stared at the arrangements for the week. Something, somewhere, had gone tragically wrong.

Eight o'clock in the morning coach transfers? All day presentations by management followed by role playing until six o'clock each evening? Then an hour's journey back to their hotel, and no time to change before a seven o'clock pick up to take them to some Godforsaken restaurant?

The problem here was serious - so when exactly was she going to get the time to wash her hair? This was hardly going to be a happy bloody holiday, was it? - trapped in a Spanish high-rise hotel listening to Pat Hardass drone on and on, followed by hours and hours of arse-achingly dull role-playing sessions. Add to that the utter tedium of managers armed with clipboards watching them for signs of negativity, and you had all the ingredients for a major nervous breakdown. 'I can't do this,' Sam whispered miserably. 'I can't go. I have to break a few ribs or contract a contagious virus. I'll die of depression if I have to go, I know I will.'

Worse still was the vision of Bernie O'Reilly skipping up to collect her sales award and thousand pound winnings. Plus all the results would be up on a gigantic screen with herself right at the bottom. Everyone would see. She might even be subjected to public humiliation. 'Bugger, bugger, bugger!' she said out loud, punching the computer keys some more. She had to get out of this, there must be a way.

She took a sip of hot tea, trying her best to erase the morning's experiences etched on her brain for all eternity: the Herculean effort of getting up and going to work for a start, trying to be more like Bernie. 'Get on the phone to Bernie O'Reilly,' the management emails said. 'If she can exceed her sales targets, why can't you? What is she doing that you aren't? Learn from your more successful colleagues. Be pro-active - pick up that phone.'

Blimey, Bernie must be busy with all those phone calls, Sam

thought, wondering what Bernie would say to the eager beavers who rang her: 'Well me darlin,' you've first to wear a really short mini-skirt, and then you've to get a little heart to heart going with your mentally ill patients. Get right up there on their beds with them, why don't you?'

Still, it occurred to her that maybe if she put some enthusiasm in and got up before ten, she might stand more of a chance. Therefore she had made a supreme effort that morning to get to a surgery where she had been told the doctors would see her if she got there by eight o'clock. She was there at ten to. Sam smiled to herself as she parked her car. Well, she couldn't work harder than this could she? She had even got up before Simon. After filling up her briefcase with loads of goodies from the boot, she walked briskly into reception, and was on the point of flashing her business card at the receptionist when a woman with a tight permanent wave suddenly burst in, shouting, 'Who the hell's that in my parking space?

Sam stiffened. She was the only person there apart from a couple of pensioners sitting quietly in the corner.

The woman with the permanent wave scanned the room, her angry glare eventually coming to rest on Sam 'Is it yours? Are you a rep?'

'I'm quite entitled to park there actually, I think you'll find,' Sam said, turning back to the receptionist and rolling her eyes in mock despair.

'Oh no you're damn well not. And you can just go and move your bloody company car out of my space right now, do you hear? And another thing - you will most certainly not be getting an appointment with me, this morning. Or any other morning, young lady'

'Appointment?' Too late, she realised the woman was one of the GPs who might have seen her ' Look I'm sorry....' she tried again, but the very irate doctor, who, now she came to think of it, looked a lot like Deidre Barlow in Coronation Street, had already gone out to wait for her to move.

When she came back in after having had to move her car onto the main road about half a mile away, the waiting room was full and there was a queue at the desk which included a couple of reps. Worse, she could hear the doctor still going berserk in the back room. She heard the word 'stupid' a couple of times and so did all the patients.

'You've done it now, luv,' an old guy in an anorak sniggered. 'She's got a right temper on her, that one. Best laugh I've had in ages, that.'

A dignified exit had been the only option. Still, she thought, marching back to her car, the day was young yet. Who could she try to see next? Determined to stay in her role as a vigorous and enthusiastic rep, Sam flicked through her notes. Ah yes, there was that new doctor, wasn't there?

She started the engine up and looked at the map - the difficulty was that his medical centre was on a rough estate she didn't know particularly well. It was in an ex-mining village and she wasn't quite sure where the surgery was. Still, she could always ask for directions when she got there.

He'll do, she thought, spotting an old man in a flat cap, coming out of the newsagents. Screeching to a halt alongside him, she called out, 'hi!'. The electric window on the passenger side purred open. 'I'm trying to find the new medical centre. Can you help at all?'

The man looked at the glamorous redhead in designer sunglasses, leaning over to smile at him from her BMW. 'As it 'appens, duck, I'm going that way meself,' he said with a grin. 'I'll just 'op in and then I can direct you right to't door. What could be better than that, eh?'

And before she could say, 'oh no you don't, buster,' he jumped into her passenger seat.

'I can't believe me luck. Hee, hee. Just wait 'til I tell't missus,' he said, gleefully. 'It's a long climb up this 'ill and I've terrible asthma, I 'ave.'

'Right,' Sam said, trying not to notice the mud caked on his boots and the strange ferrety smell.

Arriving at the surgery at twice the speed she would normally have done, she dropped the old man off at the door before going off to park. There was just one space left on the muddy, pot holed overflow area at the back. Not good, she realised, when you were wearing cream stilettos. She took a deep breath. I can do this and I will do this, she told herself. Come on, Sam, come on. You've got up, you've done the hard part - now get your ass in gear and go, go, go!

Five minutes later, she was waiting politely at reception with a determined smile on her face while the staff ignored her with well-practised expertise. Eventually a podgy woman in a tight, pink sweater and glasses, who was working her way through a bumper sized packet of crisps, said, 'there's a rep at the window,' in a bored, monotone voice to no one in particular, and not making a move herself. Minutes went by. Sam watched the woman work her way through more crisps, belch quietly, lick her finger and turn another page of her magazine.

Finally a brittle, young, blond woman behind her with a pinched mouth, sighed heavily, stomped over and threw back the glass partition. 'Did you want something?' she spat.

'Yes, I want to poke you in the eye,' Sam muttered under her breath as she searched for her business card. Then, with a huge smile, she said as pleasantly as she could, 'would you mind asking Dr Al-Khashin if he could spare me a few minutes before clinic starts?'

'Are you a rep?'

'Business Executive,' Sam said with an even bigger smile.

The girl snatched Sam's business card and slammed the glass shut. A couple of minutes later Dr Al- Khashin appeared and called her in.

'Good morning, Dr Al- Khashin. Thank you so much for seeing me,' she said, handing him her business card. He took her card and also her briefcase. She tried to pull it back from him in a reasonably dignified manner, but he held fast, waggling a chunky finger at her.

'Now, now,' he said, taking the case over to his chair before opening it up. 'Let's see what you've got for me in here, hmmm?' Rifling through her stuff with an avaricious grin on his face, he pulled out the most expensive give-aways she had, one after the other, all of which had been specially ordered for other people.

'Aha!' he said. Can I have this?' (a fountain pen). 'And this?' (a desk clock). 'And this?' (a photo frame). She tried again to grab the bag back but he held it out of reach. He hadn't finished.

'Er, Dr. Al-Khashin, I need to ask you about my product - Happylux? Look, I need my brochure....'

But by then the doctor had his head completely inside the bag. 'No mugs,' he said, eventually coming up for air. 'Ah well, it was very nice to meet you er...' He picked up her card as he stood up. 'Samantha. Yes, very nice indeed. And now I'm afraid I must see to my patients.'

Panic seized hold of her. 'But what about Happylux?' she asked him as he ushered her to the door. 'Perhaps I could just give you the prescribing information, doctor?' She thrust a leaflet at him.

Snatching it from her, he sighed heavily. 'It is too bad I don't have any time today, Samantha. But maybe you and I could go out to dinner one night to discuss this, er, Happylux, instead?' he suggested, his beady eyes settling on her cleavage. 'I know a very high class Italian restaurant we could go to - a bit expensive but I'm sure you could afford it.' He smiled broadly, revealing large, deep yellow teeth like ancient piano keys.

Sam looked down. Dr. Al-Khashin came up to her elbow in height, had a huge pot belly and a shiny bald head complete with liver spots. Hmm, she thought, even if you promised to write a hundred Happylux prescriptions tomorrow to save my career, I still wouldn't go out in public with you, buster. In fact, I'd rather go bungee jumping from a Boeing 747 jet. In a hurricane. 'Well, maybe we could discuss that next time,' she said breezily.

'I'll book it for Wednesday evening,' he replied, ushering her through the door with his hand on the small of her back.

Sam shot out of the surgery, stumbling across the pot-holed car park, pre-occupied with checking what she had left in her briefcase and cursing about having to take Dr. Al-Khashin out on Wednesday night, when she realised that something wasn't quite right. She looked across at her car. What was it? Something different about it. And then it hit her - the tyres had been nicked.

When she finally arrived home, she'd made herself a cup of hot tea, and then just cried and cried. Sometimes it was all too much - she had seen just one customer again today. It was no longer a question of *if* she would lose her job, but *when*. And then there was Simon, and that horrible chat they'd had about finances. Well, he chatted and she listened while he told her that he would be getting a bank loan for the money she owed so she would be indebted to him instead. She no longer had any credit cards or store cards because he'd cut them all up, and all the money she earned would be used to pay off this loan, so just what pleasure did she have left? It was like going cold turkey. Everything was so depressing. Right now she couldn't even get a decent haircut. Her visit to the hairdressers the day before had been disastrous - she'd asked for a 'Meg Ryan' and come out with a 'Camilla Parker Bowles'.

Eventually, she'd dried her eyes and made herself another cup of tea while the conference details downloaded. Now, after the shock of looking at those, she turned the laptop off and stared into the silence. Oh God, how was she going to get out of this mess? Could anything get any worse? And why did all these horrible things keep happening to her? It was like she was jinxed or something.

And then out of nowhere, jolting her from her reverie, came Johnny's call.

'Johnny?'

'Hi, Sam. How's it going?' He sounded odd, she thought - cooler than usual, more business like.

'Smashing - couldn't be better. You?'

'Great, yeah. So, I take it you've heard about Mel?'

'Yes. I'm really pleased.'

'I'm not surprised. Dick was a bastard to you, wasn't he?'

'You could say that.'

'Listen, did you know there's a rumour going around about you?'

'No? What rumour?'

'That you and James Harris are screwing?'

Heat shot up into her neck and face. Had the world gone mad? She gasped, struggling for words. 'Look, Johnny, I don't know where the bloody hell that's come from but it's completely outrageous.'

'So you're not then?' he asked.

'No, of course not. What's going on?'

'Search me. That idiot, Brett, got it from somewhere.'

'Brett? Oh, this just gets more and more ridiculous.'

'Don't worry about it, sweetheart. There's always someone saying something about someone else in this business. Talking about people having affairs though,' he continued, more happily now. 'Mike and his wife have split up. Apparently he's seeing Trisha - that nurse!'

'Get away!' Sam said, still reeling.

'Yeah, he caught his wife with the bloke next door, and next thing he's getting one to one therapy on the couch with Dizzy Trisha.'

'Blimey. She's got all those little kids as well, hasn't she? Isn't Mike a bit old for all that? Aren't his grown up?'

'Must be love. Still, I reckon he'll need to earn a bit more now if he's got a divorce to pay for and three little kids on top of that.'

'He'll need to get Dick's job then, is that what you're saying?'

'My God, Sam, you're a highly perceptive woman. I always said you were even when everyone else said you were a complete air head.'

'Thanks a lot. I think.'

'So anyway, sweetheart. Don't forget your bikini for next week, will you?'

'When do you want me to wear it exactly? There's no time off, Johnny. In the role playing sessions?'

'Now there's a feast for the imagination.'

Sam laughed and rang off. Maybe the conference wouldn't be as bad as expected. At least she had a good friend in Johnny.

By the time Simon came home, Sam had showered and was making dinner.

'Wow,' he said. 'The little woman at work.' He snuggled up behind her, immediately grabbing her breasts. 'How would you like to come to a party with me tonight?'

She wriggled out of his grasp and began frying onions. 'Not really. I've had a seriously awful day.'

'Again? Was it particularly crowded in the shopping mall?'

'That's below the belt.'

'Ha, ha! Come on, Sam - we need to get out.'

'Is it one of those God awful 'ward do's' where I won't know anyone but you'll be everybody's best friend?'

'I don't know what you mean. Listen, you'll love it. We're going to that new pub. You know - the one in town? The vodka bar?'

'Oh yes, the socialists' paradise. What's it called now? The Revolution? Will we need to put red stars on our heads?'

'Come on, Sam.' He reached for her breasts again. 'You'll enjoy yourself, I know you will.'

'Oh all right,' she said, wriggling away from him.

She chose a silver top and black kick flare trousers with stiletto boots. Carefully she applied lashings of black mascara and scarlet lipstick. They didn't go out together that often anymore, and it was nice to feel like a woman now and again. They should, she decided, have more fun and then maybe she could like him more. As they sped off into the night in his brand new sports car, she put her favourite CD on, noting as she did, a nurse waiting at the bus stop in her uniform, the night's work still ahead of her. There but for the grace of God...... Things weren't so bad really.

The Revolution was heaving with bodies when they walked in. Immediately Simon was collared by a gang of women in combats and strange hats adorned with bells and pom-poms. They looked, Sam decided, like characters out of some kind of medieval play. None of them wore make up, and one had on a headscarf in the style of an Estonian peasant woman. Although Estonian peasant women probably preferred Marks and Spencers these days.

'Simon,' they shouted, waving frantically. 'Over here, over here.'

Sam and Simon made their way over to the group. A couple of students slapped him on the back. 'Your round, me thinks,' said one of them, stepping between Sam and Simon so that his back was facing Sam.

'Come over here and sit next to me, Simon darling,' shouted Peasant woman.

Simon, glowing with pleasure, pressed a twenty pound note into the palm of one of the students and had been about to take his place next to Peasant woman when a blond girl in tight white jeans wiggled past him. His jaw slackened noticeably. 'Gosh, there are some beautiful women in here tonight,' he said. The two male students following his gaze, agreed with him. 'Oh, sorry darling, I meant you of course,' he said, suddenly turning to Sam and slapping her on the rump.

It wasn't, Sam decided, very nice continuously being jostled. And where the hell was that student with the vodkas? At last she spied him, the tray above his head, weaving in and out of people pretending to be poor communist brothers and sisters. With a flourish he handed out the glasses before proceeding to stand on his chair and propose a toast. Hang on a cotton picking minute, Sam thought, where's mine then? Quickly she counted the people round the table, then the glasses. Nope, she'd been forgotten.

'Simon,' Sam called, waving to flag his attention. Simon ignored her before a wall of bodies closed in, cutting her out of his view altogether. Shit! She had no money in her purse either, thanks to him. 'Bored, bored, bored,' she muttered. 'Bored and getting bloody fed up of being *pushed about*.' Louder her mutterings now. A sudden and rather painful jolt in her back decided the matter in an instant. That was it - she would leave.

The jolt had come from the babe in white jeans. No ordinary babe, Sam thought, following the wiggling, white behind towards the exit. Those jeans had gold stitching and heart shaped pockets, the top of a glittery thong peeped out at the back, and a belt dangling tiny keys and amulets bounced provocatively off one firm cheek. Babe's back was uniformly golden, it's glossy expanse broken only by a delicate, turquoise ribbon. Sam followed her out onto the street, watching as Babe jumped into her Jaguar XKR before zooming off into the night.

'Bitch,' she muttered. And what the hell was she supposed to do now, anyway? Wait in the car-park for Simon to come rolling out? She didn't even have enough money for the bus fare now Simon had taken control of all the money. All she had left was her expense account for customer entertaining and the cheque book for that was at home. He was going to give her a weekly allowance out of her own salary until the whole debt was paid off, and only then would she get her credit card back. It would take a year, he said, if they stuck to the plan. It was all her own fault - a lesson in life she must learn.

The Revolution was fronted in black glass. Sam turned to stare at her own reflection, her eyes widening in amazement. 'Fuck me, I look like Jessica Rabbit,' she said. She had big hair for goodness sake, her boobs looked huge in the tight top, and her backside was big enough to rest a tea tray on. A giggle rose up from nowhere. She fought with it, wrestled valiantly, but it was useless - hysteria had set in.

A man stopped to stare at her. 'All right, love?'

She put a hand over her mouth and nodded, silently pleading with him to push off. If only she could just go home. Why oh why did she agree to this when she knew, just knew how it would turn out? And then a wicked and brilliant thought popped into her head - hey, didn't she have a spare set of keys? She rummaged through her handbag. Aha! The keys to Simon's Audi TT sports car were at the bottom. There was a God.

Chapter 14

Johnny King glanced down at his mobile. The text message read: 'please ring Bernie O'Reilly as soon as you get this message - urgent.'

He sighed heavily. Oh God, not again. Still, he was stuck in traffic. Holding Bernie's shrieking voice away from his ear, he grimaced.

'Johnny! Would you have you heard the latest at all?'

'Er, nope?'

'Now you can't tell anyone what I'm about to tell you, Johnny. You have to promise on your mother's life. Honest to God, this is unbelievable. Do you promise, now?'

'Yep.'

'It's about Melissa.'

'Uh huh?'

Bernie squeaked excitedly. 'Yes, all my customers are talking about it today - they'll not talk about anything else. To be honest with you, I don't suppose I should be saying anything, but you know…. Anyway, apparently at one of Melissa's hospitals, the Drugs and Therapeutics Committee had a meeting to discuss the choice of anti-depressants stocked in the hospital. They wanted to have only three, so if a consultant wanted anything else, he'd have to have it specially requested, okay?'

'Yeah.'

'So anyway, they decided they would have just one from our particular class of anti-depressants, and everyone on the committee voted for our competitor's product except, guess who?'

Johnny sighed loudly. 'Nope, sorry you've got me there.'

'Only Dr Pilkington! You know - Mel's boyfriend? It seems that

Dr. Pilkington insisted on Happylux being the only one of it's class to be stocked, despite the fact that none of the other doctors use it, and since he was the only psychiatrist on the committee he got the final say, pulling rank over the Chief Pharmacist - a Mrs Popplesomebody or other - with the most almighty row braking out, by all accounts.'

'Ooops.'

'Yes, so as you can probably imagine, Mrs Poppledooda was really, really upset about the whole thing,' Bernie went on. 'She felt that Dr. Pilkington had bamboozled her into a decision that wasn't ethical. Plus she was getting a better deal from our competitor, so she was wondering what the devil was going on here, you know? So, anyway, and get this - she's walking through the staff car- park a couple of days later when she notices a Jag parked under the trees, and she sees what she thinks is an arse at the window! Ha ha!'

Johnny perked up. 'You are joking?'

'No, no, go on with you. So, anyway, she goes to look a bit closer and sure enough, it's an arse. And a big white one at that. Ha ha! She can't believe it and she stares in absolutely hypnotised. Hypnotised I tell you! And then she sees a pair of eyes staring at her in horror. Guess who? Only our Dr. Pilkington. Ha ha! And then, oh even worse...' Bernie paused for effect. 'It's only Melissa Crow on top of Dr. Pilkington on the back seat of his car isn't it?'

'Shit! Oh bloody hell.'

Bernie giggled. 'I know.'

'Did she report them?'

'Yes, at the hospital anyway. She was livid - particularly because of the drug decision, obviously.'

'So, has there been a complaint made to the company, do you know?

'I'm not sure. It's certainly gone to the top at the hospital, and it's all round the customers - they think it's really funny but some of them are a bit angry as well because of the ethics behind it, you know?'

'Well ethics are certainly an issue aren't they, Bernie, sweetheart?'

'Yes, of course.'

'Oh well, I can't say I'm too surprised, but I've got a feeling Melissa's not going to get away with this one.'

'Mmmm, well Dr. Pilkington's gone on holiday somewhere now, so I hear, but he'll be in for some serious questions when he gets back no doubt. And it's only a matter of time for Melissa - Mrs Popplewhatsit never liked her as it was and she's a vicious old trout by all accounts, so I doubt she'll let the matter go.'

'Oh Jesus,' Johnny said again. 'Poor Mel.'

'Yes, isn't it awful?' Bernie said, gleefully.

While Johnny and Bernie continued to discuss Melissa over the phone in the rush hour traffic that morning, Veronica Ball was sitting in a down market public house on the outskirts of Leeds with a middle-aged man she had never met before. The man was a private detective. She lit her third cigarette of the day and stared down at the ash trodden, swirly carpet. It was true what he had said - no one she knew would ever accidentally bump into her here.

'So what I want you to do is follow him when he gets out of the School of Dentistry, because that's when he goes off drinking with his students,' she said. 'Those are the nights he's always back late. Particularly I want you to look out for a young, blond girl with curly hair. She'll probably have her stomach exposed. You know the type?' The man nodded. 'She so fancies herself as Britney Spears. Let me know where he goes and if he goes off separately with the girl, please.'

The man took notes, promising to track her husband's movements every day and evening for the whole week she was away on conference. 'If he takes her back to my apartment I so want to know. Everything - every detail, yah? I'll pay all your overtime, anything. Photos for proof where possible. Can you do that?'

'Of course, Mrs Ball.'

'Ms Ball. I kept my family name.'

'Ms Ball. Yes, no problem. Eighteen hour scrutiny and any incriminating photographs for one week starting from tomorrow. I'll get onto it right away,' he said, pocketing the photograph of her husband and a substantial cheque. Half up front, he always insisted on it.

After the man had gone, Veronica thought - good, now she could move on to the next part of her plan. One thing was absolutely certain - and that was that she would not fail. She was so not a loser.

It was incredibly important, too, that her family didn't know about this. If she was to get Greg on adultery charges, then the divorce would be presented to them as a fait accompli. Similarly the management position. In her family, everyone was successful and they got things done. Whingeing and counselling was for namby-pambies. Picturing her brother Rupert's smirking face, himself now a leading barrister, was incentive enough, but her sister's? Oh God, no...Davina was a budding socialite engaged to a wealthy property developer, an owner of Lulu Guinness handbags, and already it was, 'well you would say that, you're a *sales* person,' and 'typical rep speak,' every time Veronica opened her mouth. Next thing Davina would be asking her to use the trade entrance. Add to that being a victim of adultery....No, she simply had to get this sorted. Think, think, she instructed herself - now she was in this business, she must get to the top. So what did she have to offer that Melissa didn't?

As she pondered this, her mobile beeped.

'Veronica Ball,' she snapped.

A nervous voice on the other end said, 'er, excuse me for bothering you, Veronica. It's Brett here.'

'Hello, Brett.'

'Er, hello, cool, yeah, right, er....'

'Did you want something, Brett?'

'Oh, yeah. Me and the lads wondered if you'd like to invite some of your doctors to our speaker meetings, d'ya know what I mean, yeah? I've set three up - the talks are called, 'Getting into the Minds of the most Sadistic Murderers in History.'

'Subtle.'

'Ha, ha! Yeah, cool. The thing is I invited five hundred doctors but so far we've only got nine replies so there's room for some of yours.' When Veronica said nothing, he added, ' If you want.'

'Mmmm. I'd need you to do all my mailings though.'

'What? Oh of course, Veronica. No probs. Cool.'

'Good - that's settled then.'

She was about to click the phone off when he asked, 'er, have you er, heard about Melissa at all?'

'Is this gossip, Brett?' Veronica asked him sharply.

'Um, yeah, I suppose so.'

Veronica sighed, but she was curious. 'Go on then - tell me.'

And so he related a story now so embellished it no longer even remotely resembled the truth.

Veronica nearly choked on her cigarette. 'Melissa was on the car bonnet, you say? Naked? Good Lord.'

'I can't believe it, can you?' said Brett.

'So who else knows about all this?'

'No one. Well, just a few of us in the team. Oh, and the customers.'

'Interesting.' She clicked off her phone and thought about what she had just heard. Well, well, well - Melissa could be out of the running if this pharmacist reported her, which she undoubtedly would by the sound of it. So, the competition would probably be from Bernie then. And Bernie would undoubtedly network like crazy at the conference, shining out like a beacon of enthusiasm and bubbliness, whereas she herself might come across as cold and rather snooty. She would so have to work on that, try to be a bit more effusive in front of management, perhaps? Although, that might mean having to look as if she was a 'people person' and do some bonding with the girls. Truly, it was just so tedious. Still, needs must.

Another question that needed an answer was - who had the upper hand, Pat or James? It could well be James. Pat liked her men, everyone knew that, and she would be persuaded by James. All of which bode very well indeed for her chances. Yes, perhaps it was possible after all.

A man with a bald head and a red face was staring at Veronica aggressively from across the bar. The pub had started to fill up with men ordering pints. The smell of frying chips permeated the stale air, and fruit machines tinkled away busily. His eyes took in her mobile phone and leather briefcase, then slowly began to appraise her body, his hostility appearing to grow by the minute.

Veronica, aware of the simmering fury in the man's eyes, shrugged. I bet he's sponging off benefits, lives in a council flat and has an ugly wife. Whatever. That is so his problem. Deal with it, she thought, flicking a brief look of disgust his way. Anyway, she was getting a text message from James:

'PRESS DOWN,' it said. She scrolled down.

FURTHER
PRESS DOWN AGAIN
FURTHER
JUST THERE
THAT'S BETTER
MMMMMM   SO GOOD
RIGHT THERE
MMMMM, BABY, YEAH
DON'T STOP
SOOOOO GOOD!
U HAVE JUST EXPERIENCED A TEXTUAL ORGASM!'

A ball of excitement fluttered inside her. In just a couple of days she would be in Spain with James. And everything was so going to go her way.

'SO CAN'T WAIT FOR REAL THING!' she zapped back, standing up to leave. She really must get on with some work if she was going to be the next manager. In fact, she looked at her watch, now would be an excellent time to go and tackle that mad cow heading up the team in the local psychiatric unit, Dr. Shelley Meacher - as yet unseen by any rep - the ultimate challenge. Yes, today is the day, Dr Meacher, that I am going to see you whether you like it or not Veronica decided, as she breezed past the man at the bar with a smile designed to permanently freeze his assets.

Fifteen minutes later, Veronica swept into Dr Meacher's office, only to find it empty. Except - aha! there was a tiny secretary hunched in the far corner. At least it could be a secretary person she supposed - hand knitted green cardigan and dishevelled hair - but then again it could be one of the patients. And why was she crouching down like that?

'Excuse me….' she called in the kind of loud and confident voice her mother used when addressing the lower orders.

The figure in the green cardigan whirled round and Veronica found herself looking into a pair of terrified eyes. The woman had on a long pleated skirt and a checked shirt buttoned up to the neck, the collar of which she was clutching. 'Yes, what do you want?' she said, backing away.

'I'm Veronica Ball from Topham Pharmaceuticals and I'd like to see Dr. Meacher please,' she said.

The woman backed away even further, her hands now grasping the radiator behind her. 'Oh, oh….. Oh no. I can't - I'm too busy, I just can't,' she said in a trembling voice while eyeing the open door behind Veronica.

Veronica hesitated. I? Did she say, 'I?'

Then suddenly the woman bolted, scurrying past Veronica into the corridor beyond. Seconds later, a door slammed shut and a lock clicked.

Her mouth still open in shock, Veronica shook her head and was just about to leave when a smart woman in glasses appeared.

'Can I help you?' she asked.

'Was that Dr. Meacher in the green cardigan, by any chance?' Veronica asked.

'Mmm. Are you a rep?'

'Business Executive actually,' Veronica said, handing the woman her card. 'I've been trying to see Dr Meacher for months and I hoped to catch her today, but she seemed terrified of me for some reason.'

The woman laughed. 'Yes, she would be.'

'Is she always like that? Or is it just me?'

'Oh no, it's everyone, love. She's a lovely person, just a bit odd if you don't know her.' The woman leaned forwards and whispered, 'she really cares about her patients though. She comes in at two o'clock in the morning sometimes just to check they're okay.'

'You are joking?'

'Oh no. She wakes them up to ask them. Sometimes she sits and knits in a chair where she can see them. Honestly love, I could tell you all sorts. Take the registrar, he's another one - I sat here and watched him one day - he crossed the road and then back again, then crossed it again, then back again maybe twelve times. It was ten minutes before he made it through the front door. Would you like a coffee, love?'

'Do you know, I'll be so glad to get out of psychiatry,' Veronica said, declining the offer.

Chapter 15

For Sam the dreaded Wednesday evening had come around all too quickly. In a pique of bad temper she found herself waiting in the restaurant car park for Dr. Al-Khashin. This was too much - he was ten minutes late already, which was particularly annoying since it was imperative the whole thing be over and done with as soon as possible. I only hope to God there's no one in there I know, she fumed, thinking that if he didn't turn up within the next five minutes then that would be the perfect excuse to just turn tail and get the hell out of there. But he did. Well, he would, wouldn't he? Had he been a handsome millionaire, George Clooney look-alike, he would have stood her up without a doubt. So, with considerable dismay, she watched as Dr Al-Khashin rolled up in his silver Mercedes, waving at her like a maniac.

'Oh, great. He's only fucking excited, the little bastard,' she muttered, through gritted teeth.

A professional smile and a business like handshake got her through the first few seconds, neatly offsetting his lunge forwards for a kiss. But after that she had no other option - she had to walk into the restaurant with him. He opened the door for her, pressing a fat, sweaty hand into the small of her back as she stepped through. To her horror, the hand remained there, dropping centimetre by centimetre, so that by the time they got to their table it was quite definitely on her backside. Bastard, she thought, quickly manoeuvring herself away from him. Sitting down quickly, she thanked the waiter for the menu and began to scan it with a fixed, tight smile, deliberately stopping herself from looking around the restaurant - everyone must think he was her date, for Christ's sake. What else could they think? It might not be possible to actually get through.

She peeped over the top of her menu. Dr. Al-Kashin grinned and raised his glass to her. She ducked behind the menu again. No, this wouldn't do, she'd have to come up with something and quick. 'Look, Dr. Al-Kashin,' she said. 'I'm afraid I really can't stay for long because my fiancé is bed-ridden and very ill. And I'm sure you are aware that we are here to discuss Happylux? It states very clearly in our Code of Conduct that the food is secondary to the meeting. And this is a business meeting, okay?' For a second she hesitated. Had she overstepped the mark?

But Dr. Al-Kashin was nodding happily, eyes glinting as they travelled from her lips to her breasts and back again. 'You know it's a long time since I had a date with a beautiful lady,' he said. 'I don't seem to meet any in this country - so many ugly women here. Tut, tut! Fat, too.'

'Date?' Sam paled.

She watched as Dr. Al-Khanin began to shovel food into his mouth - four, no five huge forkfuls before he even attempted to start chewing. Once the mouth was full, the food was slapped around like cement in a mixer. She had never seen anyone eat like that before, well not outside a zoo anyway. Slap, slap, slap, he went. Slap, slap, slurp, slurp - glug! Talking all the while.

She took a sip of water while covertly observing him - it wasn't just the fact that he was so short his feet didn't touch the floor, that he had a huge, fat belly which made him look at least nine months pregnant, that he was bald with liver spots on his head, or that he had hooded reptilian eyes and a pushed in nose. No, it was worse than that. The worst bit by far was his mouth - his lips were wet and rubbery, the bottom lip looking almost as if it had turned inside out - and the way he constantly hawked and snorted to clear his sinuses. And then there was his expression - there was something serpentine about him, something lecherous, almost malevolent - a face only a mother could truly love.

'So, Samantha,' he said. 'What does your boyfriend think about you taking rich doctors out for dinner, mmm?'

She watched him shovel a pile of tagliatelle into his mouth, sucking up the trails he didn't manage to get in first time, cream sauce spattering across his chin.

'Oh, he's cool. Do you have much of an interest in psychiatry, Dr. Al-Khashin?'

He shook his head. 'Yes. I do a clinic for Dr Douglas on Wednesday afternoons. He is a very nice man - lots of parties at the big house. Yes, a very good friend of mine.'

'I'm afraid he won't see reps.'

'I can get you to see him. I can get you anything you want, Samantha,' he said, loading a pile of yellow-green mustard onto his ciabatta.

Dessert was zabaglione for two complete with sparklers. Their spoons could not help but touch. An age passed. Then finally coffee was delivered by the smirking Italian waiter, together with the bill, which he presented with a flourish to Dr. Al-Khashin while commending him on his choice of *date.*

Sam snatched the bill out of his podgy fingers, quickly writing a cheque. 'Look, I really do have to get back to my fiancé now,' she said. 'I hope you enjoyed your meal, and perhaps next time we meet we can discuss how much Happylux you've been using, okay?' Without waiting for confirmation, she walked smartly out of the restaurant with her head held high, only breaking into a run once the doors had closed behind her.

'Do you know,' she said to Simon while she packed for the conference that Sunday. 'I'm actually looking forward to getting away now. I know it's going to be corporate hell but at least it will be a different sort of hell.' She looked up at him and smiled.

'Hmmm. I don't think you've said good-bye to me properly yet though, have you?' He cuddled up behind her, pulling her around to face him. 'I'm going to miss you,' he said, puckering up for a kiss.

Sam stared at him close range. His glasses were still speckled with something horrible and he smelled stale. He'd said repeatedly that he did not think it necessary to wash at weekends - it was his time off and if she loved him then it shouldn't matter. His lips were zooming in on hers rapidly, beginning to open as they got closer. She could see the yellowing teeth and the line of spittle that, miraculously, was still there. His hand was groping her behind, his breathing getting heavier.

With a nanosecond to spare she averted her head and patted his back. 'Poor Simon, I'm sure you'll be fine,' she said as his face smacked into her shoulder. 'Sorry, but I really do have to get on with this packing.'

He stepped backwards, putting his hands on his hips. 'Have you got enough money?'

'I've got five pounds in my purse, Simon, as you well know, and no credit cards as you also well know.'

'You've got your mobile. If you need funds you can ring me and I'll sort it all out for you.'

'I should have some money for emergencies, Simon. You're still punishing me for taking your car, aren't you?' She realised that she'd started to shout again, and stopped abruptly, forcing herself to take a deep breath and count to ten. She would not lose her temper. She would not give him the satisfaction.

'You would have money if you hadn't been such a silly girl though, wouldn't you? You were the one who went and spent it all. Still, you do need something, I suppose.' He pulled out a thick wad of notes and peeled off a couple. 'Here,' he said, handing her twenty pounds. 'That should be enough for coffees and things, shouldn't it?'

Chapter 16

It was unusually chilly in Malaga for the time of year. The palm trees lining the hotel gardens were being blown almost flat to the ground, and the usually calm sea crashed noisily onto the shore in angry, grey waves.

'I suppose a spot of wind-surfing's out of the question, then?' Johnny said, observing the stormy scene from the balcony of their syndicate room.

'I don't mind this weather,' Sam said. 'It'd be frustrating if it was scorching hot and you could see everyone sunbathing while we were stuck in here.'

'I tried it this morning,' Melissa said. 'I was out on the balcony in my bikini.'

Sam stared at her. 'Weren't you freezing?'

'I was fucking blue, Sam, but there's no way I'm coming all the way to Spain and not sunbathing. Besides, we're, like, used to it in Hull. Everybody takes a flask, a windshield and a blanket when they go to the beach.' She glanced at the clock. 'Look everyone - we really do, like, have to get some work done now, please?'

Melissa was in charge. This was her first conference as a regional manager. Unfortunately things were not going as well as she had anticipated. She'd had to scream at the top of her voice like a teacher in an inner city school with a class full of delinquents, which she thought, was not doing much for her image as a sex kitten. The region had thrown paper darts, told dirty jokes and giggled all the way through her sales presentation. At least half of them were still drunk from the night before, they reeked of stale alcohol, and by ten o'clock they'd been demanding bacon sandwiches because they were 'hypo'.

'Don't you want some hot meat inside you before lunch, Melissa?' Johnny said. And, 'do you want it *All* in, Mel?' when he poured her coffee.

The entire morning had been like an episode from a 'Carry on' film and they hadn't done a scrap of work. She just hoped Pat or James didn't decide to put in an appearance to observe the team in action. They were supposed to be putting together a presentation as a group on any topic they wanted except Happylux. This was to fine tune their presentation skills in general - things like handling objections, asking questions, and gaining commitment from key members of the audience. They had the morning to choose a topic, preferably a controversial one, put together the fifteen minute presentation and then pick a couple of people to present it to the rest of the sales division that afternoon. They were meant to prepare and research, work effectively as a team, and show the others in the division what they could do.

Ideas would then be pooled, constructive criticisms made and the principles applied to their every day situations. Later in the week they would be getting important new charts and graphs comparing Happylux with its competitors, taken from trials only recently published and heavily contested by the opposition, who had very similar trials themselves but showing the complete reverse. The company would then launch its brilliant new strategy, which was that the reps should do at least three presentations a week to their customers from now on, and the daily call rate was to go up from ten to fifteen.

The reps, as yet, were unaware of this, most of them still full of happy expectation. 'Come on guys,' Melissa pleaded over the noise of 'The Simpsons,' on television. But if she had been expecting any co-operation, she was disappointed. Sam and Johnny were still at the window, Mike and Brett were watching TV, Bernie was on her mobile phone and Veronica was flicking through a copy of the 'Tatler.' She tapped her pen repeatedly against her glass. 'Hello….Everyone, hello!'

Suddenly Bernie shouted, 'Eeek!' and everyone stopped talking. 'Would you look at the time? Jesus, we've only fifteen minutes left and we still haven't done our presentation!'

'Melissa could do it on the art of management,' Johnny suggested.

'Oh sit on it and swizzle, Johnny,' she said. 'Come on - we've got to, like, come up with something and quick - suggestions please.'

'What about fox hunting as our subject?' Veronica said, putting aside her magazine.

They all looked at her.

'Well - it's incredibly topical and controversial, isn't it? I'll present for it, and Bernie could present against it. What do people think?'

They shrugged, glancing round the room for other people's reactions. Certainly a decision had to be made.

'You two would have to work over lunch,' said Sam.

Veronica nodded. 'Well I don't mind,' she said, challenging Bernie with her eyes.

Bernie shrugged. 'No problem,' she replied, eyeballing Veronica right back. Then turning to the rest of the group, her eyes dancing with delight, added, 'I can't wait for this - it'll be a crack.'

Melissa breathed a sigh of relief. 'Well, that's, like, settled then? Is everyone happy?'

'Certainly chuffing am,' Johnny said. 'That's us lot off the hook for the rest of the day now. Well done, ladies.'

Melissa smiled uneasily. She turned her back to pack up her computer and projector, flicking her long, newly highlighted hair over one shoulder with blue nails, only vaguely aware of the sniggering behind her back.

Sam, in particular, was grateful that she wouldn't have to present anything to the whole division. What an almighty relief, she thought, still tired from last night's sleepless night in her noisy hotel room. In fact, it might be better to go and have a lie down instead of queuing up for lunch and having to make small talk. Sleep - ah, heaven…..

Her room was tiny with a spectacular view of the busy freeway, the huge billboards lining it, and the dry, sandy hills beyond. She flung herself down onto the tiny bed with it's scratchy brown blanket. Who in their right mind would pay hundreds of pounds to holiday here? The pictures they had been sent of the hotel had shown it overlooking the ocean, which it did. What the picture didn't show was that the hotel was sandwiched between two major freeways. In fact, it was on little more than a glorified traffic island. Nor did it show the lack of a beach. The pool was a mini kidney bean shape and there were maybe twenty sunloungers for a hotel which had over five hundred rooms.

Sam closed her eyes, muttering with discontent as she drifted off to sleep, her eyelids overpoweringly heavy. Oblivion, wonderful oblivion….

The sound of a loud motorbike whizzing past her window woke her with a start. She jumped up. Damn - just five minutes to go before the afternoon sessions started. They'd got a two hour slot from Pat Hardcastle to start with as well. She groaned - ugh, and this was the best day, the first one, all the others would be in another hotel so she wouldn't be able to slip back to her room. Scurrying into the bathroom, she quickly splashed her face with cold water, put some lipstick on, grabbed her bag and was about to leave when a thought hit her - oops, nearly forgot the Wank List - mustn't forget that if they'd got Pat Hardass for two hours.

Covertly she handed out photocopies of the Wank List to each member of the region just as they were shuffling into the dark auditorium, which was pulsating to the beat of Queen's, 'Don't Stop Me Now (I'm having such a good time').

Two hours of Pat Hardass, and the reps had learned that the only way to survive was aversion therapy. The List was basic grid filled with too often used words and phrases popular with the corporate world. The challenge was to tick off the ones used in a similar way to listening out for numbers at Bingo, except of course, for jumping up and shouting 'House!' And it kept them awake which was vital because everyone knew that dozing off when sales directors were talking was not a good career move, every last one of them living in fear of being that unfortunate person to fall off their chair, having entertained all those around them for many anticipation fuelled minutes with lots of head lolling and loud snorting noises. They had all seen it happen and no one wanted to go there.

So in the name of self-preservation, Dick's region sat at the back trying to scrutinise the words of the Wank List in the dark. To give the exercise more impetus, they had a bet on between the lasses and the lads. The girls reckoned Pat would win hands down. Mostly Pat used the phrases: 'at the end of the day/ go that extra mile/ top representative/ movers and shakers/ and, customer first'. But they reckoned if she mentioned: 'the big picture/ be pro-active not reactive, and, the core business,' then she would beat the MD, McCraw to Wanker of the Year. Suddenly the rock music stopped. Pat strode dramatically onto the spot-lit stage. All four hundred sales and marketing personnel from right across the company waited in silence. She was a tiny woman with a big hair. Today Pat was colour co-ordinated in black and yellow. Carefully, she placed her matching handbag on the floor beside her.

'Now,' she barked. 'I was sat in my office the other day and I thought to myself - what do I have to do to get my reps motivated? What do I have to do to get them to go that extra mile? What is it that makes a top representative? Who are the movers and shakers?'

The girls had their fingers crossed - it was looking promising. Come on Pat, talk about the core business and the big picture and we've got cocktails in the bar tonight - come on.

'So I thought to myself - Marks and Spencers vouchers!'

The reps remained silent, expecting more to come.

'Marks and Spencers Vouchers!' she barked again, louder and more slowly, as if she'd had to repeat a punch line that they hadn't quite understood.

A few weak voices bleated, 'hooray.'

'I can't hear you,' she shouted.

'Hooray!' A little louder now.

'I still can't hear you,' she shouted louder.

'Hooray!' the audience boomed.

'Good, I thought you'd be pleased. Now this is the new bonus system whereby you will all get the chance to earn £10 Marks and Spencers vouchers for every one percent you are over your sales target. It will be initiated at the beginning of quarter three in July, so you've all got plenty of opportunity to earn yourself lots and lots of vouchers before Christmas.'

'If I haven't hung myself by then,' Sam whispered to Melissa.

Melissa leaned towards her. 'Have you had any more of those phone calls recently?' she hissed.

Sam shook her head, her eyes still focussed on Pat. 'No.' Oh dear God, how on earth was she going to get through the next two hours? People smelled - there was definitely more than just a hint of body odour and stale alcohol in the air, what air there was. A slight panic gripped her

- she couldn't get out if she needed to, stuck in the middle of all these people. It was stiflingly hot, and dark too. Get a grip, girl, she told herself. Just get a grip, okay?

She decided on the power of imagination - she had once read a story where a Chinese man had existed in a box in the desert for days with no food or water because he had used the power of his mind to trick his body into surviving. If he could do that then she could survive a sales presentation. Although it was touch and go. She took a couple of deep breaths and began to imagine herself feeling cool on a yacht just off St Tropez. The boat was gently bobbing up and down. She was wearing a white swimsuit, drinking chilled mineral water, the sea breeze softly fanning her body. Someone was giving her a reflexology treatment and a dark and handsome man was smiling at her in sexy way. She was smiling back at him too. Later what would they do? They could have oysters and champagne as the sun dipped down, a midnight swim in ice cool waters maybe? A shimmer of pleasure ran all the way through her body while she contemplated this.

Then with a jolt an uncomfortable realisation struck her - her face had slipped into a dreamy, half smiling idiot expression. And something else. Someone was watching her, sharing her inner thoughts, reading her mind. She let her eyes cast a sidelong glance. Oh shit. James Harris was grinning at her from his sideline position, dark eyes glinting lustfully. Hastily, she looked away, her attention switching abruptly to the yellow and black apparition on stage, her face aflame.

Veronica had been studying the Wank List intensively when she became aware of James staring in her direction. She had already mouthed, 'hi,' to him a few minutes earlier, and they had exchanged conspiratorial smiles. She looked up now and smiled at him again, but something wasn't quite right - he wasn't responding and his eyes didn't seem to be focussing on her properly. Then it hit her in all it's stomach lurching horror - he wasn't looking at her at all. Her eyes widened. Slowly she turned to look in the direction of James' lustful gaze. Sam's face was crimson.

She would have to act fast - tonight, in fact. There was nothing she could do about it until then because Pat was going to drone on for hours, and then they had all the regional presentations to get through. Plus, if Pat pulled her usual trick - going over her allotted time by at least an extra hour - they would also lose their precious coffee break so she was unlikely to get a moment with him then. No, it was going to have to wait until tonight. This was serious - just what the blazes did he think he was playing at?

Chapter 17

By the afternoon, the regional presentations were underway. Dick's team were the last, the audience somewhat fractious. Bernie, a tiny, rather frantic figure on stage in the conference hall, began to shout to be heard. 'As you can see,' she screeched. 'There are *three* main points to consider.' Written on the flipchart behind her in huge, red capital letters it said: 'Four Main Points.' Shuffling boredom gave way to titters as one person and then another began to notice this.

Bernie grinned, laughing along with her audience for a while before having to turn her back on them altogether in order to squint desperately at the flipchart. Unfortunately she had been unable to put her contact lenses in that morning because her eyes had been too red and scratchy and she refused point blank to wear glasses. And so it was that she began to lose control. At the point where exasperation kicked in and she screamed, 'for the fox's sake,' they were rolling in the aisles because they thought, every last one of them thought, that she had said: 'for fuck's sake,' and they couldn't believe it.

Veronica watched stony faced. What an absolute shambles, she thought, glancing at James, who was sitting at the back with his hand over his face. It was a good thing Pat was out shopping and Alistair McCraw was on the golf course, or he would so be for the high jump letting this go on.

Ignoring all cat calls and the surfeit of paper darts flying through the air, Bernie finally stepped down, saying, 'and that's all I have to say on the subject of why we shouldn't be hunting foxes. Thanks, guys.' She was still smiling, although if a person looked closely it could be seen to be a little strained.

The noise level was now deafening. Someone had initiated a slow handclap and a chant of, 'why are we waiting.'

'Ban hunting!' came a shout from the back.

'Down with Toffs!' someone else called as Veronica got up to present in favour of hunting.

Veronica approached the stage with no-nonsense confidence, tucking her neat, blond hair behind one ear. She picked up the flipchart which was covered in Bernie's messy red and blue ink, and deposited it firmly behind the curtain. Within seconds her laptop fired into action and an immaculately prepared Powerpoint presentation flashed onto the large screen behind her. She looked out at the audience and calmly waited for the noise to die down.

'What,' she asked, 'is the problem, here? Don't foxes kill chickens and lambs and put people's livelihoods at stake? Has anyone here ever owned a livestock business and had an entire coup of chickens wiped out by a single fox? Seen their heads ripped off just for the hell of it, feathers and blood everywhere yet only one chicken actually eaten? Has anyone here ever struggled as a hill farmer only to find one lamb after the next murdered by foxes? Well, have you?' she asked them. 'And have any of you ever tried to shoot a fox? Did you know that only one in six attempts are successful? Have you thought about what happens to an injured fox in the wild? Well I'll tell you - it dies a slow and painful death from gangrene.'

The audience was now quiet.

'I believe it is now time for common sense, for a reality check. Time to listen to country people who are the only ones whose business it is, anyway. And besides - if this is all about love for animals then how come we have one of the highest animal cruelty rates in Europe? No, I put it to you that this is all about class, and yet the only people who would really suffer under a fox hunting ban are the working classes in rural areas - people like farriers.'

She looked slowly around the room, from face to face. ' More to the point - haven't we all had enough of being told what to do by the self-righteous? And remember - once professional fox hunters and farriers are out of business, their hounds slaughtered - it will be extremely difficult to bring that industry back again.'

No one said a word. 'Well,' Veronica said, 'Who here likes to be ordered about by someone else? Who here today, would like to be told they couldn't do something that they'd done for centuries by people who know nothing about the subject - these pipsqueaks in government? And if this isn't about class then why isn't anyone making a fuss about fishing - a hook through the mouth has been scientifically proven to hurt fish, but that was all hushed up quickly wasn't it? And what about people who keep birds in cages, reptiles in baths, or allow their children to torture the family pet?'

Still no one spoke.

Finally a lone voice shouted out, 'it's still a sport for toffs.'

'I rest my case, thank you, Sir,' Veronica said, calmly eyeballing the heckler. 'Anyone else? 'She looked straight at Bernie, who kept a rictus grin firmly on her face, clapping like everyone else as Veronica stepped down from the stage. Casting a brief glance in James's direction, Veronica noted with pleasure his expression of approval and something else - relief?

Later that evening, the reps were herded into coaches and deposited at a mountain restaurant: the Company treat. It would be a typically Spanish night with lots of red wine, they'd been promised. There would be musicians and flamenco dancers, meals in baskets, the works. Tired but excited, the reps filed into a large barn furnished with long wooden tables and benches. Vats of wine were passed around as men in sombreros serenaded them and meals of steak and chips were wheeled in on trolleys.

Veronica stared in horror at the congealed blood and pink flesh on her plate, and immediately asked for the vegetarian option. Her plate was duly removed with a flourish, and then returned a couple of minutes later with just the chips on it and a smear of grease and blood from where the steak had been swiped off.

'Oh well,' she said, with a shrug. 'I so can't take more than a couple of mouthfuls anyway or I bloat.'

'That's not what I heard,' Johnny said, giving her a knowing wink.

Veronica stared at him. How much did he know?

Bernie watched the exchange with interest. 'Oh look, Veronica,' she said, pointing excitedly. 'Doesn't that man behind you look exactly like your husband?'

Veronica swung round to look at the man Bernie was pointing out, but she couldn't see anyone who looked remotely like Greg.

'There,' Bernie squealed, still pointing. 'There, the one in the pink polo shirt over on the next table.'

But the only one in a pink shirt that Veronica could see was someone who looked uncannily like Uncle Fester from the Adams Family.

'You are joking?' Veronica said.

'No, not at all. He's the spitting image of him, don't you think?'

'No.'

'Oh well, to be sure and I thought it was the man himself.'

Veronica had tentatively just put a chip in her mouth, which she knew she would have to throw up later, when Bernie struck again.

'Where do you get your hair *bleached,* Veronica?' she asked loudly, a huge smile on her face.

Veronica twitched. 'I don't. It's natural.'

'Oh really? Well your eyebrows are quite dark then aren't they?'

The others on the table sniggered nervously, forks half way to their mouths. This was going to be good.

Veronica took a sip of wine, lit a cigarette and sat back. She eyeballed Bernie, waiting calmly for her to drop her gaze. You have so picked on the wrong one, lady, she thought. And I can keep this staring business up all night if I have to.

Eventually, Bernie looked away.

'Er, nice wine,' Brett said to no one in particular.

'Yes, yes, smashing, lovely,' the others agreed. 'Very, er, red….'

'Strange how it gets better after the first six glasses though, isn't it?' Johnny said, and they all laughed heartily as if he'd just told a great joke.

Veronica took a drag on her cigarette, scanning the room for James? Where was he? Ah, there he was and looking right at Sam, again. This was something she really had to do something about. Bernie was nothing but an incredibly irritating pipsqueak, and she would so not lower herself or lose her cool because if she did that she would have to slap her. God, how she would love to slap that woman - so much her palms itched, in fact. She watched as Bernie switched her attention to the men, thinking she had won, laughing and laughing at their inane jokes, joining in with the football banter, letting her little skirt hitch higher and higher up her matchstick thighs. She noticed with satisfaction the expression on Melissa's face as Bernie did this and smiled to herself. They were small fry, let them play their amazingly stupid attention-getting games. Who gives a rat's arse? she thought. Neither of them looked like management material acting like that, did they?

Neither Bernie nor Melissa looked exactly thrilled either, when a glamorous girl in a tight, red halter neck dress suddenly appeared at their table - circulating.

'Oh hiya, Jonnny,' the girl said, leaning over Johnny to give him an eyeful of ample cleavage. 'How are you, gorgeous?' She then twisted round to say, 'hiya,' to Brett, too. 'Isn't it great? D'ya know what I mean?' the girl said to Johnny and Brett, letting her fag ash drop onto Melissa's lap. 'Oh sorry, love,' she said. Then turning back to the lads, 'shall we go for a few bevvies later then, or what?'

'Oh right, yeah,' Johnny said, oblivious to Melissa's scowl.

'See you later then, handsome,' the interloper in the tight dress said, ruffling his hair.

Johnny and Brett grinned at each other across the girls heads.

'She's a bit of all right isn't she, mate?' Johnny said.

'Phwoar! She's well fit, yeah? D'ya know what I mean?' Brett agreed.

'What?' said Melissa, incredulously. 'That cross-eyed bastard in the red dress with a big head that's just been dropping fag ash all over me?'

Despite herself, Veronica spluttered over her wine.

'Careful,' Bernie said. 'We wouldn't want you to choke to death now would we?'

Involuntarily Veronica looked over at James again, noting with dismay that his gaze was still firmly planted on Sam. If only she could stop herself from looking at him. Why, James? Why? I thought you loved me, she thought miserably. If only she could get him on his own, find out what the hell was going on, she might stand a chance. But here she was, trapped at the dinner party from hell with no option other than to watch the inevitable.

Well, actually, I do have some choice, she decided. At least I don't have to bloody well watch. 'Would you excuse me, everyone? Just popping to the Ladies.'

Bernie let out a little giggle.

'Are you okay?' Sam called to her disappearing back, but Veronica did not look round.

Sam wore the expression of a hunted rabbit. She looked around her with dismay. There had already been a coldness and distance from Melissa following their last time out together, which she hadn't understood at the time and still didn't. And now she'd had hostile looks from Veronica too, which were even more mystifying - what was going on? Obviously she was never going to be bosom pals with Veronica, theirs would only ever be a superficial, needs must sort of relationship, but the laser eyeballing she had been getting ever since this afternoon was something new altogether.

Then there was O'Reilly over there showing her knickers and screeching with the boys, forever looking over to check that the girls were getting an eyeful, of course. Bernie was now on Johnny's knee and Sam wondered how much more she could stomach. And why was Johnny constantly looking over at her too? What was it with these people? Was she supposed to be feeling jealous of their childish antics or something? The only other person who looked like she felt was poor Mike. She smiled at him in sympathy, hoping for the recognition of a kindred spirit, but he just shook his head like an indulgent grandfather, and poured himself yet another drink.

She noticed that Mike was drinking very heavily and wondered why. Normally he was so composed and in control: this wasn't like him at all. Oddly enough, out of all the bizarre behaviour around her it, it was

Mike's drinking that got to her the most - it was, she thought, a little like noticing the pilot was shooting up drugs at thirty-three thousand feet and no one else could fly the plane. Perhaps it had something to do with the fact that Trisha hadn't turned up yet. Apparently, Trisha the nurse was lost somewhere in Europe.

'Excuse me,' she said over everyone's heads, not caring whether they heard her or not. She had to have some air.

'Oops, another one bites the dust,' Bernie giggled.

Immediately, Johnny shunted Bernie off his knee saying, 'must go and circulate a bit, ladies, you know how it is.'

The smile left Melissa's face in an instant. 'More wine, Bernie?' she asked.

'Thanks,' Bernie said, pushing her glass across. 'I need another one after this afternoon. Veronica did well though, I suppose, don't you think, Mel?'

'Mmmm. I don't think, like, anyone agreed with her, though? How can you, like, defend the murder of beautiful wild animals? I'm surprised she isn't wearing boots made from baby seal skin and an evening dress trimmed with Panda fur.'

'Still, I imagine her performance will put her in a good light for the job.'

'Oh, do you really think so?' Melissa asked, her eyes flashing dangerously.

'I suppose,' Bernie said, playing with the stem of her wine glass, avoiding eye contact. 'Which wouldn't be right would it, you know - with you having all that experience and all?'

Melissa glowered. 'Whatever.'

'I wonder where she and Johnny have got to, anyway?' Bernie said, swivelling her head around in time to see Johnny talking to

Veronica, their heads bent close as they walked out of the restaurant together.

 Melissa gasped. 'Her and Johnny? But I thought…..'

 Bernie nodded.

 'What the hell does she think she's playing at?'

 'She wants it all that one, doesn't she?' Bernie said, clamping her lips tightly shut in the manner of extreme disapproval.

 While Bernie and Melissa speculated, to a musical background of, 'Chirpy, chirpy, cheep cheep,' Veronica was leaning over the restaurant balcony watching James slip his jacket off and carefully place it around Sam's shoulders. The two of them were sitting on a bench by the lake. She could hear Sam's tinkling laughter in sharp contrast to James' deep, velvety tones. Damn, damn and damn again. Why were all the men in her life betraying her? She had kind of half imagined that she and James would run off into the corporate sunset and be executive directors together, especially now Greg was about to be removed.

 She needed James - without him she would not jump the queue. She would be left for who knows how much longer having to smile at officious secretaries and arrogant, pipsqueak junior doctors who treated her as if she was a highly suspect double glazing salesperson. Worse, she might end up having to work for one of those cheap tarts in there. Something had to be done. But what? Think, Veronica, think, think….

****

 Back home, Simon was lying on the living room floor, watching the motor racing on television when the phone rang. He sighed and stubbed out his cigarette, before navigating his way through the piles of greasy plates and coffee cups which were strewn all over the floor, to the hallway.

'Hello?' he said.

There was silence at the other end.

'Hello?'

More silence.

Slowly he replaced the handset and dialled 1471. The caller had withheld their number.

Two minutes later the phone rang again. 'Hello?'

'Did you know your girlfriend is sleeping with her boss?' the voice asked him.

He couldn't tell if the voice was male or female. It was a whinging sort of voice and the line was crackly. In fact, if he didn't know better he would say the person was holding their nose.

'Is this a joke?' he asked.

'So you didn't know?'

'Who's speaking?'

'Just thought someone should tell you, that's all.' And the caller hung up.

He looked at his watch. It was quarter past nine - well past the time Sam had been supposed to phone him. She hadn't called last night either.

Simon frowned as he replaced the receiver. Something was going on, of that he was sure. The agreement was that she would phone him at nine o'clock his time and reverse the charges. Well, there was only one thing to do: he would phone her. And he would phone her every fifteen minutes until she damn well answered.

Chapter 18

The next morning Melissa's team was in a subdued and difficult mood. There was an atmosphere and nobody quite knew what was going on as groups of twos and threes kept breaking off to gossip in whispers. Everyone appeared to have a grudge against someone else with the exception of young Brett, who remained cheerful and keen to get on with the morning's work.

'Great night last night?' he said to no one in particular. He'd downed several pints of red wine mixed with champagne at the restaurant, enjoyed jumping up and down on the tables with his air-guitar to the thump, thump, thump of Nirvana, and been shocked to discover it was nearly five o'clock in the morning when he finally fell onto his bed - fully clothed, with only a couple of hours to recover. Still, he felt great now he'd been sick, raring to go again tonight, utterly oblivious to the strange emotions and irritable expression that hovered around the team, moving from one face to another.

Nobody bothered to reply so he tried again. 'Isn't it great about the Marks and Spencers vouchers? D'ya know what I mean, yeah?'

The others stared back at him. He thought he heard the word 'tosser,' but he couldn't be sure.

They all had sunshine yellow T-shirts on with 'Happy Selling,' written across the front. Their syndicate room, stiflingly hot and thick with stale alcohol fumes, was piled high with boxes containing all the glossy, new marketing materials. They were supposed to be unpacking them and deciding how best to use them in order to sell Happylux more effectively. But raising any enthusiasm from the team was proving to be impossible for Melissa. They either moaned for coffee, repeatedly excused themselves for the toilet, or just sat there day- dreaming.

Melissa sighed loudly. Johnny had his feet on the table and Sam was gazing out of the window again. Why couldn't they get a grip? What was wrong with them? This afternoon was important - from two o'clock to six-thirty there was going to be a massive selling workshop with the new materials. This was called, 'Bedlam,' which meant they would be doing the role-playing equivalent of speed dating, on video. Marks would be given for performance and the regions would be ranked accordingly, with prizes given out to the managers of the winning teams on the last night. This, Melissa realised, could be seriously humiliating.

'Look I'm tired too, okay?' she said. 'I was, like, woken up really early this morning?'

'Why?' Sam asked her, out of politeness.

'Oh, one of the waiters was banging furiously on my door in the early hours.'

'Really?'

'Yes, it went on and on relentlessly. I was, like, really annoyed? I need my sleep more than most, you know,' said Melissa.

'Hang on a minute, he was banging on your door? That's terrible,' Sam said.

'I know. Anyway, I had to get up in the end and let him out.'

No one quite knew if Melissa was joking or not so they just stared at her.

'And my knees hurt from all….'

'On the outside or the inside?' Johnny asked.

Melissa narrowed her eyes. '…..the dancing I did last night. Right, well you've had your coffee. It's not my fault if you've all, like, had a skin full and you feel ill. We have to get on with this now, and we'll be getting a visit from one of the marketing people any minute? They're coming round to each region to, like, answer any questions we might have? And to take us through the new clinical papers?'

There was a collective groan. It seemed like the day might never end.

'Brett - would you unpack those boxes for us, please?' Melissa said.

Brett jumped up, and moments later the team were staring at their new sales brochures, emblazoned with photographs of actors pretending to be depressed people, with a mixture of cynicism and disinterest.

'I think we need more coffee,' Sam suggested.

'I think we need a truck full of amphetamines,' Johnny said.

By mid-morning there was a diversion though. The door knob to their room was rattling furiously.

'Someone's at the door, Johnny said, without looking up.

'Mmmmm,' the others murmured.

Still the person on the other side rattled away, shaking the door knob ever more frantically. The rattling went on and on for several minutes. Eventually Johnny said, 'it must be Trisha!'

'Are you mad?' Bernie shrieked. 'She can't even find the right country. What on earth makes you think she'd be able to find our syndicate room?'

'Take my word for it,' Johnny insisted. 'It'll be Trisha.'

Suddenly Mike sprung to life, speaking for the first time in days. 'He's right. I bet it bloody is.' Darting out of his chair with renewed vigour, he strode to the door and flung it wide. Trisha fell in with all her battered, well travelled luggage. She hadn't slept for three days.

'I think you'd better help Trisha find her room,' Melissa suggested to Mike. He nodded, hoisting Trisha's suitcase triumphantly onto his shoulder, unable to hide his relief.

Back in the syndicate room, Hector from the Marketing Department had arrived to run the team through all the latest Happylux selling materials. In a flurry of excitement, Melissa pulled up a chair for him, motioning for everyone to be quiet, to listen to Hector.

Hector, dressed in a Hugo Boss suit, glanced at his Rolex for several seconds longer than was strictly necessary, before holding up the new sales brochure. 'Now,' he said. 'It is *very* important that you get our new messages across to your customers, okay?'

'Yes,' said Bernie, with a grin. 'Absolutely - no problem.'

Hector looked straight at her. 'Right. Good. So, you've all had some time now to think about it - who can suggest an imaginative and innovative way to use these new graphs to best effect?'

No one spoke. Sam yawned, unintentionally loudly.

'How about we, like, do some role playing, then?' Melissa suggested.

Everyone groaned.

'I think these graphs are a bit dodgy, actually,' said Bernie, flicking though the new brochure with a disdainful look on her face.

Hector flushed. 'Dodgy?' he asked. 'Pardon me - did you say 'dodgy'?'

'Mmmmm,' Bernie casually tossed the new brochure onto the table, leaning back in her chair. 'I'm not sure I'm comfortable with them.'

'Dodgy? Dodgy?' A small purple vein stood out on Hector's forehead. 'Do you know how many months have gone into producing this brochure?' he asked her. 'Do you know how many important people at the highest level have had to sign this off?'

Bernie shook her head.

'How dare you use the word, 'dodgy,' to me! How dare you! You are never to use the word 'dodgy' again. Never. Nothing here is dodgy. Nothing.'

'Sorry,' Bernie said, with a shrug and a sly grin at the others.

Melissa tapped Hector sharply on the shoulder. 'What about doing some role play now?' she suggested.

'What?' He was still glaring at Bernie. 'Oh, yes - fine, whatever.'

'Johnny - you can, like, play the doctor?' Melissa said. 'Now, who wants to be the rep?'

No one looked at her.

'Oh, come on someone. I can't do it - I'm a manager.'

Everyone laughed.

'You said it,' Johnny said.

Still no one moved.

'Oh go on then - to be sure I'll show you all how it's done, so I will,' Bernie said. 'Even though I find these graphs impossible to make head or tail of.'

Melissa quickly moved two chairs into position at the front of the room so that Johnny and Bernie could take their places. Hector stood with his back to the wall, his expression somewhat tense.

'Ah - good morning, Dr King,' Bernie giggled as she took her seat and shook Johnny's hand.

'Top of the morning to you my little leprechaun,' Johnny said.

'So how much Happylux would you be using for me?' she said.

'Oh bucket loads,' Johnny replied, yawning.

'Oh goody - well let me show you these graphs....'

'Stop! Stop right there,' Hector said. 'What hasn't she done, everybody?'

'Established a need,' Veronica said.

'Quite. Bernie - how can you sell anything to this doctor when you haven't even established what he wants yet?'

'Oh it doesn't matter whether he wants any or not, I'll still sell him a stack,' she replied. 'Now, Dr King - as I was saying - these graphs, if I can make any sense of them at all that is…..'

The door slammed. Everyone jumped. Hector had gone.

A ripple of laughter broke out. Melissa glared at the team. 'Thanks a bunch, everybody.'

Sam turned back to staring dreamily out of the window at the now calm Mediterranean Sea. How much sleep had she had? Two hours, three? No matter, it had been worth it. This was love - absolutely the real thing. Her eye caught a seagull. She watched it ride the air currents, dipping and diving over the water, screaming with excitement. Suddenly she was right there with it. She was free, alive, powerful, euphoric. Nothing now would ever be the same again. There could be no turning back. This was it. She bit back a smile of pleasure. Oh my God, what had she done?

After James had approached her at the lake, they had chatted for a while before deciding to walk down to the mountain village to one of the little bars. The bar had been candle lit, warm, and virtually empty save a few old men playing cards. In fluent Spanish, James ordered glasses of brandy for them - a particularly rich, heady brand laced with cherries.

'Generous measures,' Sam commented appreciatively, before knocking it back in one.

James' dark eyes had flashed dangerously. He clicked his fingers. As if by magic more brandy arrived. Glass after glass passed her lips. How many had she had? Nope, she couldn't recall. They'd giggled a lot, she remembered that much. No, correction - she had giggled a lot. And then it was all a bit hazy, really. They had talked about the conference,

Spain, holidays, careers - all those sorts of things, and then, after about half an hour or so, James had slid his arm around her shoulders and said, 'shall we go back to the hotel, now?'

She'd been surprised. 'Why?'

'I think it might be more comfortable, don't you?'

'Won't you be missed?'

'Who cares? Come on - let's go.'

She had hesitated only briefly. He was much bigger close up, much darker, very in control. 'Oh, all right,' she said with a nervous giggle. Miraculously he had a taxi for them in minutes, and soon they were rolling around on the back seat as it lurched violently from one pothole to another.

'I feel a bit sick,' Sam said apologetically when they reached the hotel.

'No problem - I've got some anti-emetics in my room, come-on,' James said, grabbing her hand as he pulled her towards the lift. She hadn't resisted. Oh, how shameless - they had gone straight to his suite.

Amazingly he really did have anti-emetics. She gulped them down, recovering on the king sized bed while the room span alarmingly. What had happened next? Oh yes, he must have opened the sliding doors to his balcony - she had felt cool sea air wafting into the bedroom suite. And then how had they got from that to ….? Sam struggled to recollect the details. There were so many things compounding her memory of events - the hypnotic roll of the pounding sea, the violent rotation of the ceiling, the proximity of James' warm, masculine body. So close, so intense.

He'd been sitting on the edge of the bed asking if she needed more water when the fixation with his lips began. He had amazing lips, she thought - lips that lifted slightly at the corners in little flickers as he read the signals given out. And boy must she have been giving out come get me signals. He bent his head to nuzzle her neck.

'Mmmm,' she murmured. His skin bristled a little roughly against her shoulder, the scent of him aromatic, masculine, exciting.

He ran his hands over her breasts. She'd gasped, knew they would make love. She pulled him towards her, brushing his tantalising lips against her own, tugging at his shirt. She had always known there was more to life, that being swept away like this was how it should be. Everything had led to this moment - all the disappointments, all the rage, the fear - all of it could now be released. 'Oh James,' she sighed, then suddenly giggled at herself.

'What?' he asked, momentarily distracted from removing her underwear. 'What are you laughing at?'

'I sound like a Bond girl.'

'You look like one too,' he murmured. 'You are incredibly delicious, do you know that?'

She giggled. 'So are you.'

He nuzzled her neck again. This was unbelievable, Sam thought - she was about to be transported to heaven. Visions of long, lingering massages, a shared bath while drinking champagne, declarations of undying passion, queued up in her mind for delectation. This was it.

'Turn over, darling, would you?' he said.

She snapped back to reality. 'What?'

'There's a good girl. Come on.'

She hesitated for a moment. 'Oh, right.'

After that it had been one heck of a marathon, with James issuing urgent instructions, turning her this way and then that. At half time, he'd gone to get them some water while she lay panting for breath. 'Now let's try this one,' he said when he got back. 'You get on top of me and spread your legs wide.'

She tried.

'Oh dear,' he said, laughing. 'You were never a dancer, were you darling? My fiancée can do the splits, you know? Oh well, we'll just have to forget that one for now, I suppose.'

Still, maybe that was what real men were like, she decided, in her drunken haze - successful, rich and good looking men like James. Sophisticated sex, that's what it was. And it hadn't seemed like four hours at the time. In fact, as she stumbled back to her room, albeit a bit bow legged, it had come as quite a shock to see that it was three o'clock in the morning.

Three messages on her ansafone awaited her. All three were from Simon asking her to call him as soon as she got back to her room, no matter what the time. She stood there for a moment thinking, Simon? Simon who? Oh yes....him. Well she could hardly phone him at three o'clock in the morning when he had to get up at six, could she? even with the time difference? She would just have to say that they all went to a nightclub, and that was why she wasn't in her room. Simple! So that was one thing less to worry about then - at least with it having happened abroad, Simon would never find out.

So she pushed him from her mind. Right now her thoughts were with James, anyway. Last night had been so much more than just a shag. James was 'the one.' As she listened to various members of the team droning on and on about who said what in their hospitals or their surgeries, she closed her eyes. How on earth was she going to feel when she saw him again in the light of day with other people around? Because this was love, it really was - he was her raison d'etre and nothing else mattered now.

Brett's voice chipped away, irritating her. Like who cared if Dr so and so had this or that objection? Was she supposed to give a monkey's arse about someone else's customer? It was just never ending in this team - there was always someone bleating on and on about an unsolvable problem - warming up to the sound of their own self-important voice. Didn't they realise all this was so unimportant? People were nodding all right but she knew they were just pretending to listen while Brett and Bernie rabbitted on about fuck knows what.

She yawned. She and James would get married. They could honeymoon somewhere exotic like Fiji. Her wedding dress would be sensational - a corset style bodice maybe with a long, satin skirt. Everyone would turn to stare at her as she walked into the church. James would be waiting for her at the alter - his dark eyes alight with love and admiration. And then they would live in his London apartment, and she could shop in Harrods and Selfridges and go to trendy Boho boutiques. Maybe she would do a part time course in art and design, or take acting classes. She would take their children to school in an armour plated off-roader. Oh, the romantic possibilities were endless. No more bed pans or hospital psychiatric units for her.

Oh, but hang on a minute - what about thingy? She thought for a moment. She would have to leave Simon. Oh well….She nearly laughed. 'Sorry,' she said, snapping back into the present moment, as Johnny shot her a look. Melissa was speaking and she'd been miles away.

'I think we'll go for lunch,' Melissa said. 'It's been a long morning and we've, like, got a difficult afternoon ahead?'

A loud cheer went up. Melissa looked over at Bernie and winked. They were going to have a heart to heart at lunch time. Bernie had confided in her last night over a bottle of wine, that she wasn't going to apply for Dick's job after all as she had too little experience. She said that she would rather go into marketing, so if she supported Melissa now, then maybe Melissa would help her in return later. It all made sense. But first, Bernie said, they must make absolutely sure that Mel got the job and not Veronica. Damn right, Melissa thought, still smarting over the image of Veronica and Johnny disappearing together.

'I just cannot, like, believe the bare-faced cheek of that snooty cow,' Melissa said to Bernie once they'd got their meals. They had chosen a quiet corner well away from the masses - a table for two outside in the sunshine. As Melissa spoke, Veronica was in the process of making her way towards them with a plate of radishes.

'May I join you, girls?' she asked pleasantly. Melissa and Bernie looked at each other aghast.

'Oh I see, is it a private conversation then?' Veronica asked, taking in their hostile expressions.

'Yes, sorry,' Melissa said flippantly. And then, turning back to Bernie, said in a loud enough voice for Veronica to make no mistake about it, 'so your appraisal next year would be really important and the areas to concentrate on are.......'

Melissa and Bernie watched with narrowed eyes as Veronica wandered off with her plate of leaves, looking for someone she could sit with. They took in her endless legs, which were encased in skin tight, white lycra jeans that only she and a handful of super models could possibly get away with.

'Veronica No-Mates,' Bernie giggled.

'What she needs is a fucking good stew down her neck,' Melissa snapped.

'Yes, she needs a good feed,' Bernie agreed. 'Let's hope there aren't any cattle grids around for her to slip through.'

Melissa raised an eyebrow. That was rich - Bernie talking about needing a feed!

'So, how will we get her?' Bernie asked cheerfully. 'Will I innocently drop something in about her and Johnny to Pat?'

'Could you?'

'Oh yes. I should think so. Pat and I know each other really well now. We chatted last night for two hours, in fact.' Bernie had found out that Pat knew all about Melissa's shenanigans, that was for sure.

'Well if you could, like, drop something in subtly……..'

Bernie grinned. 'Subtle is my middle name,' she giggled. 'Tonight's the night then.' She raised her glass in a toast, but then, noticing Melissa's unease added, 'Well, it wouldn't be right for our future regional manager to be shagging one of her subordinates now, would it?'

'No, it would be shocking. Unthinkable,' Melissa agreed.

'Don't tell me you've gone and lost your bottle now. We'd be doing the company a huge favour by spilling the beans.'

'Oh absolutely.'

'And would you look at your woman now?'

'Brown nosing again,' Melissa said.

They watched as Veronica went to sit with James and Pat.

'How are you enjoying the conference, Veronica?' Pat asked her politely. Veronica opened her mouth to answer just as Pat's mobile phone rang. 'Oh, excuse me a minute, will you, lovey?' she said, scuttling off with one finger in her ear, her mobile pressed to the other, shouting, 'Hello? Hello? I'm in Spain, lovey! Hello?'

The second Pat was out of earshot, Veronica regarded James intently. 'So you're sleeping with Sam now are you, James? What about us? Are you tired of me already?'

Squish! Don't be silly. Of course not. How did you know about that, anyway'

'You really are a bigger bastard than I thought.'

'Veronica, darling, last night was just a one-off, believe me. Look, meet me in my room tonight, yah? Eleven o'clock after dinner. We need to talk, okay?'

'What about Sam?'

'What about her?'

'Well, does she know last night was a one-off as you call it?'

'She will.'

Pat was coming back.

'I so need your help, James,' Veronica hissed.

'Eleven. I promise, okay?' Then as Pat sat down he said, ' I was very impressed with your presentation yesterday, Veronica.'

Pat nodded. 'Yes, I heard about that. You obviously put a lot of thought into it.'

'Thank you,' Veronica said.

Good, so it would be tonight then. James got one more chance.

Chapter 19

All day she had looked for him. Where was he? He had to be here, he just had to be. Sam looked around the small, over-crowded restaurant as discreetly as possible. There was a dance floor, a stunning view of the harbour from floor to ceiling windows, and best of all - tonight's venue was close enough to the hotel for people to be able to walk back if they wanted to. It was perfect - yet he wasn't here. Why? Why not? All day she had been looking forward to this, expecting any moment to see him staring at her yearningly. She bit back her frustration with the evening's events. Reps were now chanting and banging on the tables, the evening having disintegrated rapidly following the copious amounts of alcohol they had all been encouraged to drink.

'Come on, you're not drinking enough!' McCraw barked at them as he marched round the restaurant, zooming in on individual tables where people were being a bit too quiet for his liking. 'You've another five bottles of red to get through over here. What are you - lily livered southerners, or what?'

Sam cringed, praying McCraw wouldn't come over to her table. She'd had four glasses of the stuff already - anymore and she'd be on the floor. Keep your wits about you, for God's sake, she told herself. There was something else bothering her too - something James had said last night, a little word that hovered and fluttered around in the fog of her memory - now, what was it? No, she couldn't think. No doubt it would come to her, probably when she least expected it, then up it would pop. There was nothing to worry about anyway - James was probably working, the poor boy. She would see him later.

A loud shriek of mocking laughter forced her to tune back in to what was going on around her. Melissa and Bernie were pointing at the dance floor, screeching and cackling with glee. Sam turned to see what it was they were looking at, and couldn't resist a slight smile herself. Bob from Accounts was swinging Veronica around to 'Mack the Knife.' Everyone knew he had a crush on her. He'd approached their table, despite the sniggering, and politely asked Veronica to dance to 'Murder on the Dance Floor,' with him. Veronica had equally politely acquiesced.

However as the dance ended, and 'Mack the Knife' came on, Bob unexpectedly made a grab for Veronica, forcing her to join him in a particularly enthusiastic rendition of the Twist. Unfortunately, Mack the Knife' seemed to be getting faster and faster, and Veronica was being whizzed about with ever increasing fervour by Bob - a surprisingly fit little guy in white plimsolls and a golfing sweater with checked trousers. He was having a fabulous time it seemed, twirling Veronica around - trying to pick her up and throw her over his shoulder. She, on the other hand, looked uncomfortably aware of the fact that the dance floor had emptied, and that she and Bob were now the floor show.

'That is *so* not doing Veronica any favours in the image department is it?' Melissa shrieked.

Then quite suddenly, the music changed tempo and it was Robbie Williams singing a duet with Nicole Kidman. Bernie and Melissa, who had been rolling around with laughter, tears streaming down their faces, watched with disbelief as Johnny materialised from nowhere to rescue Veronica. Confidently he pulled her to him, and for all the world to see, they began to smooch to, 'Something Stupid.'

Sprightly Bob, looking somewhat piqued for a moment, brightened when he noticed Sam on her own. Sam looked around frantically, but it was too late.

'That was a really sexy dance,' Johnny said when he and Veronica got back to the table.

Overhearing this, Bernie shouted across to Johnny, 'only because you haven't had a girlfriend in ages.'

'Oh right, yeah.' Johnny grabbed his drink and winked at Veronica.

'So how long have you, like, been *married*, Veronica?' Melissa asked.

'Two years. Why?'

'Just wondered. Don't you ever, like, you know, worry about him when you're away?'

'No.'

'Oh damn - does anyone have any Euros?' Johnny asked. 'I need some fags.'

'Euros - ugh!' Veronica said. 'I so don't know what was wrong with pesetas.'

'I take it you're not for us joining Europe, then?' Johnny asked her.

'No. I think we should all keep our national identities,' Veronica said.

'Well I'm all for it. I made heaps of money on our flat in Dublin after we joined in Ireland - it was the best thing that ever happened to us. I'm just hoping the same thing will happen in England,' Bernie chipped in. 'House prices rocket you know? Then I'll be zooming off to America with loads of dosh.'

'Isn't that just cashing in at our expense, though?' Veronica said. 'I mean - what's important here? I love England and I want it to stay the same - not be ruled by a pile of people in Belgium I've never heard of. And I like the pound.'

'What's so great about your country? You're not that special,' Bernie said.

'Well for a start, no one in Europe can agree about anything, or hadn't you noticed?' Veronica said. 'And the French hate us - always have. No, we should stay as we are - I don't see why we should have to have their silly rules and regulations. Our whole way of life is at risk.'

'Oooh, you're so proud, Veronica,' Bernie said in a mocking voice.

Veronica glared at her.

'Well you are proud,' Bernie said again.

'I so don't know how you of all people can talk about national pride, Bernie O' Reilly. It wasn't me that dressed up head to foot in emerald green on St Patrick's Day.'

Bernie shrugged before moving up closer to Johnny. 'Do you want to know what I'm getting for my birthday from my boyfriend?' she asked him coyly.

'Now what would that be? A vibrator?'

'Aaaah! Don't be so outrageous. Johnny King - what are you like? Don't you know I'm just an innocent Catholic girl?'

'Of course. Three Hail Marys for me again. Go on then - what are you getting?'

'So you do want to know?'

'Not really.'

'I'm getting some new black, leather riding boots - long ones.' She stretched her leg out across his lap and drew a line. 'All the way to the top,' she said, running her finger up to her crotch.

'I didn't know you had a horse,' Johnny said. 'Do you wear jodhpurs then?'

Bernie rolled her eyes. 'Why do you think I got the Landrover? '

'To take someone's kids to Sainsburys?'

'Don't be ridiculous. I have to look after Minty - he's a top class polo playing horse, don't you know?'

'You're a beautiful Irish lady,' Brett slurred.

God, weren't men thick, Sam thought, suddenly realising that the restaurant was rapidly being vacated. Hoards of drunken reps were making their way to the various clubs and bars in the area. She would have to make a decision. And soon. But what? Where the hell was he? If she went with everyone else to a nightclub, would it be the right one?

'Are you coming with us, Sam?' Johnny asked her, his arm around a tiny blonde, Melissa and Bernie in tow.

Sam did a double take. Had someone dropped something in her drink here? Didn't Mel fancy Johnny? How odd! Melissa looked pleased even, casting smug glances at Veronica, who seemed overly keen to leave. Strange, Sam thought, shaking her head, I wish I knew what the hell was going on. 'I think I'll just head back to the hotel,' she answered, picking up her bag.

Perhaps he'll be there when I get back, she thought, ignoring the cat calls and wolf whistles as she walked along the busy, night-life bright street in her killer heels and short, tight dress. He might be in the Piano Bar. Once she got to the hotel she could go in and have a gin and tonic, all sophisticated like a Greta Garbo character. He might be there waiting for her. If he wasn't, she would go up to her room and ring him from there - he could have been in a business meeting all evening, after all. Yes, that's what she would do. She picked up speed.

A few minutes later, walking purposefully into the hotel reception area, she saw him. She stood stock still. Her pulse quickened. Oh, just the briefest glimpse of him and she was happy again. She lifted a hand to attract his attention. But wait. He was walking away from her towards the crowded lift area. And there was someone with him. Who? She strained her eyes. No, it couldn't be.

'Excuse me,' someone said.

'Sorry,' said someone else as they bumped into her with a case. She should get out of the doorway, she knew, but she couldn't. Transfixed, she watched as the lift doors opened, waiting for the other person, a woman, to turn round. James and the woman walked in. The woman turned. And just as the doors began to close, he bent to kiss her. It was Veronica.

Everything around her, all the noise, the music, people's laughter, fused into a single high pitched scream. Her heart began to pound violently, rocking her whole body. She looked down - her hands were shaking, her knees felt weak.

'Would the lady like a drink?' A waiter hovered at her elbow.

'No,' she whispered. 'She would not.'

She had to get to her room, to be alone as soon as possible. She made her way across the marbled foyer towards the lifts, then suddenly stopped in her tracks. Hey, maybe she had got it wrong and James and Veronica just happened to be in the same lift together? Maybe she should ring his room anyway to make sure? It would be crazy to jump to the wrong conclusion wouldn't it? They might be old friends and he was just kissing her goodnight. He might have been looking out for her, Sam, all evening. He would be back down again in a minute. He probably expected her to call him, had no doubt been looking for her all day, in fact. He'd been involved in important business all evening. Yes, that was it - she would phone his room as soon as she got to hers.

Two minutes later she sat on her bed staring at the phone, wondering if she should. Should she? Shouldn't she? She reached for the receiver. She put it back. Should she? He would be there by now, having dropped Veronica off. Yes, she would phone. She put her hand on the receiver again. But a tiny voice was tap, tap, tapping away in the far recesses of her mind - something wrong - something not quite right. That little word, maybe? Something he had said. What was it? She almost had it. No, it had gone again.

Think, girl, think a minute. Images flashed like bullets into her conscious mind: Veronica and James having lunch with Pat, their heads bowing closer together when Pat left the table, only to spring apart again when she returned. The sales workshop this afternoon when she'd been looking out for him, only to catch a look between him and Veronica. They'd been smiling into each other's eyes like lovers - confident and familiar.

She continued to stare at the phone, at the flashing ansafone light, indecision hovering. Now she thought about it, where had Veronica disappeared to at lunch on the training day they had last month? James wasn't there either, was he? What about the off-the-cuff remarks Johnny made here and there regarding Veronica? Damn. She must have made such a fool of herself. She'd been so bloody easy as well. 'Shit! Shit! Shit!' she said out loud, plunging her head into her hands. Oh God, what had she done?

And what about Simon? She really ought to phone him back, and if he thought she sounded down then it would be for all the usual reasons wouldn't it?

While Sam was staring at the phone in her room, and Veronica and James were humping away in the shower, Bernie was making her way towards Pat Hardcastle in the Piano Bar for the final stage of her attack.

'Oh God, not again' Pat muttered under her breath when she noticed Bernie winding her way through the crowds with a pint of lager in her hand, and a huge grin on her face. Pat quite liked being sucked up to but that girl just over-did it. Last night Bernie had poked around for information until she felt sure she'd told her something she shouldn't - albeit in a veiled way. Bernie was smart, that was for sure, and full of energy. Christ, it was nearly midnight and the girl was still as sprightly as a new born lamb.

'Hi Pat, how are you?' Bernie said, clutching at Pat's sleeve as if she hadn't seen her for years. 'Will I get you a pint at all?'

'Er, no thanks, lovey,' Pat said, draining her tomato juice. 'I'm off to bed in a minute. It's a big day tomorrow and I'm on stage first thing.'

'Oh fantastic!' Bernie squealed. 'And how did you think today went, Pat?'

'The selling workshop? Yes, very well. I'm a firm believer in all my reps doing four hour selling skills marathons. It imprints the information on their brains. Plus it's on video so you can all review them at your next regional meetings, and improve your performances.'

'Oh goodeee. Oh that will be so helpful. What a fantastic idea.'

Pat began to get up. 'Right, well I really must…'

But Bernie hadn't finished. 'Pat, can I ask you something very delicate?' she said, holding Pat's arm.

Pat sighed heavily and sat down again.

'In confidence?' Bernie insisted, moving closer.

'Go on.'

'Well, you know the manager's job is coming up in our region soon?'

'Yes?'

'Well, if one of the people going for it had been in bed with one of the people in the team, would it go against them?'

'In bed? Ooh, Bernie, lovey! Who are we talking about?'

'Oh I couldn't possibly say. I don't like to gossip as you know.'

'Well it would be most serious - it would be highly inappropriate for a manager to manage someone he had a personal relationship with if that's what you're asking me?'

'Yes. God, I'm so worried about her. Maybe it's not too late if she stops now.' Bernie bit her lip.

'Are we taking about who I think we're talking about again, Bernie?'

'Not the same person as last night, no,' she said.

Pat narrowed her eyes.

'Oh dear, I feel so awful,' Bernie said, her eyes bright with excitement. 'I'm just so worried about my colleague you know, and I really don't want to see her get hurt and all. I thought I could come to you and ask your advice. Thanks so much.' Bernie squeezed Pat's arm gratefully.

'Hmmm, well, if you'll excuse me now, lovey, I must go and get some sleep,' she said, heaving herself out of the deep sofa she'd been lolling in, her linen dress a nightmare of creases. 'Good night, Bernie.'

'Sleep tight, don't let the bed bugs bite,' Bernie said cheerily. Now, where was Melissa?

Melissa and Johnny had their heads together at the bar, the little blonde still hanging around Johnny but looking a little less now like the leading lady and more like the support role.

'I'm not shagging Veronica,' Johnny said to Bernie the second she approached them. 'Jesus, whatever gave you two that idea? Me and the ice-maiden? Ha ha! Ha ha! I haven't heard anything as funny as that in ages. I'd need a chuffing stepladder to start with!'

Melissa tried to raise an eyebrow at Bernie before switching her attention back to Johnny. She tried to smile widely too, but found it difficult since she'd had the Botox. The only problem now was to offload this irritating blonde midget. Then the man and the job would be hers if Bernie had done her job with Pat.

'But Veronica's shagging someone,' Bernie insisted. 'She keeps disappearing. Would it be James at all?'

Melissa's mouth opened in dismay, but before she could speak, Johnny said, 'no.'

Both girls looked at him. Colouring slightly, he shrugged his shoulders.

'How do you know?' they said.

'Well I thought that for a while actually, but it's not the case.'

'How do you know for sure?' Mel asked him.

'Because James is riding Sam,' he said, a little too forlornly for Melissa's liking. 'I thought you knew that, Mel? You told us all.'

Melissa looked away. 'I know. Whatever. Oh well, I suppose it's, like, good news for me if Veronica's not in bed with the boss.' And neither of them were in bed with Johnny, she thought. In fact, how very satisfactory. 'Right, I'll get the drinks in, then' she said. 'We'll, like, put them all on my room? Manager's prerogative, you know. Now what are we having? Double vodkas all round?'

Chapter 20

'Veronica, which would you prefer- a cream horn or a chocolate éclair?'

Veronica, dressed as an Indian squaw, stared back at Johnny with a thinly disguised attempt at tolerance and took another drag of her cigarette. She'd had this from him all day now, and frankly it was getting to the point where clubbing him to death with a baseball bat looked like an increasingly reasonable option.

'Which would you choose, Veronica - a Mars Bar or a Finger of Fudge?' Johnny insisted.

She eyed him steadily, deciding that Johnny didn't know anything - he was just winding her up, and he certainly wouldn't be doing this if he knew she was going to be his boss in the very near future. He was a fool. She forced the corners of her lips to flicker upwards a little.

They were all in Dick's suite for his farewell party and a few glasses of champagne prior to the 'End of Conference Dinner and Dance,' which this year was on a fancy dress theme of Cowboys and Indians. It was the last day of conference, and with the exception of Sam, the team was in very high spirits, having had some of the afternoon off, their veins now pumping with alcohol, and most of them having something to look forward to. Or thinking that they had.

Dick, their leader, was dressed as Hiawatha, complete with a full head-dress of feathers which trailed almost to the floor.

'Dumpy little beggar. He's got a huge arse, hasn't he?' Sam whispered to Melissa, who giggled into her champagne.

'Oh bugger - the bubbles have gone up my nose now.'

Dick was waving his toy plastic axe around with enormous gusto just like he used to do at local children's parties when he was growing up and bullying the other, smaller kids into doing things his way. Fired up in his role as Hiawatha, he gave strict instructions to the team on how they should enter the conference hall later on. They would go in last, he said, when the hall was completely full in order to give themselves maximum impact when they entered. He would lead and run in whooping with the battle cry. They would all follow him doing the same. Was it a deal? Did they want to get noticed and show initiative? Did they want to knock the socks off the rest of the company's efforts? Were they the best region? Did they want to go for it?

'Yes,' they cried, knocking back their champagne in pint glasses on empty stomachs. Yeah, it would be a laugh, wouldn't it?

Dick beamed. A practice whooping session was what they needed now he suggested, convincing himself that his team had indeed been truly wonderful and he would miss them.

'What do you think the Queen would say now, Veronica?' Johnny asked.

Sam sighed and wandered out onto the balcony. Little boats bobbed up and down on the midnight blue sea, lights twinkling. She took another sip of champagne. How wonderful it would be to be out there on one of those and not in here. The last twenty four hours had been pretty joyless, so much so, she was actually looking forward to going home.

It had been a difficult morning and she had spent what had been left of her afternoon off asleep in bed instead of out sunbathing or doing water-sports with every one else. The day had started at eight o'clock with the MD, Alistair McCraw, delivering his all important one hour's speech, designed to frighten and intimidate. Presentations of cheques and trophies were then made to the sales league winners. Sam tried to push the image of Bernie O'Reilly holding her trophy high above her head punching the air triumphantly, out of her mind. It didn't work. Probably it would be etched there forever.

'Our most successful representative ever,' McCraw had said. 'Ladies and Gentlemen - I give you the awe inspiring - Bernie O'Reillly.'

Once the euphoria had died down, McCraw moved onto the serious business in hand. Topham Pharmaceuticals would be launching their new cardiology division within weeks, he informed them. And their new leader? Non other than that bastion of hard work and commitment, an example to us all. 'Ladies and Gentlemen - Dick Walton.'

'Did he mispronounce that?' Sam whispered to Johnny as Dick vaulted onto the stage to rapturous applause. 'Didn't he mean to say bastard?'

'Soon,' McCraw barked. ' There will be lots of exciting new job opportunities for you. But only the best will succeed. Top representatives only need apply when the time comes. Only movers and shakers will be considered. This is our core business at the end of the day, so you must be prepared to go that extra mile. You must look at the big picture and be pro-active not reactive. You must put the customer first and be prepared to think outside the box.'

Typical, Sam thought, watching him thumping the lectern as the lads in the team frantically crossed off phrases on the Wank List. McCraw had to go on and win the 'Wanker of the Year' award again. Now the girls owed the lads a drink. She couldn't even get that right. Still, that was the least of her worries.

After McCraw's speech, which was predictably followed by an arse-licking standing ovation, Pat Hardcastle got up to do hers. After three hours the reps began to fidget, with some nipping off to the toilet and, unable to find their way back to their seats in the dark, having to stand at the back of the hall for the rest of the speech. It would be over soon, though, wouldn't it? Pat was already way over her time limit. She was scheduled to finish at eleven o'clock when an extended coffee break was due. Then they'd got easy-peasy psychology sessions prior to finishing for lunch on the terrace and an afternoon off. They were looking forward to it, clinging onto the knowledge that by lunch-time it would all be over and they would be sunning themselves, drinking lager by the pool. Not long now.

One o'clock came and went. She would have to wrap up soon, surely? This was getting ridiculous. But as Pat turned another page, and introduced yet another video clip, people could be heard sighing loudly and hissing, 'for fuck's sake,' under their breath. By the time it got to nearly one-thirty there was a distinctly unhappy rumbling. Pat paused. The audience held their breath. This could be it. They could be out of here any minute now.......

'And now I'd like Bob from Accounts to come up and present his financial projections for the next five years,' Pat said to them. 'Now Bob was going to bed last night at twelve o'clock, but this is how committed he is to you all - I rang him at twelve -fifteen and asked him to get out of that bed and meet me in the hotel lounge to go through his presentation for today. Bob never hesitated. He was only too willing. Now that is the sort of commitment and enthusiasm that this company needs. Ladies and Gentlemen, may I present -Bob from Accounts!'

At two o'clock, Bob, uncomfortably aware of the lack of interest from the audience, stepped down.

'Thank you, Bob. Now finally,' Pat said as someone whispered a bit too loudly, 'thank fuck for that.' 'Finally, I want all the top representatives to give themselves a standing ovation. You have deserved it. You know who you are. Do it now!'

Bernie leapt to her feet. A few other highly embarrassed and utterly weary people had followed, clapping self-consciously.

Pat watched with satisfaction and then said, 'now I want you to forget everything you have achieved. You all start afresh from Monday morning when you get back. Everyone in this room gets a clean slate, and remember - the sooner you get cracking, the more Marks and Spencers vouchers you will earn. And for those of you who are not prepared to get up in the mornings, I have a message - you won't last long in our company. Only top representatives are welcome, which means hard work! Do I make myself absolutely clear?'

'Yes,' came the miserable response.

'Good. Now, we've worked through lunch break so off you all go directly to your syndicate rooms for the psychology sessions. Enjoy yourselves. Work hard and we'll play hard tonight. I hope you've all got your costumes!'

'Don't Stop Me Now,' then blasted out at rock concert decibel level, signalling that it really was over. There was some half-hearted applause from the managers followed by a surge towards the doors as if there had been a nuclear terrorist alert. The stampede left several people nearly trodden to death in the rush. At which point, Pat turned to James and said, 'well, that seemed to go quite well, didn't it? Pity I didn't have quite enough time to cover the new Health and Safety Data, though.'

After that the team had had several hours with a psychologist. He'd made them jump onto cards he'd spread across the floor with mission statements written on them like: 'I will be the best'.

'Guys! Guys!' the psychologist shouted. 'Listen carefully now. What you need to do is this - leap onto a card - any card - and when you land on it, shout out what colour you see in your mind as you think about the mission statement. It can be any colour - just go for it!'

'I can see red,' Sam said.

'Jump onto another one, Sam,' the psychologist said.

She jumped onto one saying : I Can Do It! 'I can see red again,' she said.

'Someone else,' he snapped. 'Bernie! What square are you on?'

'I'm on: I Will Succeed,' she said.

Johnny sniggered from the sidelines. 'Try sucking nuts, they're much tastier.'

'What colour can you see, Bernie?' the psychologist asked.

'Oooh, I'm getting a lovely deep blue,' she lied.

'Excellent! Now can everyone else see the power of the mind, like Bernie? Repeat the message you land on - I Can and I Will, or I Can Do It, or 'I Will Overcome! Try and imagine a colour as you do so, okay? Then I want you to picture your most important and difficult customer as you repeat the most appropriate phrase, and associate that colour with them.'

Sam pictured an officious little man in Pharmacy and repeated the phrase: 'I Will Avoid You At All Costs.'

What had been particularly mortifying was that everyone else said they had really enjoyed the exercise and found it useful. 'I find this such a waste of time when I should be having an afternoon off,' she'd said to Bernie.

Bernie swung around to look at her, eyes wide in amazement. 'Really?' she said. 'Oh I love this sort of thing.'

'But do you think it's useful?' Sam persisted. She'd thought the question reasonable. 'This is our free afternoon.'

'Oh Jesus, yes! Sam, you are just so negative aren't you? I can go shopping or swimming anytime. This is so much more important than having time off.'

'Give me strength,' Sam muttered, remembering her

conversation with Bernie. A light breeze caught her hair as she leaned over Dick's balcony. She had to get home to sort things out with Simon. Her phone call home had been very odd. When she had finally returned his call and explained about the late night and the tiny amount of time she had before having to go out again, she thought he would be sympathetic and supportive, but he'd been really funny with her.

'Something's wrong. What's the matter?' she asked.

'Nothing, should there be? Look, I'll pick you up from the airport, okay?'

'You don't need to, I can get a lift.'

'I insist.'

'It's seven in the morning when we get in, don't be silly.'

'I will be there, Sam.'

She'd put the phone down with a sense of foreboding. Yes, something was very wrong there. He never picked her up usually even when she'd begged and pleaded. No, his duty as a doctor came first. Always.

She could hear the rest of the team getting steadily drunker in the room behind her while she brooded on the day's events. Every now and again Brett's voice would say, 'at the end of the day, right?' or, 'd'ya know what I mean, yeah?' It probably wouldn't be long before he started saying, 'the team done well innit?' she thought. And another thing - there was absolutely no doubt that in a few minutes time she would have to see James again, not a pleasing prospect if she had to run into the room dressed as a squaw and whooping.

Reluctantly she considered rejoining the group. It sounded like the girls were doing hair and make-up, with Trisha appointed as the make up artist.

'Make me look beautiful!' Melissa said, throwing herself down onto the sofa for Trisha.

'We haven't got enough time for plastic surgery,' Mike chipped in.

'I want really heavy eye make-up like Veronica's,' Melissa said.

'But it won't suit you, Mel,' Trisha said.

'Whatever - it doesn't worry her so I don't see why it should worry me,' Melissa shot back.

Veronica heard her and shrugged. Who cared what Melissa said? She was so on her way out. Bernie was a concern though. She looked over at her now, at the big smile, the glittery eyes, the excited little dances she kept doing in front of the men. Bernie, she thought, was like one of those little birds with loads of exotic plumage that did funny little dances in front of potential mates when they were in the breeding season - look at me, look at me. Aren't I the best little bird in the jungle today?

And Bernie, she'd heard today, had been spreading rumours about her. Not to the team that she was aware of, although Johnny's teasing had been worse than usual, but straight to management. Smiling Bernie was playing games and she didn't trust her one bit. Hmmm, she would keep it to herself that she was on to her though. And so both Bernie and Veronica smiled as they watched Melissa giggle and joke around while she had her makeup done, occasionally pulling rank and reminding then who was boss. Melissa, Veronica thought, was like the Queen of Sheba on that sofa. 'Better enjoy it, lady,' she muttered under her breath. 'While you still can.'

'Who's next?' Trisha called out.

'Sam!' Melissa cried. 'Where is she? Sam? Sam?'

'I'm here,' Sam stepped back into the room. Flopping onto the sofa, she said, 'do what you want with me,' causing Johnny and Mike to raise their eyebrows at each other.

Trisha began to apply dark brown make-up to Sam's flawless skin, blobbing big freckles all over her nose in brown paint.

'Oh sorry, Sam, I must have made your eyes water - do you want a tissue?'

'Thanks,' Sam said, dabbing the corners of her eyes furiously.

'I can't believe how long your eyelashes are,' Trisha said.

'Mmm.'

'No, really! Your eyes are incredible. And your lips!' Trisha said, unaware of the fact that Johnny's jaw had begun to slacken lustfully and Melissa was beginning to scowl. 'Are you okay?'

Sam dabbed at her eyes miserably. 'Yes, just put plenty on will you?'

'Mmm,' said Trisha thoughtfully. As the others moved away, leaving Trisha and Sam alone together, she leaned towards her and whispered, 'you're very unhappy aren't you, Sam?'

Sam nodded, trying desperately to stop her eyes from brimming over in front of everyone.

'You were a nurse weren't you?'

'Yes, I was crap at that as well.'

'Oh so was I. I was so bad as a psychiatric nurse that one of my patients stabbed one of the others during cookery practice, another took a member of staff as hostage and held them at knife point on the roof, and one set the ward on fire - all when I was left in charge on my own.'

Sam started to giggle through the tears. 'Dick said you were a first rate nurse and he'd had to negotiate really hard to get you.'

Trisha laughed out loud. 'I know. Even I believed him at first, he was so convincing. And now look!' she said. 'I'm the worst nurse adviser they've ever had. But the thing is,' she leaned closer to Sam. 'I met Mike and I've been able to help him. It's made me realise what I'm good at - I want to be a counsellor. We go through everything for a reason, you see.'

'Really?'

'What do you think yours is?'

'I've never really thought.'

'The thing is - if we're not doing what we're supposed to be doing, what comes naturally to us, then everything else tends to go wrong as well, doesn't it? It's all such hard work - fighting against our true selves. And then we look to other people to put it right for us, and they never do. Do you understand?'

Sam didn't. God, Trisha was weird. 'Thank you,' she said.

'Sam, if you ever want to talk, I'm here, okay?' She laid her hand on Sam's shoulder for a couple of minutes, saying nothing.

Once Trisha had finished Sam's make-up, Sam sprung up and kissed her on the cheek. 'Thanks, Trisha. Amazingly I do feel a lot better.'

Trisha smiled. 'Good, and promise to think about what I've said? Because even if it doesn't make any sense to you just yet - it will.'

'Promise.'

'Come on now everyone!' Dick put his pint glass down amongst the eight empty champagne bottles and numerous lager cans. 'Time for our grand entrance. Are we ready?'

'Yes,' they chorused, reaching for each other to do the conga down the hallway to the lifts, Dick at the helm. 'Da da da da da da da, da da da da da da da, da da da da…….' they sang, snaking and swaying across the marbled foyer. Then, 'Shhhhh…' as they drew level with the conference hall. Piling on top of one another, they ducked behind the large stone pillar outside the wide open doors just like Dick had told them to. Dick turned to face his region. 'Now,' he whispered. 'I'll count to three and then …..' They nodded solemnly. 'One, two, three…' In a flash of feathers Dick sprang forwards.

But as the others prepared to follow, Johnny pulled them back. 'Let him go alone!' he whispered. 'We're right behind you Dick mate,' he called as his trusty team collapsed in a heap behind the pillar with hands clasped tightly over their mouths. The whole company, therefore, watched open mouthed as a lone Hiawatha waving an axe suddenly sprang into their midst, whooping and yodelling.

'Come on men!' he shouted, leaping into the middle of the amazed crowd. 'Come on!'……… He turned round to wave his team in. There was no one there. 'Oh you fucking little bastards!'

Sam thought she would laugh until she cried.

'Ooooh, watch the mascara!' Bernie said, not quite letting herself go like all the others.

Chapter 21

Turbulence hit the jet full of sales reps as it charged homewards. The people who had been running up and down the aisle, still fuelled with drink from the night before, were told to sit down and the seat belt light clicked on overhead.

Bernie, who had been trying to get a sing-along going, peered over the back of her seat at the others. 'Oh come on, will you? For the love of God, it's only a bit of wind,' she said, bouncing up and down in her seat, cheerily slurping orange juice while those around her stared nervously out of the window at the darkening sky. She was bored. What could she do? She looked at the person next to her, Sam, who was busy checking through her hand luggage. 'Oooh, what's that you have there?' she asked, snatching Sam's passport off her.

'Give it back, Bernie, for pity's sake,' Sam said.

'Not a chance. I love looking at people's passport photies,' she giggled. 'Where's yours Veronica? Come on, let's have a look.'

Veronica, completely disinterested, handed it to her.

Bernie peered at it. 'You look like an Afghan hound. 'You know - you would suit a shorter hair cut. You've such a long face. '

Veronica calmly held her hand out for the passport. But Bernie held it up high. 'Hey Johnny, get a look at this,' she shouted as the plane began to judder violently. Seconds later it dropped from the sky.

Everybody screamed. Bags flew out of lockers, crockery hit the ceiling, oxygen masks flew out. Ashen faced, people gripped their chairs, many praying, as the engines screamed, plummeting them all to earth. Seconds later, as if caught by an invisible net, the plane steadied. The lights were out, conversation stilled. All that could be heard was the sound of relief.

The moment Veronica caught her breath, realising they were still in the air, she became aware of something warm spreading across her lap. Looking down, she noticed that her cup of coffee had flown off the tiny table in front of her, spilling disastrously down her cream Gucci trousers. Frantically she tried to mop up the damage with a tiny tissue, distracted now from the alarming fact that a second ago she had been plummeting towards earth like a dart.

Bernie pointed at her, shrieking, 'oh my God - Veronica's designer trousers are ruined. Ha, ha! Oh my God - that's the funniest thing I've seen in ages. Look everyone. Ha, ha, ha!' She nudged Sam. 'Look, look.'

Sam, still gripping her chair, was praying. 'Oh God, please don't let me die with this lot. Please - I promise I will never lie, cheat or steal. I promise to sort out my job and my finances. Just please don't let me crash to the ground with Bernie O'Reilly shrieking in my ear like a mad woman.'

'Good afternoon, ladies and gentlemen,' came a smooth, English voice over the intercom. 'This is your captain speaking. Sorry about that. We ask you to keep your seatbelts on - we are expecting some more turbulence. However, in approximately twenty-three minutes, we will be making our descent towards East Midlands Airport. Thank you.'

'I thought we'd already made our descent,' someone said.

'At this rate we'll be down in three minutes time, not twenty-three, ha, ha.'

It was several hours later when Melissa arrived home. She picked up her mail from the doormat, and immediately did a double take. She stared with disbelief at the envelope with the Head Office stamp. This was significant: this was not the usual big brown envelope stuffed with messages and expense sheets and things, but a slim, white one with 'Highly Confidential' written on the front. Oh my God - this could be it.

Flushing deeply, she snatched it up and kissed it. Yes, oh yes, thank you God. But how quick - here she was only just back from conference. They must have known all along that her position as manager would be made permanent, that there wouldn't be any interviews or assessment centre crap involved - the job was quite simply hers. Oh, such delicious anticipation. But she would savour it by unpacking and making a cup of coffee first. It had been a long and tiring journey home, particularly after the action packed night she'd had last night with Johnny. In fact, she would even have a shower. That way she would open the letter feeling all calm and poised.

With trembling fingers, she put the beautiful white envelope onto the hall table on top of all the others and began to hump her suitcase up stairs, noting as she went how neat and expensive everything looked - the bed with it's fashionable mosquito net hanging from a ring in the ceiling, the polished floorboards, the minimalist white everywhere and the wide screen television set with DVD player in the bedroom.

There was no clutter in Melissa's house - she'd had it feng-shuied. I've done pretty well really, she thought. I've got a beautiful house, a gorgeous boyfriend, and soon I'll have the job I've worked so damn hard for. I knew it would happen - it had all been just a matter of time.

Tipping her bag of laundry into the linen basket, she replaced her shoes and toiletries to their rightful places, hung her jackets and then treated herself to a long, hot shower. What a wonderful feeling anticipation was, she thought, wrapping herself in a white waffle robe a few minutes later. She pinned her hair up, then casually collected her pile of mail and put the kettle on to boil. This promotion had been so hard earned. And soon she would see the precious words in black and white.

She stirred her coffee, walked through to the living room, sank into her cream, leather sofa, then ripped open the envelope. Melissa read the letter, then re-read it. Wait a minute. There had to be some mistake. A mix up. This could not be real. It said here she had to be in James Harris' office by ten o'clock on Monday morning for a disciplinary hearing.

Hang on, this couldn't be right. With shaking hands she put the coffee cup on the table trying not to spill it, then read the letter again. This letter wasn't meant for her. That was it, couldn't be. She hadn't done anything wrong. 'Oh my God, oh my God,' she said, over and over as she wrung her hands. 'What can I do? '

She got up and paced. It was cold. She was freezing. No matter. She had to do something, speak to someone. 'I know - I'll call Johnny,' she decided, suddenly scrambling for her mobile phone. 'Johnny will know what to do.'

'Hi, this is Johnny. Leave a message.' No, no, this could not be happening. Where was he? Melissa rang again, then again then again. Let him answer. Oh, please, please let him answer. After fifteen attempts with two minute intervals each time, he picked up. He'd switched on to order a pizza.

'Johnny! Johnny! I can't believe what's happening to me. I can't believe it. I don't know what's going on. I can't believe it.'

'Mel?' Johnny shouted above the noise of fruit machines and pub noise. 'Can't hear you sweetheart. What's up?'

'This! This! I've got a, a…..oh, I can't believe it,' she sobbed. 'I've only got a disciplinary hearing haven't I? It must be about all that business last month with Dick, but I thought it was all cleared up - you know that woman ringing up and saying would I stop shagging her husband?'

Johnny spluttered. 'What woman?'

'Oh I don't know - some stupid woman saying I was, like, shagging her husband or something? Which is obviously ridiculous because I, like, wasn't going with anyone's bloody husband was I? Anyway, I said she must be a mad woman because I was, like, going out with a single man at the time? Bruce Pilkington, as you know. I said it must have been one of the patients who found my business card and Dick believed me. Anyway, that's not important right now. What am I going to do about this?' she wailed. 'What's going on? What's it all about, Johnny? I don't know what to do. What would you do?'

'Hmmmm. Well, the only thing I can think of is what Bernie was telling us all, but that was before the conference.'

'Helloooo? Bernie? What was she telling you 'all' exactly? She and I are mates, you know.'

'Oh well it's probably not it then,' he said.

'What? What? Tell me!'

'Well she said that one of your hospital D&T committees had put Happylux on the formulary over and above the competition, and a Mrs Popplesomebody hadn't been too happy about that because only your Dr Pilkington wanted it, and he sort of steamrollered everyone into agreeing.'

'What? Hang on a minute - how does Bernie know about that?'

'She said all her doctors were talking about it.'

'Really? All her doctors?'

'Yes. She said that this Mrs Popplewhatsit had been very upset that she had been bamboozled....'

'Well she's a cow, she would,' Melissa interjected.

'It gets worse actually, Mel. Bernie said that Mrs Popplewhatsit had been walking through the staff car park shortly after the D&T

meeting when she noticed a bare bum in a car window. Then when she took a closer look she saw that it was you and Pilkington. So, I'm assuming she made a complaint.'

'A bare bum? A bare bum? You are joking aren't you? That must have been that Brazilian tart not me!'

'She said it was definitely you,' Johnny said, repeating Bernie's story verbatim, with the emphasis Bernie had given on the bum in question being white and big.

Melissa's mouth fell open in shock. She found it difficult to speak. 'Er, like, hang on a cotton picking minute here. Two things come to mind, Johnny: firstly I only ever gave Pilkington a BJ at work, never a full shag - and that was only once in the car, and I was most definitely not undressed - so we have, like, a vicious and untrue rumour going on. And secondly - why the hell didn't Bernie, my *mate* tell me?'

'Mel, I don't know. Why don't you ring her?'

'Oh I fucking well will, don't worry about that. And I'll be ringing Pilkington too. I never asked him to muscle Happylux in for me, I wouldn't do that, especially over Mrs Popplequick's head - she's too dangerous. Well, well! At least I know what I'm up against. Thanks, Johnny.' Then in a smaller voice she added, 'I suppose you think I'm, like, a complete slag now don't you?'

''course not. You have got some sorting out to do though, sweetheart.'

Oh yes, yes indeed. Starting with Bernie Backstabbing O' Reilly. Then after she'd wiped the floor with that little rat, she'd be phoning Bruce the Stud Pilkington at his home. They had finished with each other unofficially, using a common enough technique - avoidance. He would have to be phoned, though, to see what he knew. After all, if Mrs Popplequick had complained about her, then surely she must have been even more annoyed with Dr. Pilkington, who was, after all, the one to have publicly undermined her.

A young girl's voice answered Bruce Pilkington's phone. Melissa racked her brain. Who could this be? Did he have a daughter somewhere?

'Oh hello,' she said. 'Could I speak to Bruce please?'

'He's out. Can I give him a message?' said the little girl voice.

'Not really. When will he be back, do you know?'

'Look, who is this? This is his wife speaking.'

'Hello? Like, Bruce doesn't have a wife?'

'You aren't Melissa Crow by any chance are you?'

'Yes, I am actually,' she said. 'And I need to speak to him urgently about a work related matter, so if you could just…..' Hang on a minute. Reverse. Reverse. What was this about a wife? And how did she know her name? Melissa's heart rate shot up. Her head reeled making it difficult to think straight.

'Well I'm afraid you can't,' came the wife's voice. 'He's not at work for a while. Apparently there are some questions being asked about a drug decision and he's taken a few days off - he's gone to his parents.'

'Thank you. I'm sorry,' Melissa said quietly as she replaced the receiver. This was far worse than she'd thought. Why had she been so careless with her precious career? All that work and one BJ had seen the whole thing torn up and flushed down the toilet. She looked at her now cold cup of coffee, and let the tears flow unchecked.

And as they flowed, an annoying thought kept popping up like a piece of flotsam to the surface of a swamp. Bernie. Bernie her mate. Yes, it was all rather interesting really, how the pieces of the jigsaw were now falling into place. She and Johnny had had a zillion interesting conversations under the duvet in Spain after she'd finally managed to send that little blonde from region two spinning off into 'I- haven't-got-a-shag-for-tonight' no-man's land. But not a squeak about sly little Bernie. 'That bloody, stringy bit of gristle and bone,' she fumed, drying her eyes and blowing her nose, remembering Bernie bitching about Veronica being thin. 'She's nothing but a nasty bit of cartilage on a stick.'

And then there was Johnny. Melissa smiled through her tears. They were well matched - they both had an insatiable sex-drive and a taste for gossip. It was a good combination, she decided, and the success of their union made her question other things too. For example - did she really want to spend more and more time away from home as a manager? If she had got this job then she would be away from home pretty much all the time, spending her life in hotels or stuck on motorways - a sad and lonely figure at the window of a Little Chef eating chips and pancakes. What sort of a life was that? And also, even more importantly, they would have to keep their relationship under wraps. And what if he wanted to move in? Did she really want to be a slave to this company, never having a life of her own, especially after the way they were now treating her? Hmmm, the more she thought about it, the more she thought the answer to that was quite clearly 'no.'

A glass of whisky was called for. Knocking it back, then pouring herself another, Melissa wandered around her empty house, looking at it's perfection, at it's post TV-make-over image. Everything so hard won: the plasma screen TV bought with a Happylux bonus, the cream sheepskin throw bought courtesy of a retail competition last year. Perhaps, like her mother always said - things have a way of working out for the best and this was simply fate pushing her in another direction? To Johnny. For what were material things compared to love?

Drying her eyes, she decided to make some fresh coffee in her rarely used high tech, stainless steel kitchen. The polished floorboards felt cold with no carpets or rugs on them and everything echoed. She shivered, hugging herself to keep warm while staring out of the kitchen window. Ridiculous nonsense, she thought, eyeing the expensive decking and garden furniture she had paid over a thousand pounds for last summer and never used. The scene darkened. A few spots of rain appeared.

It would be good to go and get Louis tomorrow morning from the luxury cattery with radiators and televisions. She couldn't wait to hug him, to feel his warmth, to know he needed her and would be glad to be back. Louis was the only thing that had made her house feel like a proper home in recent years.

Oh God, tears stung her eyes again. A disciplinary hearing, though. Everyone would be laughing at her.

Chapter 22

Sam wearily pulled her suitcase trolley through customs. Please, oh please don't let Simon be here to greet her. It was irritatingly unnecessary. She had a lift back with Mel and she was going to have to travel with the window down as it was. Why oh why did she have to go and drink so much last night? Though with the plane lurching up and down like the Big Dipper, Veronica spraying the air with Escada perfume, and Bernie scoffing cheese and onion crisps and Red Bull, it was a wonder she hadn't thrown up already.

Please don't be here, Simon, she prayed inwardly, scrabbling round for her wraparound sunglasses. I just don't want to have to talk to you. I need to think. I need a bath, a sleep. Please don't be here.

He was the first person she spotted as she turned the corner into Arrivals. There he was - waiting patiently. Oh Christ, look at him - so small, grey and ugly. And he'd gone without his sleep to come and meet her. Why did he have to go and do that?

He suddenly saw her. His eyes locked with her sunglasses. 'How are you?' he asked - coolly, politely - as if she were a little known maiden aunt.

'Very tired. And a bit sick, since you ask.'

'Sam, you didn't phone me again last night. What's going on?'

'I know. Look, I'm shattered, Simon. Can we please go home?'

People were pushing and shoving from all sides. Still Simon stared at her accusingly. They had become an island in a sea of people. 'Please. I'm tired, creased and dirty,' she pleaded.

'Right, I'm afraid you'll have to carry your own bags though. My back's gone, I'm having to wear a surgical corset again,' he said, stalking off as fit as a flea. Sam looked down at her huge suitcase and hand luggage. What else could she do but pick them up from the trolley and follow him to the ticket machine?.

Simon drove home wordlessly, his mouth pinched. If she kept her head absolutely still and looked only straight ahead then it might just be possible to not be sick. The drive took an age. The car smelled of old ashtrays and take aways. It was kind of surreal, she thought, arriving home, everything as she left it just a few days ago. Yet it felt like a lifetime. Here she was - a different person. A damaged person.

While he carefully parked his car, she let herself in. The house hummed with silence, air hanging stale, dishes unwashed. There were dirty coffee cups on every surface, an assortment of ties and shoes littering the hallway. She stared at the remains of a Chicken Tikka Masala on the kitchen table and gagged. Congealed reds and yellows stared back at her. 'When did you last open a window?' she asked him before bolting for the bathroom.

How long had she been there, clinging to the toilet basin? Five minutes? Ten? It was still only nine o'clock in the morning. Simon, she knew, had a clinic to go to. So why was he still shuffling around outside the bathroom door? 'Simon - listen, just go to work, will you?' she called out in a feeble voice. 'I'm not up to a big discussion right now. I'll be better when you get home this evening, okay?'

'Are you all right, though?' he asked, rapping sharply on the door again.

'Yes, yes. I'm fine. I just need a shower and a sleep. See you later, okay?' She listened carefully, her ear pressed to the door. Only when she was certain that he had gone did she slowly and silently creep out of the bathroom and into the bedroom. The bed was unmade, but who cared? She was alone at last. Perhaps she would just have a cup of tea first, then a bath and then, oh joy, - a long, deep sleep. Time to think, to mull over everything James had said, to analyse her feelings. He had not been with Veronica last night. He'd winked at her in her Indian squaw outfit. It could just be that she'd got it all wrong…..

Kicking off her shoes, she flung her jacket onto a chair and was just about to unzip her skirt when a pair of hands grabbed at her breasts from behind. 'Have you missed me, Sam?' Simon whispered, breathing his early morning halitosis into the side of her face.

She flung him off. 'Simon, please. You have to be joking! I haven't slept for days, I've just thrown up and I'm tired and dirty.'

'Why is it like this every time you go away, Sam? What's wrong with you?' His voice pierced her head.

'Like what?'

'Well, I would have thought that after over a week apart you would have been desperate to make love to me?'

'Excuse me?' She whirled round, stared at his outraged face with it's greasy glasses. That line of spittle was still there. Obviously he'd just got straight out of bed and flung on whatever clothes were at hand before driving to the airport in all his natural splendour.

He held up his hands. 'Okay, okay. I'll see you later on then when I get home from work.' He gave her a peck on the cheek. 'Be in bed for me. Then with a sorry little backward glance 'if you still love me, that is.'

Never had the sound of the front door slamming shut behind him sounded so fantastic. That and the sound of his car roaring off - fast becoming one of her favourite moments. And no way could he be back before six at the very earliest. He had clinic all day.

Only what seemed like minutes later something woke her. Rousing herself from a muzzy headed, heavy limbed slumber, Sam rolled over and looked at the bedside clock - three o'clock. Good, hours yet. So what the hell was that noise? She strained her unwilling ears. No, it couldn't be Simon. Maybe they had burglars? The question was, did she have enough strength to get up and confront them or should she just lie here and hope they didn't club her to death while they were at it?

She stretched lazily, decided to take a chance that the burglars were not murdering maniacs, then curled up again. A floorboard creaked, a door opened, a kettle flicked on. She sat up. Bloody hell - they were making themselves at home, whoever they were.

'Hello, gorgeous,' Simon said. 'I've brought you a cup of tea.'

'You're early,' she snapped.

'You sound disappointed.'

'Well I could have done with a bit more sleep to be honest. I've only had a few hours and I haven't slept for days.'

'Is that a fact? I wonder why.' He sat down on the edge of the bed and took a loud slurp of his own tea.

'What do you mean?' she asked wearily. 'And what are you doing?'

Simon, having removed his tie, was now unbuttoning his shirt. 'Joining you,' he said with a smirk.

'I told you, I'm too tired,' she said, watching him unzip his trousers before standing up to remove them. Thank God she'd had the foresight to root out this old, full length, buttoned to the neck flannelette night dress she had on. Her Gran had given it to her for Christmas one year, much to her horror. Still, Gran had been right - it was one of those things that had come in handy after all.

Simon was down to his socks and surgical corset before he noticed it. 'You'll have to take that passion killer off,' he said, leaning over to kiss her. A rush of stale coffee and nicotine breath engulfed her as his cold, bony fingers reached for her left breast.

She turned her face quickly to one side while he fumbled with the nightdress. 'No,' she said.

He sprang back. 'What? What's the matter with you? Don't you love me anymore?'

'I've told you - I'm just too tired, Simon.'

'If you loved me that wouldn't matter. Has something been going on that I should know about?' He propped himself up on one elbow, scrutinising her closely.

'Did you know you were cross-eyed?' she snapped.

'What's the matter with you? You seem cold, distant. You would be honest with me, wouldn't you, Sam? After all - we are supposed to be getting married.'

'I know, I'm sorry.' She got up and went to the bathroom, locking herself in for the second time that day. It was as if he knew something, but he couldn't know. Nobody did. She had told absolutely no one. It absolutely could not be that.

Her reflection stared back at her in horror - wild red hair plastered back from her drawn, pale face, colourless lips, dark shadows. Her eyes were drawn to the shower unit, where a pile of long, red hairs blocked the plug hole. It was a regular thing now, her hair falling out. There were painful black things growing under her nails too. And why did she always feel as if she had the flu when she didn't? God, she needed to sleep for a month.

Shivering, she pressed her ear to the door. Where was he?

Eventually, after a lot of shuffling and sighing noises, she heard him go down stairs. Then came the sound of the TV and the repetitive drone of motor racing. Good, the coast was clear.

Chapter 23

The day was Monday. A day of change. For this was the day Dick's job of Regional Manager was advertised on the company's e-mail system, and the day Melissa came to see James. The company also posted the vacancy to a recruitment agency they had a contract with, who usually produced candidates of the highest quality. Pat and James had decided they needed to find the best person possible for this job, because frankly, Dick's team was a bit of a shambles.

They'd had lunch together in the canteen after Melissa's hearing. James expressed his surprise and displeasure at having had to discipline Melissa at all, let alone so soon after he'd arrived at work that morning with over a week's worth of paper work and e-mails waiting for him. There was, he said to Pat, nothing worse than having to do disciplinary hearings, and particularly to someone he had presented top sales awards to. She had been in on many of the management meetings recently as well. No, it had been awful, but it seemed Mrs Popplequick had made one heck of a fuss to the Human Resources Department while they had all been away on conference, and demanded that the company take action against Melissa - fast - or she would take the matter higher. In fact, she had threatened to go public.

'All incredibly tricky,' he said to Pat.

'But it's sorted, lovey?'

'Oh, yah.'

James frowned. Melissa had cast a forlorn figure in a sombre suit, staring at him pleadingly with huge eyes from the other side of his desk.

'I'm sure you'd agree that these allegations are really quite serious, Melissa?' he'd said.

Melissa nodded.

'Are they true?'

'Not really.'

'Not really? Hmmm. I'm afraid I'm going to need rather more than that. At the moment the information I have is that you were having an affair with a customer who used his senior, er - *position*, to influence a drug decision. Now, it would be amazingly helpful if you could give me your version of events.'

'Look James, I was, like, having a personal relationship with Dr Pilkington, but we were both single? At least I thought we were. And well over the age of consent. I didn't realise I needed the company's permission to date him. And I certainly never, ever asked him for any, like, business in return? In fact - I don't think I ever even mentioned Happylux - it couldn't have been further from my mind.'

'Oh terrific,' James said under his breath.

'I deny all that rubbish about a bum in the car park as well,' Melissa said hotly.

'A bum in a car park?'

'Well that's what Mrs Popplequick said - that she saw a bum in his car and him underneath the, er, bum .'

'I see. So why would he try to push our product in over the others, then? What would his motive have been, do you think?'

'I don't know, do I? Maybe he was, like, trying to teach that Brazilian tart a lesson? She was the one whose bum it was. At least I think it was hers - although it could have been his secretary's, I suppose.'

'How many women does this man have?' James raised an eyebrow.

'At least four.' She counted on her fingers. 'Five, I think.'

'Gosh.' James considered this for a moment. 'Phew. Look

Melissa, we must face facts - standards of professional conduct have fallen and a complaint by one of your most senior customers has been made, yah?'

Melissa nodded.

'Now obviously, it's completely impossible to verify the story in terms of whose, er, bum it was, as you say. But the fact remains that your Dr Pilkington had some motive for making what appears to be an unethical, unscientifically based decision in favour of Happylux, while quite clearly conducting an affair with the rep. I therefore, regrettably, have no alternative but to issue you with a formal warning. I'm so sorry, Melissa.'

Melissa's face crumpled.

At this point James hadn't really known what to do. He passed her a box of tissues, waiting for her to get a grip.

'I've worked my bloody socks off for this company and now you're all just turning on me,' Melissa sobbed, blowing her nose loudly.

James nodded, looking uncomfortable. She could be right. Perhaps he should get up and pat her on the back or something? He hesitated. No, in a minute she'd pull herself together, surely.

Melissa snatched another wad of tissues, sobbing ever louder. He swivelled round on his chair to stare out of the window. Oh God, there was never a woman around when you needed one, was there? Still Melissa howled on. Eventually he glanced at the clock and coughed. 'Look, let's get you down to Human Resources now, shall we?' he said, swivelling back to face her.

But Melissa hadn't finished and continued to sob profusely until eventually, the box of tissues used up, she dried her eyes, blew her nose again and apologised for her outburst. It was just, she explained, that it had been a shock and certain people had been gossiping about her, particularly that Bernie O'Reilly.

'Bernie? Really? You do surprise me.'

'Yes, and she's, like, gossiped to all the customers too - hardly professional to gossip about your manager like that, is it?' she said, in between sniffs.

'Look Melissa - there will be other opportunities for you in terms of management, you know that. But right now we have to protect our company's image and the image of the industry as a whole - that's the reason you're here, yah?'

'What are you saying - other opportunities for management? Hang on a minute. Are you saying what I think you're saying? That not only am I getting a Formal Warning but that I won't be able to go for the job I'm in now?

James nodded. 'And we will need someone else to cover Mrs Popplequick and Dr Pilkington, at least for the time being. Is that okay?'

Melissa looked out of the window at the rolling sea, responsibility and commitments falling away from her in lorry loads. In a funny kind of way it felt as if she'd been freed. She was light and young and ......And anyway, she had more important things in her life now - she had Johnny. Things weren't so bad.

'Can I get you a coffee, old girl?' James asked her.

Melissa managed a weak smile. 'Thanks.'

James shook his head sadly. Yes the nasty business had been taken care of. They could now move on. He looked at Pat across the canteen table with a degree of irritation. 'So,' he said. 'We can't continue for much longer with Melissa in charge, can we? Time to crack on with the short list, I'd say?'

She agreed. Yes, they would run the assessment centre as soon as possible. They always used an outside company to run their assessments, which were held in an old country house in the middle of Hampshire. And the assessment centre was legendary.

At the conference Pat had made quite a big thing about everyone having to go through one of these for a promotion of any kind, in the same way that an external candidate would have to do, and at every level in the company. That way the system was completely open and fair. What she didn't mention was the fact that after the assessments, when all the results were given back to them, they picked who they wanted anyway. Oh, and when she said at every level - she most certainly didn't mean hers.

'I had a little chat with Mike at the conference too,' James said, eyeing Pat thoughtfully.

'Oh?'

'You know he's applying for this job, don't you?'

Pat stirred her coffee, refusing to return James' eye contact. 'Mmm. He rang me.'

James' right eyebrow shot up. 'He rang you? Well, that's excellent news. So it's all resolved between you two now, is it?'

'I've waited a long time for that telephone call, James.'

'And?'

'And - we'll see.'

James took a sip of coffee. Poor old Squishy, things were by no means certain, he thought, leafing through some of the external candidate applications Pat had just handed him. Hmmm, an interesting one here - a twenty-five year old female keep fit instructor eh? James smiled. Like it, like it, even if she did have a poor degree in geography and no experience.

****

Veronica was the first to see the job advertisement on her e-mail system. She had been up early because of the mountain of things she had to do that day, starting with a nine o'clock appointment with her private investigator at yet another seedy hotel on the outskirts of Leeds. Just precisely what had her husband been up to while she was away? She had hoped very much that the answer to that would be nothing.

After the meeting she drove directly to the bank in order to transfer some more money from their joint account to an off-shore one in her own name. This, together with her personal savings account and her trust fund, gave her a tidy sum.

Following that, she'd hosted a lunch meeting with a group of doctors who were expecting her to pay for them to go to America that year in order to attend an international conference. The doctors were looking forward to the raucous nights ahead, lap dancing bars and strip joints in downtown LA, their heads bowed together discussing this when Veronica walked into the up-market bistro they had chosen, their expensive but now dumpy wives and demanding toddler children temporarily forgotten in blissful anticipation of the excursion ahead .

'Ah, Veronica,' one of them said jovially, when she arrived. 'Hope you don't mind but we've had a couple of bottles of red already. And we've ordered - did you want anything?'

She noted that they'd gone for lobster and smoked salmon, and grimaced. Bang went her twenty pound a head budget again. Declining, she ordered a glass of water and lit a cigarette while she listened to the doctors chat, in a more subdued manner now that she had joined them, about golf and house prices. Eventually the subject of the American conference resurfaced.

'Of course, your competitors took us last year,' the ring leader proffered, eyeing her shiftily.

Veronica took another drag of her cigarette.

'Fair's fair I always say,' said the one who had never used her product, but had prescribed mountains of her competitor's. 'It's Topham's turn this year.'

'I'll see what I can do then,' she said, knowing full well that there was more chance of Saddam Hussein winning the Nobel Peace Prize than Topham Pharmaceuticals footing the bill for any of them to go to America, either this year or next - Happylux just wasn't doing well enough. 'Of course one good turn deserves another don't you think?' she asked, with a wintry smile. 'You know - a few Happylux prescriptions?'

'Oh, of course, of course,' the doctors mumbled. 'Goes without saying.' They began to talk about golf again.

'So,' she asked, in what sounded to her alarmingly like her mother's booming voice. 'Can anyone tell me what the dosage is?'

They jumped apart like guilty infants. 'Ten mgs?' one suggested.

'Start on five and titrate up to forty - max. Okay?'

They nodded, about to change the subject again, when Veronica added, 'so if you write at least ten prescriptions each this month, I should, although I can't absolutely promise, be able to swing it for you. And it's going to be an incredibly exciting conference this year: LA, isn't it chaps?'

Yes, it had been a most conclusive day, she thought, scanning the job spec. before replying to Human Resources by return. Blimey, they were working fast though, with a closing date of this Friday for internal candidates. Better send a text message to James to keep him on his toes:

' WHAT DATE FOR ASS'MENT? WILL U B THERE?'

'YES, THINK SO. GUESS 2 WKS.'

'CAN U PHONE ME 2 DISCUSS?'

'SPEAK SOON.'

'WILL U B AT B&B NIGHT BEFORE?

'POSS.'

'WE COULD DO B'FAST? DO U LIKE YOGHURT?'

'NOT OUT OF A POT,' he wrote back.

Good. She had him - he would be there.

****

Johnny, clutching his gym bag on his way to the car park after an energetic workout, looked down at his mobile phone. A message awaited. He pressed for the answering service. The message said, ' please ring Bernie O'Reilly as soon as you get this message.'

'Oh fuck.' That was all he needed. He decided not to bother and jumped into his car. Immediately the phone rang.

'Johnny, hi!' Bernie shrieked. 'I hope I'm not interrupting anything important? Are you still out working?'

'Just finished.'

'Could I meet you? I need to talk to you about the assessment centre - it's urgent.'

'Slug and Pellet - I'll be there in ten minutes.'

'Great. See you soon.'

'The thing is you see,' Johnny said when they'd got the pints in. 'It's all a question of stamina. Some people just don't make it through the day.'

'What do you mean?' Bernie asked.

'Well - they break down, don't they? Can't go on.'

'Are the assessment centres really that bad?'

'Oh aye. You'll get a three hour personality questionnaire first...'

'Oh I can do those - I've a degree in psychology, not to mention the ideal personality.'

'Then you'll get a group exercise, and then you'll have to do a business presentation. Then probably an interview. Then the outdoor tests

- jumping through hoops over rivers and things.'

Bernie clapped her hands together in delight. 'Oh fantastic! I can't wait. I love doing those.'

'Well you'll probably be okay then. Most people have had enough after about seven hours of assessors with clipboards running round asking questions every few seconds. Then, at the end of the day, you get a five hour business plan to do. That's when people start crying and cracking up.'

'Oh that wouldn't bother me.'

'Some people refuse to ever go on one again - they'd rather stay as a rep for ever than put themselves through an assessment centre.'

'Fools,' said Bernie.

****

While Veronica, Bernie and Mike expectantly anticipated their forthcoming interviews, Veronica's husband decided to treat his young students to a beer or two seeing as how it was Friday evening. He reckoned they deserved a little treat. He might go further than that actually, on this warm summer evening - he might buy them all a pizza too.

He left his loud, happy students sitting outside a pub while he jauntily made his way to the cash till. The plan was to withdraw about two hundred pounds. He whistled while he waited for his cash. But hang on, what was this? Instead of getting a pile of crisp bank notes, he was politely informed that he had insufficient funds for the transaction.

He tried again for one hundred pounds, only to be again informed by the machine that there were insufficient funds. He checked the balance. It read: nine pounds and ninety-seven pence. This was not possible. Why? The little misunderstanding Veronica had concerning that girl last month was over now, wasn't it? And she had spent ten thousand pounds as her revenge. What more did she want? She had been so nice to him since she got back from conference too. They had even made love on Sunday morning like they used to, and he had brought her breakfast in bed - a glass of water and a cigarette. There hadn't been a hint of a problem. There must be some mistake.

Right, well he would have to try the building society then. He darted back to the pub, gave one of the students his only ten pound note to get some drinks in, then hurtled back to the flat for his building society book. Half an hour later he was back. He had to queue for a few minutes, no big deal, then tossing the book casually at the cashier, requested a withdrawal of one thousand pounds. He'd better grab some money while it was still there in case Veronica was planning another spending spree.

'Sorry Sir,' the cashier said. 'I'm afraid there isn't one thousand pounds in here for you to withdraw.'

'What?' He had several thousand still left in there, didn't he? 'Well, er, I see. I'll have just five hundred then please.'

'I'm sorry Sir, you don't have that much.'

'What? Well, how much do I have in there, then?'

She pushed the book towards him. Greg's eyes widened. Veronica had left him with just two pounds fifty.

Chapter 24

How bad could a day get? Because this, Sam decided, had to be the most terrible day she had ever had in the history of terrible days. And it topped a bad week. James had not called. Staring at her mobile phone, pleading with it, shaking it - nothing had worked. So what had that little wink and secretive smile he'd given her on the last night of the conference, been about then? If only she could stop herself from constantly switching the phone on - just to see if a message had been left during the five minutes since she'd last checked. It had been bad enough as a teenager waiting for the phone to ring, but this was a whole new form of torture: mobile torture, twenty-four-seven.

And then there was Simon. Ever since the episode with the flannelette nightdress, he'd been eyeing her suspiciously, checking up on her - even answering her phone calls, loudly proclaiming himself to be her fiancé: 'Yes, Samantha's fiancé here. Can I help at all?' She was sick of having to snatch the phone off him, of walking in after a hard day's work to hear, yet again, Annie Lennox singing, 'Why?' or Neil Diamond singing, 'Love on the Rocks.'

'What is this?' she asked him. 'Why all this music to slit your wrists to? What's going on?' Everything had changed and it was a total mystery. Even their arguments had no decisive point to them. She shook her head. Her home life with Simon had always been a sort of refuge from the relentless nightmare of horrible jobs and bedsits. She'd almost begun to feel like a normal person - well, safe and secure at least, if not exactly ecstatic. Now it was a battleground in it's own right.

Last night's argument replayed over and over in her head. Unforgivable things had been said. Simon had shouted at her - he was the one who did all the work and paid all the bills. He was the one who always initiated sex. What was her contribution?

'I do some things,' she said.

'Like what? Name one thing that you do other than shop.'

'I paint my own nails.'

'You are joking?'

'Yes. Oh, come on Simon. You know I clean up after you - it took me two days after I got back from conference. What's this really about?'   'Refresh my memory here - tell me what you actually do all day, Sam. What do you do for us, for me?'

'I er, um… Well, there's the er… '

'Lets face it,' he said wearily. 'One person always loves more than the other in a relationship, and in this case it's been me. I've been a fool.'

'Oh, Simon.' She looked at his grey, pinched face with it's red, watery eyes Compared to Dr. Al-Khashin he was darned attractive. She attempted to put her arm around him, to give him a hug, but he shoved her away roughly. It was too late, he said nastily. They didn't want the same things, did they? He wanted a family while she just wanted glamour and shopping. He hadn't realised, he said, how much he'd begun to resent her. It was time for her to go.

Shocked, Sam spluttered, ' but go where? Where am I supposed to go? What about the wedding? You can't mean this, Simon. You never said anything before. Why now?'

But he'd just looked at her with a wounded puppy dog expression and walked away. It was over. She'd never get her credit cards back now.

And so to today - oh, joy. Here she was, in the grip of excruciating pre-menstrual tension, obliged to pay one hundred pounds to the post-graduate centre for psychiatry. This for the privilege of putting up a small exhibition stand so that the doctors could stand around eating sandwiches ignoring her. Apart from Dr Al-Khashin. He was here as a guest GP. 'Please don't come over,' she muttered under her breath, fingers crossed behind her back. 'I just can't deal with you today, okay?'

'Can I take some pens, love?' A tired looking woman in glasses and a scruffy anorak stared up at her.

'Yeah, please do,' Sam said. Take the lot, she wanted to say, after all she had thousands more in her garage. Perhaps the woman would like five hundred mugs as well. 'Are you here for Dr Douglas's lecture?'

'I'm a social worker, love, yes. Although what *he'd* have to say that could possibly interest me, I don't know.'

'At least you get to see him.'

'Aren't I lucky? Don't you?'

Sam shook her head.

'Well that explains a lot, I suppose. He won't use your stuff or anyone else's for that matter. I had an eighteen year old last year with schizophrenia. Poor girl was from a really lousy home - one of eight kids in a rundown council house, alcoholic father, abusive mother - you know, the sort?'

Sam nodded. She knew only too well.

'Yes, well Dr Douglas injected her with one of the old antipsychotics - horrible stuff. They had to hold her down.' The woman bit her lip. 'She screamed and screamed, you know. I'll tell you, it was very upsetting. Of course it knocked her for six, and then to cap it all she got the worst muscle spasms you have ever seen in your life. Have you ever seen acute dystonia?'

'Yes, it's muscle spasms in the neck isn't it?'

'Mmm. It looked as though an invisible person was trying to

strangle her. Oh God, it was horrible. I think quite understandably she refused to have any more of it, so what did he do? He sent her home - said there was nothing more he could do if she was refusing treatment. So, of course, she just got worse and worse. He then had to re-admit her, by which time she was so paranoid she lashed out at one of the nurses. And what did his nibs do next, do you think? Refused to have anything more to do with her because she'd attacked one of the staff.

'But why couldn't she have one of the newer drugs? They don't give such nasty side effects. I know of kids who've gone back to university after treatment.'

'He won't touch them. Says they're just the same as the old ones and too expensive.'

'In terms of efficacy, yes, but not in terms of side effects, and that's what stops people taking the drugs. Oh, for goodness sake. So that poor girl's finished really isn't she? She'll be on the streets until she gets locked up for knifing somebody or something.'

'What can you do? He's all powerful isn't he? His own kids are at Oxford and Cambridge, himself a well paid professional with a country home. He's all right, isn't he? Do you know, it makes me so angry?'

Sam shrugged. 'It's just down to his own politics, I think. Well, I'll have a go,' she said. 'But I can't promise he'll listen to me.'

The social worker nodded despondently. 'I thought I might manage to grab a sandwich here at least, but look....'

Sam looked over at what her one hundred pounds had bought - and noted two plates of very ordinary sandwiches and a small dish of crisps. A lightening flash of fury shot through her. Right - someone was going to answer for this.

'Is that it?' she asked, marching up to the Post Graduate Administrator, a young girl with a pineapple style hairdo.

The girl glared at her. 'What do you mean, 'is that it'?'

'Well I paid a hundred pounds on the understanding that there would be enough food for twenty-five doctors, and frankly, that wouldn't feed five.'

'The profit goes towards books. That's what the doctors want. Dr Douglas said!'

'Quite a big profit then?'

'Do you want this meeting or not, because there are plenty or reps that do if you don't?'

'But they're going to think I've been mean,' Sam said. 'It doesn't reflect very well on my company, does it - this excuse for a lunch?'

'Yeah well, like I say - take it or leave it,' said the girl, walking away.

Sam gritted her teeth. 'Cow,' she muttered under her breath. She had to calm down. She'd wanted to slap the girl very badly indeed. Deep breaths, deep breaths, she told herself.

'I have to say,' a voice behind her said. 'Your company has barely provided us with enough to live on. The food is disgraceful.'

Sam swirled round, a dangerous glint in her eyes. 'I couldn't agree more. I was just asking the Administrator, in fact - exactly what my one hundred pounds had been spent on. Perhaps you would like to go and discuss the matter with her?'

'One hundred pounds you paid? Good Lord. Yes I most certainly will.'

Yeah, good. Go and whinge to pineapple head, she thought - do her good to get an earful. Glaring at the doctor's retreating back, still muttering, it was a second before she noticed a pleasant looking man staring at her.

'Hi,' he said with a smile. 'How are you?'

'Oh hello, Dr Harvey.' Whoops - time to put her nice person hat back on. Sam recognised him as a consultant psychiatrist from another hospital she covered. He was sweet, she remembered. Pity then, that he had that sour faced old trout in tweed with him - a woman psychiatrist who had consistently refused to see her, although Sam knew she saw the male reps. Oh well, she was *so* in the mood for a challenge.

'Have you met Rosemary?' Dr Harvey asked her.

Sam held out her hand and said brightly, 'no, we haven't met, have we? I'm…'

'What time is the lecture, Marcus?' the woman said, turning deliberately to face Dr Harvey.

Dr Harvey smiled nervously, eyeing Sam's outstretched hand.

Sam smiled too. Right, well two could play at that game. 'Oh, Dr. Harvey,' she said loudly, turning her shoulder to exclude the woman in tweed. 'Look, I have that clinical paper you wanted. Do you remember? It's the new one comparing Happylux with our competitors - it's got all the latest comparative data on side effects and efficacy.'

Dr Harvey grinned happily. 'Ah - thank you, I've been trying to find tha…'

'Good God! I really can't think of anything more boring than having to read all that drivel, can you, Marcus?' Tweed woman asked him.

Dr Harvey flushed and stammered. 'Er, well - it's kind of you, Sam.' But Tweed woman's black eyes were on him. 'However, as you say, Rosemary, quite, er, er….. boring, yes. Quite.' He shuffled off.

'Would you like a Happylux leaflet?' Sam asked Tweed woman, keeping the huge, now unnaturally bright smile on her face.

The woman psychiatrist slowly, rudely, looked Sam up and down, keeping her arms firmly folded.

'It tells you all about Happylux,' Sam insisted. 'Really - all the main points in a nutshell. Bit of bedtime reading, perhaps?' She prodded the woman's folded arms with the leaflet. 'Go on - be a devil - take it,' she said. 'Live a little.'

Tweed woman continued to stare at her and then, with quiet deliberation, turned and walked off.

Sam glared at Tweedy's retreating back, imagined beating her to a pulp with a Happylux leaflet, before slumping down onto the plastic chair next to her exhibition stand. 'Bitch,' she muttered under her breath. 'What a bloody massive cow. I wonder how many people have gone to her with depression and then topped themselves?'

Surveying the room full of customers, she thought - what a load of bastards. If Superwoman micro-mini Bernie was here, she'd be out there networking, getting to know them all. Bernie would be enjoying this, wouldn't she? She would be chatting and grinning and selling, selling, selling without a moment of introspection on what her life was all about and whether it meant anything or not. She looked over at the doctors she was being paid to get to discuss Happylux with, and for a moment hatred gripped her soul.

Still seething, her eyes came to rest on one of the foreign doctors - a young man from Iraq who had been very kind to her the last time she visited the hospital. He looked over at her and smiled, before turning back to his colleagues. He'd had a hard life - such an uphill struggle to get his qualification - and now here he was up at all hours in this depressing place that smelled of cabbage and disinfectant, with it's locks on all the doors and security systems. The day she saw him he'd had only two hours sleep after spending the night trying to treat a patient who had tipped into a psychotic frenzy, running round the hospital threatening staff and refusing all medication. Yet still he had found time to see her the next day, and he always managed to talk to the nurses and receptionists with respect. A wave of shame washed through her. Thank God for people like him. Anyone of us could end up in here, she thought. It could be me. In fact the way things are going, it probably will be. I only hope I get him and not Dr Douglas.

And talk of the Devil - wasn't that the man himself, over there with a circle of ardent sycophants around him? Aha, she thought, ignoring her nagging period pains, the frustration with James and her fury with Simon - Aha! Why not do something about this utter bastard right here and now - in front of all his peers and juniors? May as well, seeing as she was on such a roll.

She scrutinised him through narrowed eyes. Dr Douglas was a small man in a crumpled, ill-fitting grey suit. He had little hair left, his face was ruddy with broken veins and he had an alarmingly mad glint in his eyes. He must be in his late fifties, she guessed. He was the Medical Director, Senior Consultant Psychiatrist and Head of the Drugs and Therapeutics committee, which made all the decisions about which drugs were stocked and used for the whole hospital and the entire surrounding area. He was also vehemently anti-industry and never, ever saw or even acknowledged drug company representatives. He was known not to use any drugs unless he had to on his patients and was currently setting up a national study to show that the newer drugs for depression were all a complete waste of time and money.

Dick had told her to devise a strategy for him - well this would be it - it would be called - ta-da! 'the surprise strategy.' A tiny spurt of adrenaline began to fizz around in her stomach. Without further thought regarding possible outcomes, Sam sprang from her chair, and strode purposefully towards him.

'Good morning, Dr Douglas,' she said loudly.

He spun round in surprise, glaring in an outraged manner at her outstretched hand. Instinctively, the crowd around him began to draw back. 'Yes?' he snapped.

Sam dropped the attempt at a handshake. ' Hi, I'm Sam Farmer, the sponsor for today's meeting. As we haven't met before I thought I would come over to introduce myself. I really wanted to ask you if you had tried our product yet because it has an excellent side effect profile and the patients really like it.' She forced a pleasant and confident smile.

There were a few nervous titters. Dr Douglas' face darkened. He spluttered for a moment. 'Your company,' he spat 'has done nothing, absolutely nothing useful in in the past fifty years. The entire industry has done nothing worth a penny for my patients. I don't use drugs at all if I don't have to and the only thing worth even discussing is psychotherapy, which is the only area to have made any significant advances.'

He turned away. Did he click his heels? Sam couldn't be sure.

'Permission to argue the case for defence?' she asked. Out of the corner of her eye she could see the Iraqi doctor shaking his head very, very slightly. No matter, she must press on.

Dr Douglas spun round on his heel, pointing a finger in her face. 'Your industry is wrecking the planet, young woman. It is evil and I have nothing more to say on the matter, understood?'

Sam wiped his spit from her shoulder, clenched her fists to stop them from shaking and took another deep breath. My, my, what a nest of vipers she'd unleashed. 'But that quite simply isn't true, is it, Dr Douglas?' she said to his retreating back, in a surprisingly calm voice. Was that her voice? 'Whatever you may think of the industry as a whole, and I might agree with you on a couple of points, the fact is that some of these very expensively researched drugs offer real hope to some very ill, very vulnerable people. And how much more vulnerable can you get than desperately poor and mentally ill too? What about those people? It would be a different story if it was one of your kids wouldn't it? If it was yourself or your son? What would you want? I bet you'd get the best treatment and hang the cost.'

But Dr Douglas kept on walking, his entourage scurrying after him into the lecture theatre. She watched the double doors open, then slam shut, leaving her suddenly alone in the room. A second or two elapsed before the full extent of her own fury hit her. She whirled round, knocked her exhibition stand to the floor, and kicked it. Then, in the middle of throwing videos and books aggressively into cardboard boxes, she stopped. This really was not the job for her, was it? What was it Trisha had been trying to tell her on conference? She'd forgotten all about Trisha, but there was something she'd said about coming to realise it later? Of course....

But what could she do? Thousands of pounds in debt and soon to be homeless again? Oh Christ. Well one thing was for sure - she'd had enough of sticking her head in the sand. She had to do something, anything. And another thing - she would call James to find out just exactly what was going on there. She would not be some kind of sitting duck, a victim. Had he really just used her for one night? Impossible as it was to believe, she must know. Grabbing the rest of her things she shot out to the car park, ignoring Dr Al-Khashin who was knocking on the window, waving at her frantically from one of the offices, and drove off without a backwards glance. She was going to find a quiet country lane. She needed to think.

Half an hour later, parked on a muddy, grass verge by a farm gate, the ideas came thick and fast. When she got home she would be telling Simon that she would leave as soon as she had worked her notice. Then she would be packing her bags and going to London, where she would stay with her sister, Hannah, until a flat of her own could be found. She would work as an agency nurse to pay the rent and Simon back for the loan. And maybe she would take those acting classes she'd promised herself.

Good, that was decided. Now for James. She had already put his name into her mobile phone. She stared at it. James, James, James…. Oh dear God, what would she say? Remember me? Yes I'm the one you shagged at conference in thirteen different positions. Oh, you don't remember? Oh never mind then, my mistake, so sorry to have bothered you….

Her finger hovered over his name. Should she? Shouldn't she? Hang on though, there was something he'd said, wasn't there? Some reason why she couldn't hold out any hope. What was it? She leaned back and closed her eyes, her mind travelling back to that last evening of the conference when Trisha had asked her if her if she was happy. And it was then that those little words she'd been searching for zoomed into her conscious mind: what was it James had said now exactly? Ah yes, 'my fiancée can do the splits you know?' My fiancée.

Well that was that then, wasn't it? She had her answer. A couple of raindrops trickled down the windscreen of her lovely, comfortable BMW. It was going to be hard waving good-bye to the creature comforts she had grown used to, but hadn't she been more miserable than she had ever been in her whole life just trying to hold onto them?

It was kind of sad though. She'd miss this car. Still, the time had come. And as she started up the engine, her decision finally made, the relief came in torrents.

Chapter 25

Sam's news spread rapidly around the rest of the team once she had told Melissa. Veronica, however, already knew. She had been busy buying every book available on how to pass psychometric tests, numerical tests, and understanding corporate assessment techniques, in preparation for the assessment day, when James called her.

'Bunny, where the blazes have you been? I've been trying to contact you for simply days now.'

'Squish! Darling, don't worry. I just had to nip over to Bangkok, that's all.'

'Bangkok? Why?'

'Oh, for the most incredibly boring meeting....'

'Did you see Katrina?'

'A bit. So, why the panic, Squish? Is it about the assessment centre? I told you, it's amazingly simple.'

'That is so not what I've heard, James. Look, I need to know exactly what happens on the day. Even with you on the panel, I'll still have to perform amazingly well.'

'Squish, don't worry about it - it's an absolute breeze. You'll get an interview, a few questionnaires and a group exercise. I think that's it. I'll tell you, darling - it's so incredibly tedious. And we pick who we want anyway.'

'Is that all there is? Are you sure there's nothing else?'

He thought for a second. 'You might have to do a business plan.'

'What about outdoor things? You know - team work and initiatives?'

'Don't recall.' James yawned. 'Nope - pretty sure there's none of that.'

'So I don't need to bring my gym kit?'

'Gym kit you say? Mmmm - oh I think you should definitely bring that, you know - just to be sure, ha, ha!'

'Do you know if you'll be there the night before yet? At the hotel?'

James laughed. 'Hotel? Is that what you've been told? Well, I intend to be, Squish. Look - good luck, old girl. Just do your best. Oh, by the way - did you hear about Sam Farmer?'

Veronica froze. 'What about her?'

'She resigned this morning.'

'Because?'

'Because she was crap at her job, I suppose. Anyway, must dash Squishy. Ciou!'

'Hang on a mo. Did you hear any more about Mike? You know, there was some issue between Mike and Pat, wasn't there?'

'Oh yah. What the hell was it?' He yawned loudly. 'Nope, can't remember. Sorry, darling. I really do have to go now, Squish. Love you.'

Veronica clicked off her phone seconds before Melissa called to give her the same news about Sam. Well, that was just fine, she decided. It seemed her only serious competitor for the job was Bernie. If there was an unresolved issue between Mike and Pat then she herself stood a pretty good chance. And with James' undivided attention there was everything to play for. Especially now that the other matter had been dealt with.

Her husband had arrived home very late on that Friday evening he found he only had two pounds and fifty pence to his name. Drunk and seething with fury, he had staggered up the luxuriously carpeted, private hallway to their apartment and, fully charged up for a fight, rammed his key into the lock. 'Veronica?' he shouted. 'Veronica?' But, the more he struggled, the more obvious it became that his key no longer worked. Veronica had changed the locks.

Of course she heard him rattling around impotently with his key. After about ten minutes she'd opened the door just a fraction with the newly fitted heavy duty chain on. Just long enough to calmly inform him that she would be suing him for divorce first thing on Monday morning.

'You can't do this,' he shouted.

'Oh but I can, Greg' she said with an enigmatic smile, calmly shutting the door in his face. She then hired the sharpest divorce lawyer she could find, providing him with photos, dates, times, names, and whatever money it cost to act brutally and swiftly.

She smiled to herself, thinking about the future - golly, she was so ready to move on in her life. In fact she had already had the apartment valued in anticipation of her new start - she'd had it done on the same Friday evening she had the locks changed actually - and what a pleasant surprise that had been - an added bonus. Yes, she was in good shape: the assessment day simply could not come soon enough.

And finally, after what had seemed like months of waiting, it was suddenly upon them. It fell on the most sweltering day of the year - the hottest day in June since 1957, in fact. All the candidates were forced to spend the previous night in airless rooms above a rickety, old pub situated by the side of a dual carriageway, a situation made infinitely worse by the unpredictable and vitriolic showers, which shot out scalding water one minute, followed almost immediately and without any warning, by an icy cold blast. Then no water at all. The wholly inadequate shower curtains allowed what water there was to swamp the tiny square of linoleum on the bathroom floor, and the one threadbare towel available so small it wouldn't have dried a hamster. All those who had arrived travel weary and sweaty, just dying for a long, cool shower and a hair-wash, were therefore somewhat disappointed.

Veronica's room, above the kitchen, got extra heat together with spectacularly colourful language from the pot washer and the chef, well into the night. She lay on her bed, flushed and perspiring, dressed only in her underwear. Opening the window wasn't an option because of the busy dual carriageway beneath. Sleep eluded her. The night would be long. And there was something else worrying her - James hadn't checked in yet. She had only spoken to him a few days ago - he 'probably' would be at the assessment centre, he said. If so, he really should be here by now.

She reached for her phone and sent him a text:

'WHERE ARE U?'

Mike had fared little better with his room, which was above a bar full of teenagers singing football songs. He had a bath but no shower, and the walls were so thin it was possible to hear every juddering tap and toilet flush, even the bloke next door snoring soundly. Bastard, he thought, as he lay staring at the ceiling, waiting for sleep to come. When finally it did - fitful and mind-racing, somewhere around midnight - a group of drunken girls suddenly burst up the stairs screeching hysterically, banging on all thebedroom doors as they ran down the creaky corridor.

Everyone woke except Bernie, who had ear-plugs in. Only Bernie came up trumps, with the largest room at the Inn and a relatively cool view of the garden at the back where there was a fountain. Bernie slept soundly.

The following morning they each arrived separately at the large, rambling country house where the selection would take place. Veronica drove slowly up the long, winding drive in her black BMW, Chanel sunglasses shielding her eyes from the already brilliant sunlight. She looked out over the grounds, and then immediately did a double take. Set out in little clusters were parallel bars, rubber tyres, green barrels and planks of wood. She checked the signpost. Yes, she was in the right place, this definitely wasn't a Territorial Army Headquarters or anything. Her heart did a little flip - oh dear Lord - outdoor group activities.

'You bloody bastard, James Harris,' she said, thumping the steering wheel. 'You bloody well told me....' And then, drawing up outside the main entrance, her mouth dropped open in horror as she noticed a couple of men fixing a blue nylon rope to a tree above the river. Veronica glared at them. 'I so hope all this isn't for us because if it is I'm going to look like a complete tit swinging from that in my suit and high heels.'

Bernie bounced up and down in the seat of her Landrover as she arrived, whooping with excitement. 'Oooh, goodie!' she shouted. 'Oooh, would you look at that - parallel bars and all.'

She had brought her size six, low-rise mini shorts and a white T-shirt to change into for the outdoor events. And, ooops, she had forgotten her bra again. All she had to do now, she told herself, was loads of positive thinking, keep smiling, fix the psychometric profile to fit what they wanted, and the job would be hers. With a bit of luck on her side, Pat Hardcastle would be on the board of assessors too. They hadn't been told in advance who would be there on the day. They may actually get a whole load of strangers, but as long as the final decision would be made by Pat and James, that may not matter. The assessors were just there to give them marks for the tests, that was all. She was very hopeful. After all - she was their star. She had been told.

Mike reached for the rescue remedy Trisha had given him, his forehead already dripping with sweat. It was still only eight o'clock in the morning. 'I can and I will,' he repeated to himself, picturing the colour blue.

'I will win,' Veronica repeated to herself, as the assessors filed in and she realised with a thumping heart that James wasn't there but Pat was. Where was he, the bastard? 'No matter - I will win,' she said under her breath. She felt she didn't need to imagine a colour. James said he might not be here for the actual assessments, so it was okay. As long as he was around afterwards to discuss the results with Pat, he would make sure she got the job. He so wants to work with me not the others. I know he will make sure I get it, and I will definitely get the top marks for today, so there'll be simply no excuse, she told herself.

James had also reassured her that the external candidates were not any more likely to get the job than the internal ones. The keep fit woman he fancied interviewing had turned out to be about four foot two and the same again in width. As soon as she'd walked into the room James had decided she would not be getting the job. Fat arse, he told Veronica - no chance. He could barely be bothered to ask her any questions. Veronica looked over at Bernie, who had just finished giving Pat a little wave. Their eyes met and Bernie grinned.

'May the best man win,' Bernie said.

'Touché,' said Veronica.

The day began with psychometric and numerical testing, followed by various assessments. But by coffee break tragedy struck - Keep fit girl could not go on. Bernie found her sobbing in the library.

'You've got to give yourself the best chance,' Bernie told her in an upbeat voice. 'You can't just give up, now. Come on, will you?'

Keep fit girl glared at her through red eyes. Not only had the others ganged up on her in the group exercise, but she'd then been utterly humiliated in the role play section by Bernie. Bernie had been supposed to play the part of an incompetent rep who needed to be disciplined. Keep fit girl was supposed to be the manager doing it. People with clipboards had stared at her throughout. It had been bad enough. But then Bernie had decided to toss away her script and make another one up as she went along. Bernie had morphed into an ambitious rep who had been overlooked for promotion, and what was she, the manager here, going to do about it?

'This isn't in the script,' Keep fit girl had said.

'What script?' said Bernie, staying firmly in role play. 'You're my manager and I want to know why you've broken your promises.'

Keep fit girl flushed. 'No, no - you're being disciplined....'

'May I remind you that you're in role play, here,' an assessor chipped in.

Bernie nodded, folding her arms defensively. 'So what are you going to do about it?' she repeated. 'Call yourself a manager!'

'This isn't fair,' Keep fit girl said, her lip beginning to tremble.

The assessors scribbled furiously. 'Stay in your role,' they snapped, rolling their eyes and looking at each other with outraged expressions.

'I, er.... Well, I'm sure I didn't promise you anything,' the girl said to Bernie, realising she had little choice but to play along.

'Oh yes, you did,' said Bernie, before launching into the full scale attack that was to be keep fit girl's undoing.

Keep fit girl, suitably annihilated, had retired to the library for a moment alone, to recover, not suspecting for a moment that Bernie would follow her to finish off the job.

'Where's the other girl gone?' Veronica asked Bernie, over coffee a few minutes later.

'Couldn't take the pace,' Bernie said with a shrug.

'What, she's left?'

Bernie nodded cheerfully. 'Oh well - one less.'

They had lunch with the assessors in a formal dining room, complete with silver service, white table cloths, and waiters attending to them in hushed tones. They sipped their soup as quietly as possible. No one spoke.

Eventually, Bernie broke the silence. 'What will we be having this afternoon, Pat?'

Pat sighed and put down her soup spoon. 'You've got your interviews, and we'll be doing the outdoor team activities I think, lovey. Have I got that right, Neil?' she asked the small, wiry looking man with a bald head, seated at the end of the table.

Neil nodded, a strangely malevolent gleam in his eyes. 'Great fun it is, too,' he said, rubbing his hands together.

Veronica grimaced.

'Oh I can't wait,' Bernie said, bouncing up and down in the seat. 'So, Pat - will it be very different for me being a manager to being a rep?'

Pat took a quick slurp of soup. ' Yes - very,' she snapped.

'How did you become a manager? Did you have to go through one of these in your day?'

Pat put her spoon down again. 'No. I had to do it the hard way and stand in for people at short notice all over the country. I did that for eighteen months before accepting a position in Scotland.'

'Ugh - Scotland! You must have been desperate,' Bernie chuckled.

Pat stared at her. Neil, who was Scottish, stared at her.

When the day was finally over, each candidate was seen privately and asked if they had any questions.

'Just one,' said Veronica. 'When will we know?'

'As soon as we've made a decision based on today's results,' Pat told her. 'Usually it's at least a week.'

Veronica drove home deep in thought, her car so thick with cigarette smoke she could barely see out of it. By the time she was level with Nottingham she decided it must be foggy and put her fog lights on. Certainly it was very irresponsible, she thought, ignoring yet another idiot flashing her, that no one else had.

It had been a long and difficult day. And it may well be a fact that the worst bits would now be permanently etched on her brain. If only there was a way to delete unpleasant memories, she thought, like you could on a computer. Particularly that part of the day where they had been given, as a group, two planks of wood, a ball of string and a football, and been told to get the ball from one giant stone toadstool to another without them or it touching the ground. She had had to do this in high heels and a suit while Bernie had skipped around in skimpy shorts. At the point where she had been straddled between two toadstools on a flimsy board in a hard hat, a person with a clipboard had asked her exactly what her strategy was and she had very nearly lost her temper. Her extremely expensive tights were ripped and she'd torn a nail.

At four o'clock, the outdoor assessments were declared to be over. Someone noticed that tall glasses of orange juice with ice had been laid out on wooden tables on the lawn, and they ambled towards them, beginning to relax. It would be nice to have a cool drink, they agreed, before their drive home.

'Er guys, guys….sorry.' Neil had burst forth from the direction of the French windows, marching towards them in a somewhat agitated manner. 'No, no, Sorry. Those are for the other group. You need to be heading for the library to pick up your business plan assignments.'

They made their way to the library. in silence Three hours had been allocated to the task. They must find a room and work alone. They would then present their work to a panel of assessors. And only then, when the sun had begun to sink in the sky, had their ordeal finally finished. It was over.

Weariness engulfed Veronica. Gratefully, she slid into her BMW for the long drive back to Leeds. She flicked on the air-conditioning, relishing the icy blast on her face. Thank God it was all over - just please, please, let it be worth it. If only she could speak to James, though. Where was he?

In response, as if by magic, her mobile phone beeped. She looked down at a new text message. It was from James, and it read, 'GOOD LUCK.'

Chapter 26

No, it was far too soon. This could not be. Hurtling back from her day's work in Harrogate the following day, Veronica looked down at her car phone and gasped. Pat Hardcastle's name was flashing repeatedly. Surely the decision could not have been made already? It just wasn't possible - they said a week. She wasn't psychologically prepared - this was outrageous. No. She would let it ring. She could not and would not take the news, good or bad, while doing eighty miles an hour on the A1 trapped between two lorries.

Ten minutes later, composed and safely in a Little Chef car park, she tapped into her messages. She was to phone back as soon as she could. This was it then - the start of her new life hopefully.

'Veronica, lovey,' came Pat's voice. 'I wanted to speak to you personally to say that you did exceptionally well at the assessment centre. You were a credit to the company, but I'm sorry to have to tell you that we can't offer you the position on this occasion.'

'I see. May I ask why?'

'Of course you can, lovey. There were two other candidates who also did very well and we had to choose one of you. I decided in the end to offer it to Mike. We all felt that your team needed somebody who had management experience and the maturity that goes with it, and Mike was the only one who could offer us that.'

'Mike? Mike got it? But I thought….Oh, right. I see, of course.'

'Now, Mike will be starting pretty much straight away so I hope that you will support him and continue to do the excellent job you have been doing for us. If it's any comfort I can reassure you that you won't have to do a further assessment if you re-apply within the next two years for another post. And Melissa's position as regional trainer is due for renewal should you wish to go for that.'

'Regional trainer?' Veronica thought quickly - that would be on top of her existing job for no extra pay, wouldn't it? 'I'll think about it,' she said. 'Thank you, Pat.'

She switched off her phone, leaned back and closed her eyes. Good God, there hadn't even been enough time to go through the results properly. In fact, it must have been a foregone conclusion all along, and that bloody assessment centre, as people had always muttered about under their breath, was but an exercise in humiliation. She decided to ring James at home without delay - he must have known. And surely he would be back from Bangkok by now.

'Sorry, he's away on business,' the foreign sounding voice informed her.

'Still? I see. May I ask when he's due back?'

'Who's calling?'

'Oh, I'm so sorry, didn't I say? It's Veronica Ball, his colleague in Leeds.'

'Ah, his colleague! Hi! I'm Katrina - James' fiancée. It's such good news, isn't it? We're very excited about his new job.'

'Er, new job?'

'Didn't you know? He just got the Sales and Marketing Director's position for Asia. My father is the MD. So, James will be in Bangkok until some time next week. Can I help at all? '

'No. No, I'm so sorry to have bothered you. Congratulations. Thank you.' Veronica clicked off her phone. Well, thanks a million, James. He must have known that he wouldn't be there for her assessment review. No wonder she hadn't got the job - without his input everything had been down to Pat. It must have been completely fair after all.

She squeezed her eyes tightly, defying the burn of threatened tears, yet still they oozed - treacherous and hot, ruining her mascara. Blast them all. Every last one of them. Her patronising brother would be sheer torture this Christmas, and her smug, little sister with her new diamond engagement ring, the rock so heavy it had to be lifted on to her finger by crane. Oh God, it would be simply awful. And herself alone this year too. All fantasies of James helping her to decorate the tree while they bragged to the family of their prowess in the company had now been cruelly dashed. A divorced sales rep - what could be bloody well worse than that? At this latest thought, her tears erupted unchecked. She ranted, thumped the steering wheel and screamed until her throat hurt.

And then she picked herself up. It was a rejection, common enough. And at least she still had all her arms and legs. Pressing a tissue to her eyes, Veronica told herself to get a grip, 'come on - mustn't be a big cry-baby. What would mummy say if she saw me snivelling like this?' She rummaged in her bag for a lipstick. 'And anyway - I did the best I bloody well could. I did incredibly well at the assessment centre so I won't have to go through one again, and I've been consistently successful ever since I joined Topham. There will so be a next time, and I will be in amazing shape when that next time shows up. They have to give me a manager's job, they simply have to. I'm management material, for God's sake - look at me!'

In fact, wasn't Dick recruiting soon? Yes, of course - she would ring Dick next week. He was a pussycat, after all. And anyway, cardiology was far more high profile than mental health.

Back in Sheffield, Bernie was pacing. She paced and paced. What had gone wrong? She had the best sales results in the company. She had done brilliantly at the assessment centre, managed to portray the perfect personality, networked to within an inch of her life, and annihilated the competition. So why hadn't she got the job? And worse - what in the name of Jesus and Mother Mary was she going to do now? Everyone had expected her to get this promotion. She was the high flier in the company and most people knew that if you didn't make it into management within the first five years then you never would. She couldn't be the dreaded plodder, she was their star. And then there was all that other irritating business bubbling up, too. She had recently been barred from two of her hospitals, and now three GP surgeries, having been overheard saying to patients as she worked her way round the waiting rooms, 'go on, you should ask him for Happylux. It's the best one on the market. He'll probably put you on one of the cheap ones unless you ask for this. You've your rights, you know.'

She had really banked on moving up, leaving her trail of destruction for others to deal with. How could she possibly clear it up herself? And wouldn't her activity and sales records start to suffer if she was barred from so many places? Hmm, she really would have to act fast.

Picking up the phone, she dialled the sharpest recruitment agency in the business, told them she was the top rep and wanted a career move. Topham had not rewarded their star player well enough - big money, a better package and more of a future was what she required. It was all to play for. And with her mind now focussed, Bernie began to photocopy month after month of sales results.

Brett sat with his mouth open while Johnny filled him in on all the gossip. He had just got back from two weeks in Majorca. It was almost September and the days were hot, long and lazy. And as his team seemed to be falling apart, that had seemed as good a reason as any to call a lads meeting at the Slug and Pellet, the fact that there was a match showing, purely coincidental.

'So, Sam's gone now,' Brett was saying. 'And Bernie too?'

'Yup. Sam couldn't hack the job - nobody knows where she went to though - someone said she'd gone to London.'

'Cool! London. Well I suppose, at the end of the day, with her looks she could do anything she wanted…..' Brett said.

'Yeah. She couldn't do the job though, could she? And she had the advantage of riding the boss too. Which just shows doesn't it - their looks can get them in but they can't do the job for them?'

'Riding the boss? Really? Which one?'

'James Harris, of course.'

'Oh yeah. That's what Mel said, wasn't it? Funny that - I thought she was just stirring things up.'

'Apparently not.'

'Blimey! It just shows you dunnit? D'ya know what I mean, yeah? Well, I hope she's not, you know, on the streets or anything.'

'On the streets? You mean wrapped in a blanket, living in a skip and swigging gin?'

'Well, yeah.'

'Don't be ridiculous.'

'But Simon chucked her out and she hasn't got a job. She hasn't got any parents either, you know?'

'Yeah, but she wouldn't be on the streets, would she?'

'She might be…'

'She won't be,' Johnny snapped. 'And as for Bernie - well she was up to all sorts. She got banned all over the place. Anyway, she landed a new job in London with a massive salary and a Mercedes. She's on Fifty K last I heard. '

'Cool! She was a brilliant sales person though, d'ya know what I mean?' Brett said.

'D'ya reckon, mate?' Johnny laughed. 'One of her customers

rang Mike about her after she left, did he tell you?'

Brett shook his head.

'Yeah, he was really upset.'

'What, that she'd gone?'

'No, that she sold him her horse before she did. Turned out that old Minty wasn't a prime polo player but an old nag with fleas and a bad back. Enormous vets bills, apparently.'

'Ooops.'

Johnny sniggered. 'Anyway,' he said. 'My guess is she'll fly right to the top - her sort always do.'

'Cool,' Brett said, and then thought for a minute. 'How are you getting on with Mike?'

'Really well, You?'

'Yeah, he's cool. I couldn't believe it about him and Trisha though, d'ya know what I mean?'

Johnny laughed. 'Mike gave her such a load of bullshit, did he tell you?'

Brett shook his head.

'Oh yeah - our Trisha's *healed* him, mate. Ha, ha! It's a right laugh, I'll tell you. He gave her this complete hard luck story about Pat doing him over all those years ago. He told Trisha that he'd had an affair with Pat and then chucked her when his wife found out. So, you know, a woman scorned and all that? Pat had set out to destroy his career and blocked his path ever since. Anyway, Trisha counsels Mike and gets him to 'get in touch with his feminine side', apologise to Pat, buy her lunch and the like. Meanwhile he's busy telling Pat all about Veronica and Bernie's squabbles at conference, and all about Bernie talking to the patients and getting barred left right and centre. Next thing - the job's his. Apparently he did crap at the assessment centre.'

'So what really happened then, between him and Pat?'

'Oh you don't want to know, mate.'

'I do.'

'Well, they were having an affair, that bit's true. And they were both married at the time. They were regional managers together and always away at hotels and things. Anyway, it was during one of the mergers when several top jobs were up for grabs. Pat, it seemed, presented some of Mike's ideas at the managers meeting and passed them off as her own. Mike was incandescent with rage - took her to one side and called her a fat cunt. They had a right old barny - no big deal you might think. But - one of the other managers overheard, and when Mike dumped Pat, this manager persuaded her to complain about Mike's verbal abuse - said he'd make it worth her while. So it went to a disciplinary hearing and this other manager gave evidence, mentioning the 'fat cunt' comment. Word had it he even taped some of their conversations. Mike was demoted immediately.'

'But why would this other manager be so malicious, d'ya know what I mean?'

Johnny laughed. 'You don't know fuck, do you, Brett? Mike was his main competitor for the sales director position. With Mike off the scene, he was free to shoot up the ladder with a very loyal Pat in tow.'

'What a bastard.'

'Yeah, and poor Mike was blocked every time he tried to go for promotion after that.'

'Blimey.' Brett took a slurp of beer and thought for a moment. 'So, who, er …. who was this other manager?'

'Alisdair McCraw.'

'Fuck me.'

'Brett! You never swear.'

'I fucking do now.'

'Ha, ha! So you see - nothing's fair, mate. What you've got to do is play the game, see? Arse lick big time at conference and then you can be as much of a lazy git as you want the rest of the time. Still, it seems little Trisha came in handy. At long last Mike's got shot of the wife and he's moved up again. Pat must have bought the apology business hook, line and sinker.'

'He's lucky to have met Trisha, isn't he?'

'She's lucky to have him. If he wasn't the manager she'd have been sacked by now. And her with three kids as well. She must have seen him coming, the dozy sod.'

'She's well attractive though,' Brett said, out of fairness.

'Yeah, if you like ageing Lolitas,' Johnny said.

Brett looked at him - Johnny seemed to be a lot more cynical and touchy these days.

'Anyway, I've got some news of my own,' Johnny said. He took a swig of Old Speckled Hen, and watched Brett carefully for his reaction. 'I've got the Product Manager's job on Dick's team - starting next month. I'll be moving to Southampton.'

Brett swallowed hard, struggling to find the words. 'But you're always in the gym. How....?'

Johnny narrowed his eyes. 'Nobody went and told you that hard work paid off did they, Brett, mate?'

'Well, yes, I mean no... Cool,' he said, in a wobbly voice. 'At the end of the day, right? Yeah? Well done, d'ya know what I mean?'

'Yeah, it's great. I'll get to work in the office with all those office babes. I'll get a load more money and I'll get an apartment overlooking the sea, and go to the beach at weekends. No more white coat chasing for me, mate.'

'What about Mel? I thought you two were living together?'

'Not living together exactly. I just spent a bit of time at her place, that's all. It was never serious, just a shag,' he lied.

'Cool,' said Brett.

Johnny frowned. Melissa had actually been heartbroken. Melissa had screamed, shouted, wept and threatened to castrate him with the kitchen knife. Everything was going wrong for her, she said, and it was all his fault. The last he'd heard Mel had been seen out on drunken, over-emotional nights out in town with various gaggles of girlfriends telling her he 'wasn't worth it,'. She'd had a boob job too, he believed, seemingly unaware that this had contributed further to her image as a massive joke amongst senior management. He'd been at one of their dinner parties the week before.

'Did you see her parading around in her thong when we were on conference?' one of the managers asked, hooting with laughter.

'Oh, and how she kept leaning forwards at meetings in that low cut suit so you could see her silicone boobs,' another one sniggered.

'And fancy all that writhing around on a car bonnet in the nude! Did you hear about that? She wanted to be a manager apparently....'

'Aw, mate,' Johnny said, noticing Brett's expression. 'She wanted kids. She started bleating on about a baby, and I'm far too young for all that. It's just not me, mate.'

'She lost her training job to Veronica as well, didn't she?' Brett said, making Johnny feel even worse. 'Mel must be well pissed off.'

'Yeah, she is. She's taken it hard,' Johnny said, omitting to mention the fact that Melissa had bought a punch bag and stuck a photo of Veronica on it. 'I think it was Mike's strategy to stop Veronica going off to Dick's team. He told her - oh God, this is pure genius, mate - he told her that she would never get a management job unless she did at least two years regional training on top of her sales job. That way he gets to keep his one decent, hard working rep for a bit longer and he gets all his training work done for him.'

'Nice one. Hang on a minute - what do you mean 'one decent rep?'

'Sorry mate, no offence. Tell you what though,' Johnny said, leafing through, 'What Car' magazine. 'I think I'll get myself a BMW Z4 now I've opted out of the company car scheme and I get the money instead. What do you reckon? Nice or what?' He flashed a picture of a black metallic model at Brett.

Brett's pleasant expression faded a little. 'All right for some,' he said in a dull voice.

'You still got your Vectra, mate?'

'Mmmm.'

'How much longer have you got that for?'

Brett looked at the floor. 'Three and a half years,' he muttered.

'Never mind. Come on, sup up. Your round.'

Chapter 27

<u>Six Months later.</u>
<u>In a Private London Hospital: The Operating Theatre Recovery Unit.</u>

'Girl, girl!' The old woman snapped her bony fingers. 'Girl!'
Sam scowled, pretending to be busy.

'Girl! Oh for goodness sake. Are you deaf or something? Girl! Girl!' Narrowing her eyes, the old lady spied the Ward Sister, 'Sister - over here please.' She began to cough. ' I wish to complain - your nurse simply isn't good enough. I've been calling and calling.'

'I'm so sorry, Mrs Robinson-Smythe,' Sister said, plumping up her pillows, rubbing the old lady's back. 'There, there. Nurse? A word, please,' she called to Sam.

'What now?' Sam muttered under her breath, noting the old woman's smile of satisfaction.

'Why aren't you looking after your patient? She says she's been calling you.'

Sam sighed. 'Yes. Sister.' She stopped checking the drug cupboard, locked it and walked wearily over to her patient. 'What can I do for you, Mrs Robinson- Smythe? Again.'

The old woman scowled at her from her sick bed. 'I want a toffee.'

'There you are,' she said, passing the old lady a sweet.

'I want it unwrapping,' the old lady snapped.

Sam unwrapped it. 'Here,' she said.

'No, no, no. You stupid girl. You've touched it now. Get me a drink.'

'Water?'

'Tea - I want tea.'

'Right.' Under Sister's watchful eye, Sam fetched a cup of tea and held it to the woman's lips.

'Aaagh! You stupid girl. She's burnt me. Sister, Sister - she's burnt me. Help.'

Sam, red faced, began to dab a tissue over the old lady's chin but was smacked away. 'Get away from me, you idiot girl.'

'I'll take over here, Nurse,' Sister said, her lips so tight they almost disappeared. 'Have you written up your reports, yet?'

I can't take much more of this, Sam thought. Please, please let me pass this audition on Saturday. I have to get out of here. They'll sack me soon, I know they will and I can't stay at Hannah's place for ever.

She bent her head, trying not to cry, and began to write the day's report for the night staff. There were no windows in the underground recovery unit, and the air conditioning droned noisily. Thank God there was only one more hour to go. If she had to mop the brow of just one more spoilt teenager having silicone implants, or one more Arabian princess having a rhinoplasty, each one carrying on as if they'd just had major life saving surgery, whingeing about the pain, she'd have to run screaming from the building. She'd seen nothing of London other than this basement hellhole, her back ached from sleeping on her sister's sofa for the last six months and everyone here treated her like some kind of servant.

After a couple of minutes, the phone rang. Sam snatched it up, 'Sam, I mean, Staff Nurse Farmer. Can I help you?'

'It's Sister on Ward Nine. I'm ringing to check if it's okay for my patient's husband to pop down and see his wife? Is she out of theatre yet?'

'Oh is that the Italian lady? Well we have a patient on a ventilator at the moment so I'm afraid it isn't convenient. She shouldn't be long though. She's only had a bit of liposuction, hasn't she?'

'That's not the point, Nurse. He's desperate to see her. He's crying.'

'Sorry, but no. Tell him she won't be long - fifteen minutes at the mo....' The phone had gone dead.

Two minutes later, Sister from Ward Nine brought the Italian husband into Theatre Recovery. He was wearing a full length fur coat. Swooping past patients still on oxygen masks, and the one on the ventilator, he rushed to his wife.

'Darling! Darling!' he cried.

Sam glared at the Sister from Ward Nine. 'I said 'no' for a good reason, Sister.'

'Two minutes will not do any harm, will it Sister?' she said addressing Sam's superior.

'Times up then,' Sam replied to her back. 'And that coat is unhygienic.'

'I'm not sure I like your attitude, Nurse.'

'Rules are rules,' said Sam, marching over to the Italian man. 'Excuse me, Sir...'

He whipped round, his long coat knocking a tray of urine pots off the Nurse's desk. 'Oh thank you, thank you, beautiful lady,' he cried, clasping her hand.

'Yes, well I'm afraid you must go now. We have some very ill people in here,' she said hotly, before returning to her desk. Honestly, the rich think they can break all the rules and do anything they want - champagne demanded the second they opened their eyes, some of them. She would never get used to it. Now, where was she? Ah yes - the old trout and her in growing toe-nail...

Deeply engrossed in her report writing, it was several minutes before she realised that something had fluttered down in front of her face. It was a fifty pound note. 'Grazie,' called the Italian over his shoulder as he swept out of the room.

****

A couple of weeks later, Johnny King was on his way home from an all night rendez-vous with an attractive brunette from the office. The attractive brunette, Emma, had been wearing tight, white tops and doing lots of unnecessary bending over in the office for weeks, hoping to get his attention. But she had been one of dozens since he came to Southampton. And she wouldn't last much longer than a week.

On the way back to his flat that morning, Johnny stopped at the local newsagents to get a paper. Casually, he sauntered back to his car, glancing only briefly at the blonde in the G-string on the front page of the tabloid. But a brief glance was enough. His brain had already computed the tiny photo in the bottom right hand corner of the page, and was just in the process of relaying the information to his conscious mind.

By the time he sank into the driving seat of his brand new BMW Z4 sports car, he had already snatched up the paper and turned to the page that went with the photo. It was Sam. 'Bloody hell!' He spread the paper out against the steering wheel and stared.

Sam was to be the new face in a regular soap on TV, the article said. She would soon be a household name - you heard it here first. It seemed she would be on his TV screen every night of the week. He read and re-read the words - her beauty, her natural talent, her intelligence, living in Chiswick, a boyfriend in films, a key role.

Johnny put the tabloid down onto the passenger seat and stared out at the rolling, winter sea. Little drops of seawater splattered onto his windscreen in a sudden gust of wind. He hadn't thought about her for days now. In fact, he thought yesterday might have been the first day he hadn't thought about her at all for over six months. He'd been just beginning to get over her, to come to terms with what he had done.

Really it had all gone horribly wrong. What had he been thinking of that night in Spain? She was only supposed to have had a row with Simon, leaving the way clear for himself. He would have been her shoulder to cry on, provided the sofa for her to sleep on, and then who knows how things would have progressed? How was he to know that she would flip and make such a dramatic decision to disappear off to London without so much as a word? And where had she gone? No one seemed to know what had become of her. What if his interference really had resulted in her sleeping rough?

There hadn't been a day or night for months when he hadn't fretted, even spending entire weekends looking for her. Would she be in a shelter for street people? Would she be working King's Cross?

Oh Sam, Sam. He looked down at her photograph, tracing a finger down her face. 'Sorry' really didn't cover it. He really had been a bad, bad boy. If only he hadn't had to go and fall in love with her. Still, he thought, looking down at his bleeping car phone, there was at least one wrong he could put right. 'Hi, Mel,' Johnny said softly.

THE END